I0671819

The Aether

A journey to the other side

By Lani Moku

The Aether

A journey to the other side

Lani Moku

Copyright

Dedication

To Stanley and Florence

The Aether

A Long Day

Dr. Bruce Rollin is working late in his lab, waiting for the results from the satellite. Years of research are now on the line. The test results will determine if the project is a complete success or an absolute failure.

Sitting all alone in the dark, all he can do is watch the monitor display information coming from the deep space survey satellite. The data continually scrolls down the monitors, being analyzed by a supercomputer in some distant building.

Bruce grabs the last of the cold pizza, tossing the empty box up on the table. After thirty-two hours, it's almost over. As the project leader, he hasn't been able to go home. Sleeping on a cot in his office for the last several days, he longs for his soft, warm bed.

At 3:30 in the morning, everyone else had already gone home. Extremely tired, Bruce is ready to shut down for the night. Having to wait for the data download is extremely boring. With everything completed, there is nothing else to do but wait for the satellite to send the final signal.

* * *

A loud, beeping sound wakes Bruce up. The satellite finally sends the signal indicating the data transfer is complete and has gone into the sleep mode to recharge the batteries for the next batch of tests. The only thing left is to save all the data and make sure everything is backed up.

After years of work, he couldn't resist taking a peek at the data. He is not going to get any sleep wondering if the test is a success or a failure. After entering the backup command on the keyboard, he runs a program to view random samples of the data.

When the first image appears on the screen, he is so shocked. The new sensor is performing better than anyone anticipated. The data shows results well in the ultraviolet and deep in the infrared areas. The resolution is far better than anything currently available. Zooming in on one of the test stars, it displays information in such detail that no one has ever seen before. He knows this is going to make the front cover of Scientific America. All those years of hard work have finally paid off.

* * *

Driving home on the empty roads, Bruce can't stop thinking about his future. It will be a big boost in his career with more grants, a larger lab, but mostly notoriety among his peers. Analyzing the data will probably take a year or more. He knows there will be some groundbreaking discoveries just from the initial spot checks.

His phone is ringing nonstop from fellow researchers to congratulate him on the results. People around the world are already sifting through the data. The next few days will be a nightmare, with everyone wanting interviews. All he wants to do is sleep after working nonstop for the last three days. Luckily, everyone else on the team is home asleep. He can rely on them for all the press releases and dealing with the news media.

Looking down the road, not one person is out on the streets. The traffic lights are all green. He wishes it was like this all the time. Usually, during the day, the roads are packed with cars, bumper to bumper, all the way home, having to stop at every streetlight.

The phone rings again. Recognizing the number displayed on the dashboard, Bruce's old friend from Germany is calling.

He presses the receive button on the steering wheel. "Hey, Martin!"

"Congratulations, Bruce! Well done! We're going through it now, and it's very impressive. You got some fantastic images here."

"Thanks! Yeah, I think we got a winner. I took a quick peek, and damn, it's more than we were hoping for."

"You still at the lab?" Martin asked, hearing some strange background noises on the phone.

"Nope… On the way home."

"What time is it there? It must be late?"

"It's almost four in the morning. It's been a long day, or should I say a long week. I'm going to do nothing but sleep for the next day or two."

"No way, Bruce! You got to get them when it's hot. Everyone is calling asking about you. I was going to set up a few interviews with the press. You think you'd be up for a few questions? It won't take long."

"Sorry, I have to pass… I have been up for a couple of days now. Can't really think straight. I'm so tired, just call Bill. He'll be ready to deal with the news people. He is scheduled to be at the lab at six. That's a couple of hours from now. He'll have some sample data by then."

"Bruce, we need you! This is your baby! Don't let someone else take the glory!"

The phone starts beeping again, with another call coming in. "I got to go… I'll talk with you in a day or two."

"All right… Good job!"

Bruce glances down to press the receive button to take the other call. In the corner of his eye, he notices some blue lights flashing up on the building as he approaches the intersection. The street light is green, but the flashing light is getting brighter. He takes his foot off the gas pedal to slow down, getting a little cautious going through the intersection.

Once in the intersection, he sees two police cars racing toward him on his left. They are far enough away but are coming toward him really fast. Blinded by the bright headlights and flashing blue emergency lights, he can't see anything else. He made a big mistake slowing down, then stomps on the gas pedal to get out of their way.

Keeping an eye on the police cars, he is having a hard time trying to figure out which part of the road they are on. All he can see is the bright flashing lights. For a fraction of a second, something blocks the headlights of the police cars. Right away, he knows what it is. The police are chasing someone, and the car they are chasing doesn't have any headlights on.

Knowing the other car is going to hit, Bruce leans over to the right as far as he can. Time slows down, waiting for the impact. He looks at the clock, noticing the seconds are going by so slowly.

The speeding car slams into the driver's side of Bruce's car. All he hears is a horrible crunching sound. He is violently tossed about, and then his car starts rolling over. All the airbags inflate, but they are not much help when lying across the seat. The passenger airbag slams into his arm, making matters worse. The seatbelt holds him in place, but his head slams up on the roof of the car. The pain is excruciating.

After the car rolls over several times, it eventually comes to a complete stop. Everything is quiet. Glass is everywhere. Smoke slowly fills the car. Bruce is lying across the seat, staring at the dashboard. The front windshield is smashed, and the roof of the car has caved in on top of him. He can't think straight and does not remember anything, having no clue why his car is so mangled.

After about a minute, he starts to comprehend things a little better. With all the smoke in the car, all he can think about is getting out. Unable to move his arms and legs, he is starting to wonder if this is the end. Just to get the seatbelt unfastened takes forever. There is no way to crawl out of the windows since the roof has been crushed. He tries to sit up, but the pain is unbearable.

A voice comes out of the darkness. "Are you OK?"

He looks up, seeing a police officer. "I think so… A little banged up… The smoke is getting bad. Hard to breathe."

A huge billow of white smoke fills the car. "It's just a little fire in the engine. Don't worry about it. We got it under control. We'll get you out in no time!"

Bruce hears sirens in the distance. The smell of burning oil and rubber makes it hard to breathe. With all the white fumes from the fire extinguishers filling the car, it's not helping much.

With all the flashing emergency lights illuminating the inside of the car, Bruce can now see everything. Looking down at his arm, he quickly closes his eyes. Seeing his left hand covered with blood is more than enough to make him queasy.

So disoriented, he starts hearing voices. Most are incoherent. A rumbling noise is so loud that his ears feel like they are about to explode. Slowly opening his eyes, the car is surrounded by people. The roof of the car is being cut apart. The passenger door is pulled open and then cut off with a large circular saw. That is the source of all the painful noise.

"How we doing?" the medic asked.

"A little tired, but I am hurting all over."

"Don't worry... We're going to get you out in just a few minutes. I need to check your vitals and get a neck brace on you."

"My neck is OK, but my arm took a hit. Oh shit!"

"Are you OK?" the medic asked, noticing he was so pale.

"Getting tunnel vision..." Bruce mumbles, trying to get the words out. "Feel kind of woozy," then passes out.

* * *

Visions

Bruce slowly opens his eyes. His vision is so blurred, and all he can see is a bright light going back and forth. Odd shapes and shadows are moving in front of him. Unable to move, the pain is shooting throughout his body. All he can hear is a horrible, loud, screeching sound, confused about where he is and what is happening. It feels as if he is having one hell of a bad dream.

"Come on, Bruce! Stay with us! We're almost there!" a strange voice shouts out.

He opens his eyes again. Unable to move his head, all he can do is stare straight up. His vision slowly clears, realizing he is in an ambulance. A strange person appears right in front of his face and is smiling trying to say something. The noise from the siren is drowning out everything. Looking down, he sees an oxygen mask on his face and a big white neck brace down below his chin. That's probably the reason why he can't talk or move his head.

Bruce constantly slips in and out of consciousness. Every time he opens his eyes, he is in a different place. At first, he was in an ambulance. Now, he is standing in the middle of a field surrounded by green grass and tall trees. It is like a bad dream where nothing makes sense. So confused, he has no clue what is happening.

There is a painful flash of light, and everything goes dark. His vision is blurred for a few seconds, blinking his eyes several times, slowly adjusting to the darkness. Looking around, he is lying on his back, surrounded by nurses and medical people racing down a long hallway. Hearing voices of encouragement and not feeling any pain, he is starting to wonder if maybe it's not that bad. A warm feeling goes through his body. Getting so tired, he can feel himself nodding off.

He is jolted awake, hearing a strange high-pitched noise. The noise is so loud it drowns out all the voices. Surrounded by people, he can see their mouths moving as if they are screaming something, but there is no sound. Looking up, he is so surprised to see a medic pounding on his chest. From the looks on their faces, something terrible has happened. Getting tunnel vision, he is unable to make out what is going on as everything goes dark again.

* * *

Feeling an excruciating pain in his chest, Bruce is jolted awake. There is so much commotion going on around him. Now, he is surrounded by people wearing blue smocks, masks, and protective eyewear, all yelling out to each other. His clothes are being cut right off his body. Seeing all the red stains on everyone's hands, he starts to panic, knowing that is his blood.

A strange man starts slapping his face. "Bruce! I'm Doctor Wagner. Keep still. We need you to stay awake and don't keep fighting us."

Bruce struggles to talk. "What's happening? Where am I? I thought this was over. Why am I still here?"

"You are at Memorial Hospital. You've been in an accident. We are here to take care of you, and we have a few tests to do. So, just bear with us for a few minutes."

"Give me something for the pain… It's getting worse!" with everyone pulling on his arms and legs.

"We are… Just give it a minute or two. We need you to be awake for a while. Can you feel this?" reaching down, pulling on Bruce's left index finger.

Bruce cringed. "Yeah! That's not helping."

"How about this?" the doctor asked, running a metal pen along the bottom of Bruce's foot.

He screams out loud. "I think I've had enough! No more…" feeling light-headed.

A loud buzzing sound is drowning out all the voices. Nothing makes sense anymore, and the pain is slowly going away. His entire body starts feeling warm, as if someone put a blanket over him. Feeling so tired, all he wants to do is sleep.

The bright operating room lights are so painful. Bruce tries to close his eyes, but the light is still there. So confused, he keeps blinking, but nothing blocks the bright light.

The blinding white light slowly fades away. Everything is quiet. There is no more pain or people shouting at him. He feels a strange sensation, like floating in the water. Everything is blurry, making it hard to distinguish anything, but he can see shadows moving around him.

Slowly, his vision starts to clear. The dark shadows are people wearing blue outfits, frantically moving around a table. The strange thing about it all, he discovers that he is looking down. Then, he realizes this is the emergency room that he was just in. He can't see what's happening because the big operating lights are in the way.

The pain is gone, and everything feels OK. He can move his arms and legs without any problems. He can breathe normally, even though it feels like he is floating on top of the water. With no idea what's going on, this must be another one of those strange dreams.

The weird sensation of floating is like the snorkeling trip he had while on vacation. Bruce loved snorkeling in the warm, calm waters of the Caribbean, looking down at all the fish and coral. It is almost the same, but this is more like being in a room filled with warm water and not much of a view.

There is also a current slowly pushing him along. Floating across the room, he notices a couple of signs on top of a cabinet. The signs are in bright, bold colors. Each one reads 'Ask for Karen Brown' in large print. It's an odd place to put a sign, but he figures someone probably tossed them up there long ago.

Approaching the end of the room, he tries to stop. Frantically swinging his arms back and forth, but it doesn't help. Still moving along, one last big cabinet attached to the wall slowly passes underneath him. Again, he sees another of those strange signs, 'Ask for Karen Brown,' on top of the cabinet.

Reaching the wall, he puts his hand up to stop. To his surprise, his hand slowly passes right through it. He can touch the wall, and it does have density, feeling more like Jell-O. The wall slows him down a little, but the current is pushing him through to the other side.

He goes through the wall, floating into the hallway to the nurse's station. People walking around don't seem to notice him. Odd little lights slowly drift about, moving along with him. Some of the floating lights turn, running up through the ceiling or down one of the other hallways.

Floating just below the ceiling, he has no control over anything. Trying to move his arms back and forth, but it doesn't help. The current keeps pushing him along. At least he could swim in the water, but this stuff is really weird.

He approaches a large room filled with chairs. Only a few people are here. Then it dawns on him. This is the hospital waiting room, and he has been here before when his friend broke his leg. Getting close to the small group of people, he is so stunned, recognizing every one of them. His girlfriend, Debbie, is here. Also, his brother, mom, and dad are here as well. He sees his best friend, Wayne and Mark. He yells out, but no one hears him.

Bruce tries everything to stop. Flinging his arms and legs about doesn't help at all. He slowly flips upside down out of control. With his legs up in the ceiling, he is finally able to slow down. Grabbing onto a trellis below him, he comes to a stop.

He quickly learns to grasp things slowly, so his hand doesn't move right through. Still upside down, he pulls himself to the floor using the trellis. Luckily, the current is not as strong near the floor. Righting himself, it feels like standing at the bottom of a pool, feeling almost weightless. Unable to walk, he grasps the back of the chairs to help get to where his family is sitting.

Standing in front of his friends and family, he is so shocked. His girlfriend and his mother are crying. The look on their faces is so disturbing. They are all grieving for some reason. He keeps yelling out, but no one can hear him. He doesn't understand what is happening, but most of all, why is everyone here?

He tries to grasp Debbie's hand, seeing she is so upset. Again, his hand goes right through. He notices a faint glow around his hand for the first time, like a light bluish glow around his arms and legs. Putting his hand up to his face, he can almost see right through it.

Looking right at Debbie's face, he notices something odd about her. He keeps blinking his eyes, trying to get a clear view. For some reason, she has this strange faint bluish glow on her face, as if someone is shining a blue flashlight on her. Glancing over at his brother and parents, they also have the same faint blue glow. The light is not on them but coming from inside. He can't see through them, but everyone has this blue light just inside their heads for some reason.

Everything is so strange. Nothing makes sense anymore. All Bruce can think about is waking up from this horrible dream. Getting so frustrated, he yells out. There is no reply or even a reaction from anyone. Going from one person to another, it's all the same. No one can see or hear him. He doesn't understand what is happening or why he is here.

Bruce is starting to get scared. Something is not right. He sees an old man standing behind the next row of seats, staring at a woman sitting in one of the chairs. He also has this bluish glow all over his body, but the woman only has a bluish light just within her head.

"What is happening here?" Bruce cries out.

The old man turns, looking right at him, slowly shaking his head.

"You can hear me!" Bruce yells out.

"Yes, I can," the old man said, then turned back, looking at the old woman.

"I don't understand any of this," Bruce said. "They can't hear me… They don't even know I'm here."

The old man slowly gets down on one knee. "I think we're here to say goodbye…" putting his arms around the old woman who has her hands up to her face, crying profusely.

"Oh my God!" Bruce gasped, glancing over at his friends and family.

He remembers the accident and being in the ambulance. Looking down, he sees no injuries. He can stand and walk with no problems, although it feels as if he is standing at the bottom of a swimming pool. People are walking about, acting as if nothing is unusual. This is like one bad dream, but it feels so real for some reason.

More of those tiny glowing lights appear. It reminds him of fireflies that he collected when he was little. These are brighter and constantly lit, flying up and down the hallways. Some of the lights even travel right through the windows, going outside.

One of the glowing lights comes so close that he tries to move out of the way, but it's too late. The small glowing object hits the side of his face. He feels a jolt of energy. Suddenly, he is in another room, a small wooden shack, all dark and dusty. Three little Asian children are standing next to a wooden box. A woman sitting on a mat is breaking up small twigs, tossing them into a wood-burning stove.

The image is so real. Bruce can even smell the fish cooking in the pan. The woman and the children are dressed in strange outfits. Everything looks old. There is no electricity, and the windows are open with wooden shutters and have no glass.

The scene quickly changes. Now Bruce is standing in a field surrounded by dozens of Asian people, tilling the soil with old farming tools. Others are planting tiny seedlings into the soil. He can smell the soil and even feel the heat from the sun. The cool breeze feels so good on his face.

In the distance, he sees the snow-capped Mount Fuji. Since he has never been to Japan, how can he see things so clearly, as if he is really there? Everything is so real, not like any normal dream.

The visions quickly go from one location to another. Bruce sees different people and their families growing old together. Almost like seeing his life flashing in front of his eyes. What makes it so odd, this is not his life but someone else's life.

He feels another jolt of electricity. A little stunned, he realizes he is back in the hospital again. He is wondering what brought on all these strange dreams. Seeing the glowing light moving away from the right side of his face, he reaches up with his hand trying to touch it. As soon as his hand gets close, faint blue wisps of light jump to his finger. His mind is filled with more of those strange visions of Japan.

A few seconds later, there is another flash of light. He is back in the waiting room again. The small light slowly moves away, eventually going through the window.

His mind is still a blur with all these little glowing lights darting around him. He is wondering why he is having all these strange visions that are so real. Everything is so odd that he is having a difficult time trying to figure out this weird dream.

He sees a woman standing all alone next to the nurse's station. Just like the old man, she has a bluish glow covering her entire body. They are the only two people that look different. Everyone else has that strange faint glow as if they all have a blue light bulb just inside their heads.

"Can you hear me?" Bruce asked, waving at her.

She nods her head. "I don't know what to do... Where am I supposed to go?"

"I'm not sure..." Bruce replied. "I don't know what I'm doing here. This is like a bad dream that won't end!" so glad that she could hear him.

"Am I dreaming?" she asked, "Can you help me get back home?" trying to reach out to a nurse walking past her.

"I don't think they know we're here," Bruce said, seeing how the nurse just ignored her.

The look of absolute horror on the woman's face is so disturbing. She loses control, going into a rage, flinging her arms about, trying to grab anyone who walks by her. The scene is just too painful to watch.

Three nurses, walking at a fast pace, slam into the woman, but they pass right through her. The woman slowly starts tumbling out of control, floating down the hallway. Eventually, the woman disappears right through a wall. Bruce knows there is nothing he can do to help, feeling so useless.

Bruce glances back at the old man. The old man stands up and reaches up with his arms. The woman starts crying uncontrollably. Then, the old man slowly fades away until he is nothing more than a bead of light. The glowing light pulsates a few times, slowly circling the old woman. Eventually, it moves away, going outside through the window and then up into the sky.

Bruce shakes his head. "Oh, God! No, I'm not ready for this! This is not right!" understanding now what is happening and why he is here.

He turns to his family, so angry, not wanting any of this. Now, he knows why they are so upset. They are here for him, and that's why they are all in so much pain.

"No!" he yelled. "I'm not giving up… It's not my time! I'm going to fight this!"

He stares at his girlfriend and his family. "No! I'm not leaving!" getting so angry. "I don't have to do this! It's not my time. It's not my time!"

The room slowly gets brighter, and he is having a hard time seeing anything. Bruce reaches out to his family as he feels himself being pulled away. Everything is turning white as if a bright light is shining in his eyes. He starts hearing voices and strange noises. A horrible pain shoots through his entire body, and then he feels a surge of heat and electricity shooting through his chest.

* * *

"OK! Clear!" the medic yelled, making sure everyone stepped back from the patient.

Placing the two pads on each side of the chest, she presses the trigger on the defibrillator pads. The patient's chest heaves as the electrical charge surges through the heart.

"We have a pulse! Strong! There's another. I think we're good!" the Anesthesiologist shouted.

Bruce gasps, trying to take in a breath. The pain is excruciating. A surge of air is forced down into his lungs. He is unable to speak with an oxygen mask over his face, and something stuck down his throat. Lying down on a table, he is surrounded by people wearing blue smocks and masks. He wishes this nightmare would be over.

* * *

Recovery

Four days later, Bruce slowly awakes. For a few minutes, he is so confused, having no idea where he is. Seeing all the tubes sticking into his arms, he must be in a hospital room, starting to recall glimpses of the accident and being in the emergency room.

Lying in bed all alone, he is starting to wonder how bad it is. There are plenty of his vital signs being monitored with all the medical instruments next to the bed. He can see his heartbeat and blood pressure are normal. With a temperature of 96, everything looks OK.

Since no one else is in the room, he tries to figure out his condition on his own. The cast on his left arm tells him a lot. He can lift his arms, and moving his fingers is a good sign. Looking down at his feet, he can move his toes, but his left leg feels odd. Pulling back the sheets, he sees the full leg cast, but at least the right leg is still good.

Reaching up with his right arm, he feels a huge bandage wrapped around his head. Just touching it makes his head hurt even more. He has vague memories of the car hitting him, trying to recall what happened. The cast on his left arm and leg is making sense now.

After waiting over fifteen minutes for someone to come into the room, he looks for a call button. There are so many wires and tubes going to all the instruments. He is scared to move. Already getting tired, he quickly falls asleep.

***

Bruce is standing underneath a huge oak tree, watching the sunset. He feels so warm and content watching the clouds turning orange. The gentle breeze never felt so good. He always enjoys spending time at the park. It is the best place to rest, getting away from all the turmoil from work and the big city.

After watching all the birds flying about, a strange feeling goes through his body. The wind feels as if it's flowing right through him. The sensation is so weird, almost like having no weight at all as if being in the water. Bending his knees, he kicks up from the ground. To his surprise, he slowly starts floating up in the air.

Drifting along with the wind, Bruce goes higher and higher. Floating above the trees, he is starting to get scared, wondering how to get back on the ground. Moving his arms and legs about seems to work, and it's almost like swimming. He finds it such an odd sensation to swim through the air with the birds.

After a while, he is starting to get the hang of it. In a way, this is so similar to being in a swimming pool. Face the direction you want to go, then start doing a breaststroke. Just like in the water, when you stop moving your arms, you slowly come to a stop. Flying about like the birds is so easy.

Exploring the park, he is having a lot of fun weaving through all the trees. People walking about didn't seem to notice or care. With the sun halfway below the horizon, Bruce slowly descends to the middle of a crowd. Standing on the grass, he quietly watches the final moments of the end of another day. The clouds slowly change from orange to a brilliant red glow as the sun slowly fades away.

With the sun beneath the horizon, everyone slowly gets up then starts walking away. He turns to see a woman standing all alone, and she is staring at him. She looks a little odd. No one else has noticed him, but this woman keeps on staring right at him. He slowly moves away, but the woman is watching his every move.

As the darkness sets in, he notices a strange bluish glow around the woman. For some reason, he knows something is not right with her. He goes into a panic, trying to get away but finding it difficult to move. Every step he takes feels as if he is so heavy that it's almost impossible to walk.

Someone is shouting out his name over and over. Looking around, he sees no one else in the park but the woman. He has never been so scared in his life. Everything starts to go dark, and then he hears a loud bang.

* * *

"Bruce! Come on! Are you awake? Are you hungry?" a strange voice yells out.

Bruce is jolted awake. All he can see is a brilliant light. He reaches up to cover his eyes, trying to block out the painful light.

"It's OK... I'm just checking your pupils," putting the small flashlight in her pocket.

"Who are you?" Bruce asked.

"I'm Doctor Anderson... It's good to see you're finally awake. I know you probably have a lot of questions, but I need to check on a few things here," jotting down some notes in the chart.

A nurse walks in. "Hello, Mr. Rollin... Would you like something to eat?"

"Sure... I'm starving! What do you have? I can go for a good cheeseburger! I want some fries, too! Is there a Fatburger near here?"

She laughed. "I don't think so... How about some chicken strips, rice, and a salad? If you're good, you might get some applesauce for dessert."

He cringed. "Sounds as if I don't have a choice."

The nurse smiled. "I'll be back with your meal in a few minutes," walking out of the room.

"Well, I'm glad to hear you're hungry," the Doctor said. "That's a good sign, but your eating habits are going to change."

"So, how bad is it? I don't remember that much."

"You were in a bad car accident. The impact was mostly on your left side. You have a fractured femur and fibula in your left leg. Your left humorous is fractured, too. You have a lot of bruising on your left hip, but luckily, you didn't fracture it. Our biggest concern is the fractured skull. You had some swelling on your brain and have been in a coma for a week."

"It's been a week?"

"Yes, a week... Overall, you're doing pretty good. It looks like you're going to pull through this without any problems."

"That explains the throbbing headache. That's what hurts the most."

"I'll give you something for that... We'll be keeping you here for another week for observation. We're going to put you through a few tests. If everything is OK, then you can go home!"

"I'm stuck here for a week... Damn, so, where is everyone?" looking around the empty room.

"The nurse is calling your family now. They'll be here shortly. So, do you have any questions before I leave?"

He thought for a moment. His mind is going blank. The only thing he really needs is food.

"Nothing at the moment... Maybe later, when I have more time to think about all this."

She smiled. "Good... Have a nice dinner. Remember to eat slowly. It's been a week since you've had any solid food. If you need anything, just push the call button," pointing it out to him.

"Oh, so that's where it is," reaching over to take the white box. "I thought this was the TV remote."

"It serves that purpose, too. Just push the red button if you need anything."

As the Doctor is about to step out of the room, Bruce yells. "Oh, there is one thing! Who is Karen Brown?"

The Doctor immediately stops. "Why do you ask?"

Her reaction startles him. She gets really serious all of a sudden, slowly stepping back into the room.

He shrugged. "I don't know why... I guess it struck me as odd."

"How?" she quickly replied.

"Why would I ask for Karen Brown?"

Her eyes widened. "Why would you? Do you know her?"

He slowly shakes his head. "No, never heard of her. I just can't get that vision out of my head."

"What vision? Did you see something?"

"Yes, I did! I saw all those signs with 'Ask for Karen Brown' on them. It's like they're plastered all over the place."

The Doctor is a little shocked. "I see..." jotting down something in her notes.

"Is there anything wrong?" Bruce asked.

"Oh no, it's time for your dinner," the doctor said, seeing the nurse walking in, pushing a trolley. "I'll be checking on you later," then quickly leaves the room.

Bruce just shrugs it off. Seeing the food takes his mind off of everything. He is so hungry. Even the hospital food looks good.

* * *

Just as Bruce finishes dinner, his parents, brother, and girlfriend run into the room. Debbie grabs him and then starts kissing him. His mother is on the other side of the bed, hugging him as well.

"Bruce, are you OK?" Debbie asked, wiping away the tears.

"Yeah... Not too bad. Just a few aches and pains."

"Oh, we've been so worried!" his mother cried out. "We've been here every day. I'm so sorry. No one was here when you woke up!"

"It's OK... Don't worry about it..."

"I was so scared," his mother said. "I thought we lost you."

"Naw... The Doctor told me it was just a few bumps and bruises. No big deal," not wanting to get everyone worried.

"A couple of casts, too!" his brother said. "Check out that helmet you're wearing."

Bruce reaches up, feeling the thick padding around his head. "Yeah, it does feel like a helmet."

"Are you doing OK?" his father asked. "You have been through some bad times."

"It's not that bad," wondering why everyone is overreacting.

"Haven't they told you?" Debbie asked, kissing him again.

"Told me what? The only thing I know is I have been out for a week. I think that's got something to do with my head," gently tapping on the bandages.

His mother took his hand. "Bruce, it was really bad... They told us you had to be revived several times," then starts crying.

"What do you mean?"

"Son, your heart stopped," his father explained. "When you were in the ambulance, then a couple of times in the emergency room."

"What? You got to be kidding!"

"No, your heart stopped for almost three minutes," his mother added. "Bruce, you died several times."

"They told us you're lucky to be here," Debbie explained. "We thought we lost you," her voice starts to break up.

"Oh, don't worry about it… I feel fine. Just a little tired," not wanting to get his family upset.

He is so shocked to hear all of this for the first time. He had no idea. His injuries are minor, except for the skull fracture. Now, he is wondering how much the doctors aren't telling him.

* * *

Late into the night, more friends and co-workers are showing up. Everyone is bringing flowers, boxes of candy, and fruit baskets. At times, the room is filled. The nurse is always coming in to escort a few out when it gets too loud.

Peter Smith walks in. "Hey, buddy! Good to hear you're up. How are you doing?"

"Not bad…" Bruce replied, glad to see his good friend. "Want a chocolate?" handing him the box.

"My God! You got enough chocolates here to last a few months," seeing all the boxes in the room. "I got some good news for you… Check this out," handing Bruce a large envelope.

Bruce opens it up, pulling out a few sheets of paper. He is so shocked seeing his photo and the review of his work.

"Yep, you're real famous now! I just got this off the Internet. It's all over the news, too. You ought to see the images."

"Are they that good?" Bruce asked.

"You bet! These things are going to rewrite the books. Already, after one week, we see resolution like never before. Congratulations!"

Bruce quickly reads the review. "The preliminary tests are outstanding. I can't wait to get back to the lab to check on the numbers."

"We've been running around ragged with all the press. Everyone is asking about you."

"Why so soon?" Bruce asked. "We just got the numbers. It's going to take a while to check things out."

"That was last week… We checked the numbers. Paul did a press release, and it went all over the world. It's been on TV and the front page of every newspaper."

"I keep forgetting…" Bruce said, confused about what day it was. "I wasted a whole week in here."

"Well, things have been in motion for a week. Once the news people heard about your accident, it made it worse. We got them camped out in front of the lab."

Bruce laughed. "Sounds like a slow news day."

"When you get back up on your feet, you're going to be doing a lot of interviews."

"I can't be bothered with them. You guys can handle that. I got more important things to do. I need to get back to the lab to check things out."

The nurse walks in. "Sorry, visiting time is up. He needs to get some rest," seeing Bruce is getting tired.

Everyone slowly gets up. All are congratulating Bruce, wishing him well. The last ones to leave are his family. They have been here all day long. After many hugs and kisses, the only one left is his brother.

"Maybe they can let me stay?" John asked.

"Go home and rest…" Bruce replied. "Not much to do here. I'll probably sleep for a while."

"Is there anything you need?" John asked. "I can bring you something to eat or maybe a book to read."

Bruce laughed. "I got enough chocolates and fruit here to last a week or more. Although there is one thing you can do for me."

"Sure, what is it?"

Seeing how his brother is looking a little too serious. "It's a little embarrassing, but can you change my bedpan?" trying not to laugh.

"You want me to get the nurse?" so startled by the strange request.

"Oh, no, they're too busy. You can do it. It's no big deal. I have been working on it all day long, and it might be full. You may have to take it in there and dump it out. You'll probably need to wash it out, too," pointing over to the bathroom.

Bruce is fighting hard not to laugh. The terrified look on his brother's face said it all. John is hesitant, not knowing what to do. He keeps looking at the door, hoping a nurse will walk in. Slowly, he makes his way over to the bed.

Bruce can't hold back any longer, laughing out loud. "Oh, the look on your face... I got you good!"

John almost collapses. Sweat is running down his face. He smiles and then starts laughing.

"Yeah, you're back to normal," leaning over, hugging his brother.

Bruce is shocked, seeing how his brother is getting emotional. "There is one thing... The next time you come to visit, stop by Fatburger. I can really go for one of those cheeseburgers. I want the big fries, too."

John laughed. "You got it! I'll see you tomorrow at lunchtime."

"Don't tell the nurses. You may have to sneak it in. You should see the crap they are making me eat here. It's all healthy food!"

The nurse comes in. "OK, time for you to go. We need to do some tests on him."

"Oh, great!" Bruce said. "More poking and prodding."

John laughed. "Take good care of him... Make sure he gets a sponge bath," winking at the nurse as he walks out.

"Thanks for stopping by... See you tomorrow!" Bruce shouted, waving at his brother.

The nurse smiles at Bruce. "Oh, I'm glad you're looking forward to a sponge bath. It just so happens that you are scheduled for one."

"So, when do we start?" not believing his luck.

She starts giggling. "Oh, no... Not me. You're scheduled with Nurse Roberts."

A man walks in, pushing a cart, wearing orange and yellow scrubs.

"I guess I'll leave you two alone. Mr. Rollin, this is Nurse Roberts. He'll be giving you your sponge bath. I'll check back with you shortly," then promptly leaves the room.

Bruce cringes, not seeing that coming, wondering how much longer he is going to be stuck here. Feeling much better, he is ready to go home. Especially now, with this guy preparing to give him a sponge bath.

* * *

Discovery

Bruce wakes up early in the morning. He is not looking forward to another day lying about in bed. Feeling a lot better and much stronger, he can at least get up and hobble to the bathroom on his own. At least there are no more bedpans or sponge baths from here on out.

While eating breakfast, a woman walks in. "Mr. Rollin, how are you doing?" looking over his medical chart.

"Not too bad... Actually, I'm ready to get out of this place. How much longer will this be? I want to go home."

"We have a few more tests. With the head injury you received, we're going to monitor you for a few days."

Bruce notices something odd about this woman. He has never seen her before and is wearing a strange, colorful outfit. Most doctors wear white lab coats with a stethoscope around their necks. Just by her disposition, he knows she is a doctor, doing nothing but flipping through his medical charts.

"Mr. Rollin, have you experienced any unusual dreams?"

Before he can answer, Dr. Anderson walks in. Right away, he could tell that she was not too happy with this other doctor.

"Excuse me, doctor... You have no right to be in here!" taking away the medical chart.

"I have every right!" the other doctor yells out.

"Not until the administrator approves it. This is my patient. Please leave!"

The doctor turns to Bruce. "I'll be back..." then promptly leaves the room.

"What's going on?" Bruce asked.

"I'm sorry, but she is not allowed to see you until it's been approved," Doctor Anderson replied.

Bruce doesn't think too much about it. He is so tired of these doctors making him do the same old tests over and over. The whole hospital thing is getting old. After reading the information he got from Peter, he is ready to go back to the lab. After years of work, he finally has a major breakthrough, and now he is wasting time in a hospital room.

* * *

For the rest of the day, friends and family have been dropping by to cheer him up. More flowers and even an illegal cheeseburger are brought in. Debbie, Bruce's girlfriend, never leaves his side. Someone is always with him.

The big cheeseburger and fries make Bruce's day. His brother John pretends to eat it when the doctors and nurses are in the room. Although, the nurses were getting suspicious and made John take it all out to the hallway to finish eating. Bruce is mad, but at least he could eat half before they took it away.

Peter finally shows up with Bruce's iPad from work. Being in the hospital, Bruce is oblivious to what's been happening to all of his research. Right away, he is on the Internet. To his astonishment, the test results have spread worldwide.

After checking his email for the first time in a week, it'll take a month to go through them all. There are also dozens of requests for speaking engagements from all over the world. With all of this going on, he is stuck in the hospital. Now, more than ever, he wants to get out of this hospital and back to his lab.

With all the commotion going on in his room, Bruce occasionally sees that strange doctor out in the hallway. Constantly pacing back and forth, she never enters the room. At one point, he sees her with a group of other doctors arguing about something. Somehow, he knows he is the topic of this heated conversation in the hallway. He is starting to wonder if they have told him everything.

***

Days later, Bruce is scheduled for another batch of tests. He is wheeled down to the examination room again. Every day, he has been going through the same test over and over again. More CT scans, MRIs, eye and hearing tests. He figures all this must be for the head injury.

Once the tests are over, Bruce expects to return to his room. This time he is going somewhere different. At the end of the long hallway is a group of doctors and nurses huddled together, discussing something. From their posture, some look somewhat irritated.

"Bruce, we have someone here who wants to talk with you," Doctor Anderson said. "This is optional. You don't have to participate. This has nothing to do with me as your doctor."

"So, what's this all about?" he asked, seeing all these official-looking people standing around.

A woman walks out of the room. "Hello, Bruce... I'm Doctor Brown," reaching out to shake his hand.

"Oh, Hi..." Bruce said, shaking her hand. "Is this a new test or something?"

Everyone is looking awkward for some reason. There is nothing but silence.

Doctor Anderson approaches Bruce. "Do you recognize this person?"

He looks up at her for a few seconds. "Yes, I think she was in my room a few days ago," remembering the unusual hospital clothes she had on.

The doctor smiles at him. "Is there anything you would like to ask me?"

He just shrugs his shoulders, having no idea why he is here, then sees her name tag. "Holy shit! You're Karen Brown! Yeah, I got a big question. What's the deal with all those signs?"

She glances over at the other doctors, "If you don't mind, I have a lot of work to do here," motioning to the nurse to bring Bruce into the room.

Doctor Brown quickly shuts the door and can't help from smiling. The other doctors constantly ridicule her and her work, but occasionally, she gets lucky. She has been waiting for someone like Bruce for a long time.

The nurse pushes the wheelchair in front of the desk. She is no ordinary doctor. Seeing all the strange posters on the wall, Bruce is getting very curious about this.

A man walks in with a video camera mounted on a tripod. "You're just in time," Dr. Brown said. "Put the camera in the corner. We'll be ready in a few minutes."

"So, I guess you have some questions for me?" Dr. Brown asked, sitting down behind her desk. "If you don't mind, I'll be recording this session," pointing over at the camera.

"As long as you don't put it on the Internet," he replied.

"Oh, we don't do that… I have a very strict doctor-patient relationship. Everything you say will be kept within these walls."

"We're ready!" the man said, operating the camera.

Dr. Brown gets very serious. "This is Dr. Karen Brown talking with patient Bruce Rollin. This is the first discovery session," then motions over to Bruce.

He glances over at the video camera, feeling awkward. "So, where do we start?"

"Tell me why you are here?" not wanting to feed any information to him.

There is a long pause. "I guess the first thing is... Why all the signs? Why do you want someone to ask for you?"

"Where did you see the signs?" she asked.

He thinks about it for a moment. "It's still a big blur, almost like a dream... Those signs in bold colors really got me to notice them in the first place. Why do you put them up on top of those cabinets and bookcases? No one is going to see them up there."

"You did! Actually, I have a few in here. One is on top of my bookcase over there, and more is on that top shelf."

Bruce thinks this is odd. "Why? No one is going to notice them unless they're eight or nine feet tall."

She smiled. "But, again, you did... You are barely six feet tall. So, how did you see them?"

The question got him thinking. If the signs are up so high, how did he see them? He has been trying to recall what happened. The accident is still one big blur. With all the drugs they have been giving him, he is having a hard time distinguishing what is real and what is a dream.

He hesitates before answering. "I think it was a dream... A really weird dream I had. I was swimming somewhere. It was hard to focus. Everything was blurry."

"Think back... Where were you?" she asked.

There is another long pause. "I was in a hospital... It's odd when you think about it. I was just floating around, almost like swimming in the ocean. It was a really strange dream. I remember these people who were covered in blue clothes and even had blue hats on. I was floating on top of the water, just watching it all. They were all around a table. There were a lot of lights. The next thing I knew, I was drifting along. That's when I saw the signs."

"You were looking down on everything?"

"I guess... It was like floating face down in a swimming pool."

"So, if this were that room, where would you be?" she asked.

He looks up at the ceiling. "I guess it would be about a foot under the ceiling. That's about how high the water would be."

She picks up a wooden stick with a mirror attached to the end. She holds it up over the top shelf and then angles it to reflect the image of the red sign.

"So, is this what you saw?"

He leans over, seeing the reflection of one of the signs, 'Ask for Karen Brown.' "Yep, that's about it... Looks just like one of those I saw."

"For you to see this sign, you had to be up there, floating up near the ceiling. You saw this in a dream?"

"I think so..."

She puts the mirror away and then places several photos on her desk in front of him. "Does this look familiar?"

He gasped. "That's the place!" seeing the photo taken from above of several doctors standing around a table.

He leans over to look at the other photos of various colored signs on top of the shelves and cabinets. "Yeah, saw those too."

"You saw all of this in your dream?"

"Yeah, strange dream..." then starts feeling a little odd after seeing the photos.

"Bruce, these photos are from one of our emergency rooms here. It wasn't a dream. This was the room you were in after the accident. You lost a lot of blood and then went into cardiac arrest. Your heart stopped for several minutes.

Actually, it occurred three times before they were able to stabilize you."

Bruce didn't say a word, starting to recall the images from that night. Everything has been strange since being in the hospital. So doped up with all the medications, he doesn't know what is real or not.

"Do you want to stop?" she asked.

He shakes his head. "No... I need to know why this is happening. How do I know all this? Basically, what you are saying is that these weird dreams I had were not dreams. I was dead at the time?"

"Technically, no... Your heart stopped, but the brain will continue to operate for up to four minutes before the cells are damaged from lack of oxygen. The entire time, they were pumping oxygen into your lungs while they were trying to resuscitate you. You had what we call an out-of-body experience."

"You got to be kidding?" surprised to hear that, but now it's all making sense.

"You're not alone... That's why I put those signs up there."

He laughed. "So, I died in the operating room, then started floating around?"

"How do you feel about that?" she asked, leaning back in her chair.

He had to laugh again. "I thought it was one hell of a wacko dream... I have been so drugged up. I didn't know what was going on. That was all real?"

"I think so... Tell me what you experienced."

"Now, I think back, it was like floating on top of the water, and I was pushed along like being in a river. You have a floor plan of this building?"

She grabs a rolled sheet of paper from the shelf, unrolling it on top of her desk. "Does any of this look familiar? This is the room you were in," pointing it out to him.

Looking at the floor plans, he sees the path he took across the hospital. "Yeah... I remember being here and then going to the next room. I ended up in this big open area here. Then I went all the way to the waiting room."

"That's pretty much going in a straight line... You said it's like being in a river?"

"Yep, a river with a slow current... The weird part was hitting the walls. It wasn't solid, but it did have density. It slowed you down a little, and I could almost feel it. It's like putting your hand in Jell-O that's not fully set. A lot thicker than water."

"So you drifted to the edge of the building?"

He pauses for a long time. "Yeah… That was the scary part. That was the nightmare of it all. That's one thing I never want to go through again."

"What happened? Can you talk about it?"

He drops his head, burying his face in his hands. "I saw my family out there... They were all hurting. It was like I could feel their pain. Debbie was there, and my mom, dad, and brother. My friends were there too. They were all crying, and it was so sad. It was a horrible thing to see. I tried to talk to them, but it was like I wasn't really there. No one could see or hear me. When I touched Debbie's hand, that's when I noticed something was odd. My hand was almost translucent. It was there, but then it wasn't."

"How do you mean? You could see your hand?"

"In a way, yes... I could almost see right through it. There was also a strange light blue glow all around me," looking down at his left hand.

She reaches down, pulling out a sheet of paper from her desk. "Was it something like this?"

He lit up, seeing the drawing. "Yes, that's it! Where did you get this?"

"Another person who had a similar experience just like you gave this to me. Luckily, he's a good artist. So, did everyone look this way?"

"Not really... I had this blue glow on my arms and legs, like in the picture. But everyone else looked different. It was bizarre. They all had this faint blue glow, more like a light inside their heads. If I wasn't dreaming this, then what was it?"

She pulls out another picture. "Look familiar?"

"That's what I saw! Why does everyone have a blue light inside their heads?"

"That's the big question. Everyone has been debating that for years. People who experienced what you went through saw the same thing."

"Now, I think about it... There was one old man, and he was different. He had this bluish glow around his entire body. That's how I noticed him. There was something else too. At first, no one else could hear me, but then I found out he could. He even talked to me."

Dr. Brown is stunned. "My God! You were able to communicate with another person?" then she glances over at the cameraman, so shocked at what she is hearing.

Bruce just nods his head, staring at the floor, getting emotional. He now remembers the absolute horror of that strange dream and what it meant.

"What is it?" the doctor asked, seeing him getting upset for the first time.

"I can remember now... It's the old man. He was the one that really scared me."

"The one that talked to you?"

"Yeah, at first he was like me, not knowing what's happening... He was standing in front of an old woman who was crying. Then he knelt down, putting his arms around her. When he told me that we were here to say goodbye, it all

41

made sense. When I saw him slowly fade away to a point of light, it scared the hell out of me!"

She gasped out loud. "Wait a minute... You saw him dissolve to a point of light! You actually witnessed this?" frantically jotting down notes trying to record every word he said.

He nods his head. "Yeah, it was really weird... All of a sudden, he was nothing but a bead of light."

After writing down a few notes, she continued. "What happened after the old man turned to a point of light?"

"It was so sad... The light circled the old woman a few times. Then it slowly went through the window and up into the sky."

"Did the woman react to it?"

"No, it was like she didn't know he was there. No one knew we were there. No one could see us."

"So, you actually saw this light floating about, going right out the window?"

"Yes, it was like one of those fireflies or lightning bugs going through the room. Now I think about it. I remember seeing other lights just like it floating up and down the halls. Some were going through the walls floating outside. They were so tiny. Some had these little trails following behind. It was like those sparklers we used to have as kids. When you waved them about in the air, they left a trail of light behind. I wonder if those lights were people, like the old man I saw."

"That's a good question... How do you feel about this? Seeing your family and not being able to talk with them?"

"At first, I thought it was just nothing but one bizarre dream. When I saw the old man disappear like that and float away, it struck me. I was like him. I'm standing there in front of my friends and family. I guess I was there to say goodbye," trying to hold back the tears.

The nurse is becoming concerned. "Bruce, you want to go back to your room?" seeing him getting upset.

"No, I'm OK..." wiping away the tears.

"You knew why you were there?" Karen asked.

There is a long pause. "Yeah... It took me a while to figure it out. I was in a hospital waiting room, and I was like the old man. I must have died and didn't know it. I was there to say goodbye to my friends and family."

"How did you feel about that?"

He looks right into the doctor's eyes. "I was mad as hell! I wasn't ready to die. There are a lot of things I want to do with my life! I wasn't going to take it either and basically said no!"

"What happened?"

"I remembered yelling and screaming out loud. I was so pissed off. Then I got this horrible pain in my chest. It was like being on fire. Things started getting blurry, and everything got so bright. I thought that was the end for me."

Karen leans forward. "Then what happened?"

"The next thing I knew, I was on the table with all these doctors around me. That's when I felt this horrible, excruciating pain over my entire body," starting to shutter just thinking about it.

"Do you remember waking up in the emergency room?" the nurse asked.

"Yeah! It's like waking up in the middle of an operation, and you feel everything that they are doing!"

"That's enough!" the nurse said, turning to the doctor. "This is too much for him. He needs to rest," seeing the sweat pouring down his face and looking pale.

"No, we need more time. This is a major breakthrough!" the doctor shouted.

The door opens, and two burly orderlies rush in. "Take Mr. Rollin back to his room," the nurse ordered.

"I'll be needing more sessions with him!" the doctor said, getting mad.

"We'll leave that up to Doctor Anderson!" a man said, entering the room. "We allow you to interview patients, but it's at our discretion. This is a hospital. Our goal here is to treat our patients."

Bruce looks up at the tall man. Wearing a white coat, he thinks this is just another doctor. Seeing the word administrator on his name tag, he knows this guy is in charge.

"Thanks, Doctor Brown!" Bruce said. "I want to talk to you again about this... Let me get some rest first. I'm getting tired."

As they wheel Bruce down the hall, he can hear a big argument going on behind him. Apparently, these people weren't getting along. Whoever this Doctor Karen Brown is, he wants to talk with her again. More than anything, he wants to get to the bottom of this. Being told that he had died several times and after all the strange dreams he has had, it's all starting to make sense.

* * *

Research Lab

After months of recuperating, Bruce finally returns to work after his accident. As soon as he walks in, he is so shocked. Everything is different, and he doesn't even recognize his old lab. Now, it's twice the size and more than doubled the staff.

"Surprise!" everyone yells out as he enters the huge room. "Welcome back, Bruce!"

Bruce is shocked to see the big crowd. "Thanks... Wow, this is a little different from when I was here last," glancing around the room.

The entire room is filled with balloons. Glitter and streamers are showering down from all the Champagne Confetti Poppers. Welcome back banners hang from the walls and ceiling. The tables are filled with an abundance of food and drinks.

"Congratulations!" Paul Anderson shouted, shaking Bruce's hand. "This is all yours. You deserve it. We brought in the best of everything. Anything we missed, just let us know," the administrator boasted.

Bruce is almost lost for words. "This is impressive," somewhat in shock with the changes, especially in Paul's attitude.

For years, Bruce had been begging Paul for more money. They have always been working on a tight budget. He was always scrounging around for anything that could be used. Most of their computers and equipment had been bought from Goodwill or second-hand shops. At times, he used his own money to purchase equipment or supplies.

One by one, everyone comes over to congratulate him, shaking his hand and patting him on his back. He has no clue who these people are. Some of them probably work in other departments, getting in on the free food and drinks.

The worst ones are those wearing suits and ties. These are the grant people or from the government. The big military brass is also here, all dressed up in their uniforms, with their medals and ribbons across their chests.

The new sensor Bruce designed was intended for Astrophysics to explore the universe. He hoped some of the sensors would be given to NASA for the next generation of space telescopes. With all the new investments coming in, Bruce knows much of his work will probably end up in some future spy satellite looking down on the people of Earth.

The celebration has started. Champaign is passed around, with plenty of food to last for hours. Bruce finally sees the five people who made it all happen. Peter Smith, Tom Harris, Lisa Phillips, Sarah Evans, and Maria Garcia are all standing together in the center of the room. Bruce runs over for a big group hug. Everyone applauds and cheers, seeing the big reunion.

For the next couple of hours, Bruce and his team explain how things work. With so much new equipment, Bruce is also learning a few things. Huge monitors display the latest deep-space images. No one would have noticed how far advanced these new images are until the current image is shown first. The before and after images of distant galaxies are astounding. Even the non-technical people are amazed at the brilliant colors and detail.

* * *

Initially, Bruce is thrilled to get back to work. With all the new equipment and unlimited money supply, the lab can produce the sensors in days instead of months. The prototypes were created with obsolete machines, but there is no limit to what they can do now. Unfortunately, he feels that the excitement is over. Even with the new lab and all the extra people, for some reason, none of this seems important anymore.

After all those years of struggling to design the sensor, he can now see the results from all that hard work. In a way, he has accomplished his goal. Now there is a big push to mass-produce the sensors. He loves the creative part, designing something new and revolutionary. Being a factory worker was not part of the plan.

After the accident, Bruce sees life a little differently now. He enjoys being outside more than ever, taking long walks through the forest or on the beach. At times, he spends hours just watching the trees move as the wind gently blows through. Even the sunset is now something he never misses.

The sessions with Doctor Brown enlightens him about the out-of-body experiences. He had read all of her books and attended weekly meetings with people who had gone through similar situations. Part of his therapy is to learn how to deal with it and to put it all in perspective.

Bruce is discovering so many new things in life. He never gave much thought about angels, the afterlife, reincarnation, remote viewing, and the well of souls. Now, he is deep into the metaphysical world, and it's all he thinks about.

* * *

The first test is scheduled for the new production sensor, and Bruce is late as usual. Everyone is patiently waiting, not saying a word.

"Sorry, guys!" Bruce shouted, rushing into the room. "I stopped by the coffee place, and there was a big line today."

47

Tom is getting a little annoyed. "We were just about to start without you..." turning off the lights.

Lisa sets up the program. "So, this is the first low light sensitivity test for unit number RE-105. We're going to start at 0.000001 Lux and move up the spectrum."

They are all looking at Bruce, waiting for his command. "OK, let's see how it does… Go for it!"

Lisa hits the enter key. The program starts sending out signals to the box. The box, as they referred to it, is a ten-meter-long rectangular test chamber made of lead. The box is designed to prevent any interference from local electromagnetic radiation or stray neutrinos striking the sensor, creating false readings. At one end, there is the new sensor, cooled down to minus 270 degrees Celsius using liquid helium. At the far end, the emitter generates electromagnetic radiation at precise increments through the entire spectrum.

The test is long and tedious. The computer is going through the spectrum at various levels. The results are immediately displayed on the big monitor.

"That is amazing!" Bruce shouted. "It's already detecting the faint light levels."

"This is what we were predicting," Maria said, handing the chart to Bruce.

"It looks as if we're doing better than the prototype," Bruce said. "It's a shame we didn't have all these expensive toys years ago."

"Tell that to Paul!" Peter shouted. "We could have gotten the assembly completed a year early. We've wasted so much time scrounging around for equipment instead of working," getting so frustrated with the management.

"That's all in the past…" Bruce remarked. "We're here now, and it's paid off. If we can come up with results like this from all that old obsolete junk we've been working with, just think what we can do now!"

"It's going to be a long wait," Maria said. "I got some other work to do. You want to help me?" glancing over at Lisa and Sarah.

"Sure..." Lisa said. "We'll let the boys watch the clock," walking out of the monitor room.

Peter nudges Bruce's arm. "So, you were just standing in line for coffee? Yeah, right..."

Bruce smiled. "I had a nice big bagel too. You ought to see the clouds out there today. Big white, puffy cumulus clouds slowly move along with the wind. That was a sight for sore eyes. It doesn't get any better than that!"

Peter just shakes his head. "We're rewriting science here, and you're out looking at the clouds!"

"Some of the brass was here yesterday," Tom added, feeling somewhat awkward. "They're asking a lot of questions..."

"Yeah, Bruce..." Peter said. "They're getting concerned about you."

Bruce just shrugs it off. "I'm not going to worry about it. We're a team, and we'll be knocking their socks off," pointing over at the monitor.

"Still, they want to make sure you are OK," Peter said. "It's only been a few months. If it's too much, you can always take a few days off. Maybe a vacation," knowing full well that Bruce is not interested in the project anymore.

"I have had a vacation... Months of sitting around doing nothing," leaning back, slowly closing his eyes.

Peter and Tom look at each other. They know it's getting bad. Bruce designed the most advanced optical sensor in the world. He still has not done any interviews, papers, or anything. Because of the accident, people left him alone to let him recover. With millions of dollars coming in from investors, people with power want results. They also want someone to parade around, and from the looks of things, Bruce is not interested in any of it.

* * *

Late into the night, the tests are over. The results exceed most of their expectations. Bruce slept most of the day in his office so he could spend the night reviewing the results. He is always at his best, working late when no one else is around, no phone calls, or people coming in wanting something. He can concentrate on one thing and can get more things done.

With all the tests completed, he can now do some of his own. He designed this for deep space research, not for spying on people. The main batch of tests is to see if it meets the military's requirements, but he has his own personal tests to perform. He wants to push the envelope on the sensor to see how it really works.

Bruce readjusts the emitter to see how the sensor can detect the lines in the hydrogen emission spectrum. Playing with the settings, he realizes he can filter out the light down to a narrow wavelength. No filters would be required. The sensor can electronically be set to detect any range, but mostly, it can be configured to view an extremely narrow bandwidth. It is something that he wasn't expecting. This feature is more of a mistake, not by design, but it will give them even better results.

* * *

After spending hours with the emitter and sensor, he is curious to see how this will work in a regular digital camera. He remembers they had an old Hasselblad. He finds what he is looking for after rummaging through the cabinets. Luckily, the Hasselblad camera has a removable digital back. With a little bit of work, he might be able to replace the camera CCD with his new sensor.

Removing all the tiny screws, he pops out the original sensor from its backing using a big screwdriver. He cringes, knowing that he has just destroyed a $17,000 camera they bought a few years ago.

After wiring the camera to the input cables, he starts up the program. With the camera up on a tripod, he just points it across the lab. With everything ready, he turns on the camera. After adjusting the light range and sensitivity, the monitor lights up. He is surprised that it actually works. With a little adjustment on the aperture and focus, the image quality from the sensor is fantastic.

He attaches one of their GoPro cameras to the top of the Hasselblad to do some comparative visual tests. The small portable camera makes a perfect viewfinder. Now, he can see where he points the camera before running back to the control room to experiment with the settings.

Bruce plays with the camera settings for hours. Seeing the lab in the different light spectrums gives some impressive results. The heat signature from all the equipment is like looking at a rainbow. The water pipes can be clearly seen behind the walls. Even the stars can be seen through the window. After seeing all those stars, he knows what to do next.

Finding a long cable, Bruce crawls through the window, putting the camera outside and pointing it up at the stars. After getting the cables hooked up, he sees the image on the monitor. This is what it was designed to do. Astronomers throughout the world will be fighting like mad to get this. Unfortunately, the military will be getting the first batch and will probably make sure no one else gets to use these.

Playing with the settings, Bruce realizes he can boost the signal. The monitor flickers at first, and then the image is locked in. He has to blink a few times, not believing his eyes. The image is so clear. It's the kind of quality you get from a huge telescope and not from a little camera. The glow from the Milky Way galaxy can clearly be seen. With the high-resolution sensor, he can zoom in and still see so much detail.

The M81 galaxy is so clear, and the detail is fantastic, and all this is from a standard 90 mm lens.

He finally brings it back in, getting tired of crawling through the window to change the camera position. The one thing he needs is to be able to pan and tilt the camera remotely.

Walking around the lab, Bruce is not finding anything that will work. Not knowing what's in his own lab is getting frustrating. In the last few years, he installed every piece of hardware. He knew what he had and where he bought it. Since his accident, the lab has been filled with so much new equipment he has never seen before. Most of it is still in its original boxes.

He sees what he is looking for, an old security camera that can be operated remotely on the ceiling above the door. Grabbing a ladder, he quickly tears it off the wall. Luckily, the security camera has a standard USB interface. In no time, he has it mounted on top of the tripod.

Bruce sets up the camera with the improvised remote control mount in the middle of the lab. Dragging the long USB cable into the control room, he hooks up the other end of the cable to his laptop.

Using Google, he searches for the driver software. He has the software downloaded within a few minutes and starts operating the camera. The improvised camera mount works perfectly. Now he can point the camera in any direction, all controlled by his laptop in another room.

He is about to put the camera outside but notices the time. Looking out the window, he knows it's too late. The sky is bright, and the sun should be up soon. To his surprise, he has worked all night long.

Another day just started hearing the front door slam as someone walked into the lab. He adjusts the sensor back to the visible light range, and the monitor flickers a few times showing Lisa walking across the room. Bruce rotates the camera keeping her in the frame. He is so amazed by all the details.

After adjusting the sensor to the infrared range, everything giving off heat appears white on the monitor. He can clearly see Lisa sitting in her chair, generating an enormous amount of heat. The sensor even picks up the heat rising above her, looking like smoke from a fire. Even her footprints can clearly be seen where she walked across the room.

Playing with the settings, Bruce's curiosity is getting the best of him. He adjusts the settings from infrared through the visible region, then into the ultraviolet. He is so intrigued by seeing how someone looks through all the wavelengths of light. At the far end of the ultraviolet, everything turns dark on the monitor. He expected this because the air blocks the high-end ultraviolet.

Hearing another loud bang, he knows someone else just came in. He boosts the signal, trying to get something to show up on the monitor. A very faint glow moves across the screen. Then he notices another faint glow where Lisa is sitting.

Staring at the monitor, he doesn't understand why everything is dark after boosting the signal. Glancing down at the controls, he forgot it was at the end of the ultraviolet range. Moving the settings back to the visual spectrum, the monitor lights up. Lisa is sitting in her chair with Maria standing next to her.

He couldn't stop thinking about the weird ultraviolet image when Maria walked in. Nothing should be detected at that range, even after he boosted the signal. He resets everything back to the ultraviolet. The two faint glowing dots reappear. After seeing the visual wavelength image, those faint glows are at the same place where Lisa and Maria are. Zooming in a little, he discovers those faint dots are right on their heads.

Noting the wavelength, he wonders if it's something in their shampoo, or maybe it's their makeup reflecting the ultraviolet light. With a little tweaking, he narrows the wavelength a little more. The faint glow is still there, and it's not feedback or a burned-in defect on the monitor.

Then he sees movement. Maria walks toward the camera, coming to the control room. The faint glow is more prominent, surrounding her face. The glow is following her every move.

"Hey, Bruce!" Maria said, a little startled seeing him in the office.

"Good morning, Maria!"

"When did you get here?" she asked.

"I was up late looking at the data. Then I got sidetracked."

"You were here all night? Is there a problem?"

"No... It looks good. I put it on the shared drive. I think Lisa is checking it out now."

"Oh, good... Here, I got some breakfast tacos," handing him one.

"Perfect! Just what I need."

She sits down in one of the chairs. "It's been a long time since you pulled an all-nighter. What are you up to?" seeing the cables on the floor leading out to the lab.

"Check out the monitor!" moving the settings back and forth through the light spectrum of Lisa sitting out in the lab.

"Is that one of ours?" she asked, staring at him.

"Yep... I have been testing it out. Call it a little freelancing project."

She gasped out loud. "What? We're supposed to give those to the military. They're first on the list. They paid a hefty price for that and expected them to be delivered on time!"

He just glares at her. "Oh, that one was flawed. It didn't pass the first batch of tests."

"Oh, great! Well, you just put that in the logs. I'm not! This is all your doing," pointing her finger at his face, not believing his story.

"I had to do some extra tests just to make sure they were working. I retrofitted one of the cameras I found."

She looks out the door seeing the cables leading up to the camera. "I hope you didn't damage it. That is a very expensive camera out there!"

"No... Just a little modification. I attached one of the sensors to the back."

She gets real close to the monitor, examining the resolution. "This is at room temperature?"

He smiled. "Yeah... Pretty good, wouldn't you say? I also got it hooked up to a remote-controlled mount," reaching over to his laptop to change the camera position.

She laughed. "I see you've been a busy little bee. Oh, I love to see how it works on the telescope!"

"That's the first thing I thought about!" reaching over to the keyboard. "I had it outside for a while. Check out these images."

Maria's mouth drops wide open, seeing the images. "We got to send these to the astrophysics department."

He nods. "These things are way better than we thought."

Hearing voices in the lab, she looks up at the monitor. "Well, they're all here. You better hide your little experiment. You don't want Paul finding out about this."

"I know... Go out and get their attention. Maybe put the breakfast tacos on Lisa's desk so I can hide the camera."

The plan worked well. Putting the rest of the breakfast tacos on the far side of the lab gives Bruce a chance to put the camera away without anyone else noticing. With the military watching over things, all personal experiments are now forbidden. Everything has to be pre-approved and justified. He knows the worst part of accepting money for research. You eventually end up losing control of your own project and end up being an employee.

* * *

Group Therapy

Bruce arrives early for his therapy group. With Dr. Jack Steward as the guest speaker giving a talk about reincarnation, Bruce knows there will be a big crowd today. Initially, he thought all this was a big scam, but his experiences after the accident may give him some answers.

After reading a few of Dr. Steward's books, Bruce finds it all so fascinating. Learning about life after death is one thing, but finding out that one could live many lives gives him a new outlook on things. Hearing how some people could speak in ancient dialects or foreign languages and describing old villages that no longer exist is something he is really interested in learning. Even more fascinating is learning how some of these people recall all the details about their past lives and even how they died.

"I'm glad to see you're here today!" Karen shouted, walking across the room to meet her famous patient, Bruce Rollin.

"Hi, Karen! I didn't want to miss this one. There's a big crowd here tonight," noticing more people are here than usual.

"Oh, he's good! He is going to show us some of his new findings. We also get a preview of his upcoming book."

"Yeah, I read his last one. That was about four years ago. I can't wait to see what he's got in his new book."

She holds up the same book. "I brought mine here today, and he signed it! His new book is going to be even better."

"Oh, I didn't think of that... I wonder if I can get him to sign this?" holding up his iPad.

She laughed. "You may not want his autograph in permanent ink on that fancy toy of yours."

"Well, I brought my iPad today to show you something. You may find this right up your street."

"What is it?" she asked.

"You remember how I was telling you about this new device I am testing?" looking around, making sure no one else was too close to hear.

"Oh, the top-secret one we ain't supposed to know about?"

He glares at her. "No, the other one... Anyway, I was playing around to see how it works in a regular camera. When someone walked past it, I got some strange images up in the ultraviolet range," holding up the iPad to show her.

She is confused, seeing the dark image. "I don't see anything."

He turns up the brightness. "One is here, and there's the other," pointing it out to her.

She leans over to get a closer look. "It's very faint whatever it is… All I see are two faint blue smudges?"

"Check this out..." swiping his finger across the screen to display the next image. "This is a composite of the ultraviolet on top of the normal visible light image. Look where those two glowing things are."

Her mouth drops open. "It has to be a fluke. Is this the only one?"

He moves his finger across the screen again. "There's plenty more. This was a live video feed. You can watch the video, too, if you want. I didn't think anything of it until later.

Initially, I thought it was detecting their makeup or shampoo, but as you can see in the other images, it's not the case."

"It looks as if it's following them around… What exactly is it?"

He shrugs his shoulders. "Not sure... This is unusual. I thought it was a heat signature, like the infrared images. But, the infrared will show heat from the entire body. For some reason, it's only around their heads."

"Maybe you're detecting the brain's EEG. Normally, to detect that, you'll need direct contact with the skin using electrodes. That will be fantastic if that's what this is!"

"I don't think so…" Bruce said. "Those frequencies are way down low. Maybe 250 to 2,500 Hertz."

"So, what would these be at?"

"Oh, these are extremely high frequencies. It took me a while to figure out the wavelength, but it's precisely 299.704458 nanometers. It's a unique wavelength."

"What's so special about that number?" she asked.

He tries to explain it so that she can understand. "It's an extremely narrow range. It'll be like listening to an orchestra playing, and then someone drops a pin on the stage. You would need to filter out a lot just to hear that pin drop. Since the pin emits a sound at a precise wavelength, most sensors would never pick it up. Too many other sounds would mask it."

"So, how did you detect this?"

"It was just the way we designed the sensor that made it possible. You may be right. It was just a fluke."

She watched the video several times. "You do know what this means?"

He smiles, nodding his head. "If it weren't for the accident, I would never give it a second thought, but I have seen this before."

"Do you think it's the same thing?"

He shrugs. "It could be… It is hard to say. I think we need to do a lot more tests to find out."

"Can we get our hands on that camera?" she asked, getting excited.

Again, he smiles. "I sort of borrowed it for a short time. It's at home, hidden away. Hopefully, no one will find out it's missing from the lab."

Karen notices Dr. Stewart is getting ready for his talk. "We need to get some people to view this," handing back the iPad. "I think you've stumbled on something very important here."

The room is packed. Usually, only about a dozen people attend, but today, there are over a hundred. Bruce thought it would mostly be the old hippie crowd, but a wide range of people are here. Dr. Jack Stewart is famous, and reincarnation and past life regression is a big hit.

* * *

Bruce is up all night thinking about Dr. Stewart's new theories. Hearing about old souls and reincarnation is so intriguing. He is fascinated by the subject, reading all the latest research about multiple lives and how people are able to recall details under hypnosis.

A lot of it is starting to make sense after reading up on the out-of-body experiences. To his surprise, many people have gone through the same thing. Initially, he thought he was having a bunch of weird dreams. Now he is wondering if this all might be for real. Talking about it is helping him come to terms with it all.

The group sessions are helping. Talking with other people who also went through the same near-death experience makes it a little easier to deal with someone who can relate to it. The floating about and seeing family, and worse, other people who had died, are common to everyone.

The glowing orbs are the most intriguing of them all. Having one of them move through his body and then seeing someone else's life experiences is something he can't get out of his mind. Were these glowing orbs someone's spirit or soul? Seeing the old man dissolving into a point of light seems to confirm the theories. There have been many heated discussions trying to explain it.

Bruce knows it's just his word, but there has to be a way to prove it. No matter how many times he tells the story, there are always people snickering behind his back, not believing any of it. The proof is what he needs. He is not interested in proving it to others but mostly to himself. There are so many unknowns and unanswered questions. Finding the answers will be his life's goal from here on out.

* * *

Word spreads fast about Bruce's secret experiments with his new sensor. He made sure to keep it all anonymous, but some of the images were sent across the world to the paranormal society.

Karen Brown sets up an impromptu meeting with the leading researchers to view Bruce's test results. Nothing like it has ever been seen, and it could be the evidence they all have been searching for after all this time.

Bruce drives to the University for the big secret meeting. He makes sure no one is following him, always driving about to various places in town. His project is Top Secret, and if the military finds out about his little experiments, they will fire him in a minute. He knows the people at work are already suspicious of him after the accident.

Parking in front of the science building reminds him of the good old days. He has fond memories of his college days, but he hated every minute of it during that time. The tests were the worst of it all. The tests were not designed to see what you had learned but more of a way of filtering out the top five percent of the students. As far as he was concerned, the test scores really reflected how the instructor was able to teach the material.

Bruce always had problems with the professors at his college. They always put themselves up on pedestals, constantly telling all the students how superior they are. Years later, after working in the real world, Bruce now knows how incompetent those professors were. None of them ever had a real job and wouldn't last one day in the real world.

Walking down the hallway, Bruce is starting to wonder if anyone is going to show up for this meeting. No one else is around. The halls are empty. He expected to see some people standing about, but the place is deserted. As soon as he steps into the room, he is shocked to see the huge crowd.

"Hi, Bruce!" Karen shouted. "I thought you got cold feet and weren't going to show up."

"I wouldn't miss this for anything!" hugging Karen. "I had to take the long way to make sure no one was following me. Also, I got some more video and images," holding up his iPad.

"Good... I'll get them to set up the big screen," waving at one of the assistants to help.

Bruce notices a lot of people that he has never seen before. He is getting a little suspicious. Any of these could be a plant. He is always wary of spies and espionage, which is a big problem in this new high-tech business. Once he got the big military funding, he was paranoid, but after the accident, it's worse. Now, he always has this feeling that big brother is watching over him.

Karen escorts him over to a small group of people at the front of the room. "Bruce, I'd like you to meet some of my associates. This is Bill Davis, Dr. Jason Lee, Linda Clark, Dr. Laura Scott, and the infamous Dr. Mark White."

Bruce shakes everyone's hand. He is stunned, recognizing all their names. These are some very famous people, and many have published books and been on TV. Even more intriguing, these people are all here to see him.

"It's nice to meet you all," Bruce said. "I read all your books and your research. It's an honor to be here."

"The honor is all ours," Linda Clark said. "I read about your work. The last article in Scientific America was astounding. It looks like you might be rewriting a lot of science books."

"Yes, it was brilliant!" Bill Davis shouted out, shaking his hand again. "I can't wait to see these images! I heard so much about them. I'm curious to know why this new camera sensor is so different from what's currently being used."

Bruce has to think of an easy way to explain it. "Let's see... As you know, most camera sensors are nothing more than a small half-inch silicon wafer that's filled with little buckets called pixels that gather light. Most cameras today are about 3,000 by 5,000 pixels, giving you over 15 million-pixel resolution. They work by the light hitting the pixels, giving you the image. Since light is nothing more than electromagnetic radiation or waves, I took a different approach."

"Similar to radio waves or even sound waves?" Linda asked.

"In a way, yes... They are all waves, and that's the problem. Visible light has many wavelengths, but we see them as colors. Most camera sensors just gather the red, blue, and green wavelengths. From those base colors, you can generate all the other colors. The trouble with that is it does leave out all the high-end ultraviolet, the low-end infrared, and a lot more. We wanted the entire spectrum, as much as we can get."

"So, how did you do it?" Bill asked.

"Can you believe it was initially an accident? I discovered a way of detecting light at the molecular level. With a little experimenting, I was able to create these ultra-thin layers to detect a very precise electromagnetic wavelength. By changing how close the molecules are packed together, it changes the wavelength it detects. So, I just made a whole bunch of them and stacked them up. Each one will detect a different wavelength with a little overlap. That overlap will get all the ones in between."

"Sounds like one of those sand screens," Linda said. "We used those on the beach in Alaska looking for diamonds. Each layer has different size screens that filters out the big stuff at the top."

Bruce smiles. "That's about the way it is. That's a good way to describe how it works."

"It's three-dimensional?" Jason asked. "Don't the ones in the front block the other wavelengths coming in?"

Bruce shakes his head. "Nope... That's the best part. We put the short wave layers up front so the long waves pass right through. Each layer does not impede the other waves. There is no deterioration at all. Think of each layer as a tuning fork. It only vibrates at its designed frequency."

"What about the envelope?" Mark asked. "What is the quantum efficiency?"

"It's a straight line across the board, about 92%. We went from 50 nanometers down to 50 micrometers."

Mark is shocked to hear that. "You got to be kidding?"

"Nope... We centered it on the visible light range but didn't expect the results that we got. It's well beyond the specs."

"Damn, that will make one hell of a good space telescope!"

"That was the plan... Unfortunately, the astronomy people don't pay that well. The military and a few others that

I can't mention bankrolled it. Those test satellites cost lots of money. Hopefully, we'll get one or two out of the deal."

"How were you able to build up the layers?" Jason asked.

"Simple… It's like spraying paint on a car. You just keep adding more and more, and it's all automated, too. We got the process down now, so we have about an 85% success rate."

"That's pretty good," Jason said. "I also heard you can adjust it to filter out certain wavelengths?"

"Yes, that's the best part of all. The sensor can be controlled electronically. We can adjust the envelope to cover the entire spectrum or down to an extremely narrow wavelength. We can also move it up and down the scale."

"I don't understand," Karen remarked. "What's this envelope?"

"Think of a piano with 88 keys. You can put your hand down and hit five keys at once, and that would be the envelope. You can move up and down the scale by pressing five keys at a time. Maybe you want just one key, or you can push all the keys down at once. We can do that to the sensor by using a computer. That allows us to filter out the light we want to see. We can also adjust the sensitivity of each layer, boosting the signal to pull out the faintest level of light."

"It still sounds like gibberish to me," Karen remarked, shaking her head, still not understanding all this technical jargon.

"Dr. Brown, we are ready here," the assistant said. "Bruce, all you have to do is set your iPad Wi-Fi to this account," handing him a slip of paper.

In less than a minute, Bruce has the huge flat-screen monitor mirroring the screen of his iPad. He is a little nervous. These are some industry leaders here, and he is about to make a presentation to them all. His research with his new sensors goes back only a few years, but this group they have been doing research for decades.

Bruce starts, clearing his throat. "Again, I'm honored to be here. This is a first for me, especially talking about this new discovery. As you know, our new sensors are working better than expected. Here are some of the published images we got from the deep sky survey," displaying a few of the samples that went out to the public.

"These are impressive!" Mark White said. "It's remarkable how you're able to record infrared all the way up to the ultraviolet. Is this a composite image?"

"Oh no, this is one image. I think this is about a five-minute exposure. We had this wide open to cover the entire light spectrum."

Mark is shocked. "You can get all this from one exposure?"

Bruce smiled. "Oh yes... It can even go beyond that. These are just the published ones. The next batch of images is from the ones they don't want people to know about," opening the next folder on his iPad.

Looking out at the crowd, Bruce can see they are all absolutely stunned. "As you can see... It's far better than what's been made available to the public," showing the first image.

"Unbelievable!" Mark shouted out. "Will they release any more of these? Are the satellites going to be available to the universities for research?"

Bruce shrugs his shoulders. "There is only one satellite now that we're using to test things out, maybe after a few years. Most likely, the military will have a dozen up there pointing down at the earth for their little spy games. It'll probably be like the space telescope where we just get the one. NASA has a few people on the team to make sure the astronomy people don't get left out."

"What about the images Doctor Brown told us about?" Laura asked.

"Ahh, yes, the good stuff," Bruce boasted. "I have done a little experimenting on my own. I hooked one of the sensors to the back of a regular camera. I just attached it with duct tape, but it works. It wasn't cooled down like the satellite, but it works just as good," tapping his finger on the screen, opening the folder to display the next set of images.

Everyone gasped out loud, seeing the images.

"I was just playing with the settings going through the entire light spectrum when I discovered this," Bruce explained. "These are images of one of my co-workers when she came in. What you see here is the faint blue glow. It's superimposed over the regular image to show how it's oriented right where her face is," pointing to the screen.

"Notice the blue, glowing things are right where their heads are," Karen said. "See how it moves with them as they walked about," as the various images are displayed on the screen.

"Could this be a reflection of something?" Laura asked. "Are you sure they are emitting the light?"

"From some of my other recordings, I get this from all angles."

"You have a video of this, too?" Dr. Lee asked.

"Yes, I have several videos. Most of these are still images from the video."

"So, this only shows up at 299 Nanometers?" Bill asked.

"Precisely 299.704458 Nanometers!" Bruce answered. "It's such a narrow bandwidth. The wavelength is so precise. Of all the ultraviolet sensors I tested out, not one will even pick this up. It's like going out fishing with a casting net with a four-inch mesh. You may catch some big fish, but anything under four inches will flow right through. So, in a way, most people don't know about this because they've never seen or detected it. We just got lucky, but if it weren't for my accident, I would never have thought twice about it."

"It looks like a little blue light bulb inside their heads," Linda commented. "Could this be heat we're looking at?"

"No... That would show up on the entire body," Bruce explained. "I suspect it's a form of energy, as you can see. I panned the camera around at all the equipment, and there was nothing else that emitted this wavelength. The weird part is that it's always at the center of the brain. No other part of the body has this. Also, this does not show up in animals, just people."

"You think this is the same as what you saw after your accident?" Dr. Scott asked.

Bruce hesitates. "The more I think back about it, maybe... Most of the people I saw in the waiting room also had this faint blue light just inside their heads. I was only a few feet away and could clearly see it."

"I understand that you had the same blue glow," Dr. Scott added.

"For me, it was different. I could see it was around my hands, arms, and legs. I never saw myself in a mirror, so I assumed it was all over me. Only two other people had the same glow all over their bodies. Everyone else, it was only around the heads. It was weird. Then, when I saw this. Yeah, it's not as clear but similar," pointing up to the screen.

"So, everyone has this blue light?" Linda asked.

"At first, I thought that was true. I had the camera pointing out my apartment window one day. I was recording people in the playground across the street. I noticed that kids under three or four years old, for some reason, don't," displaying a few images.

"Why is that?" Linda asked, looking over at Karen.

"Your guess is as good as mine," Karen said. "There are a few theories, but we need more test subjects."

"One of the possibilities is that they're too small, and it's not bright enough to detect from that distance," Jason suggests. "Maybe, if we get a little closer, we can pick something up."

"Maybe, or maybe not," Bruce said, with a sheepish smile on his face. "We'll let you look at all the images and video, then you decide for yourself."

"You said you still have access to the camera?" Linda asked.

Bruce nods. "Yes, I have been reluctant to take it outside, but as Karen said, we need more test subjects. Most of what I have is friends coming over or, as you can see here, people walking down the street or in the park. We need more of a controlled environment. Also, not everyone is the same. Some people are brighter than others. Why? I'm not too sure…" displaying more images.

Bruce hits the slideshow button to display the rest of the images and videos. He knows it's going to take a long time to understand all of this. These people are the best in their fields of research, and he can't wait to start working with them. Unfortunately, if he gets caught, he will lose everything, his research, job, and reputation.

The screen goes blank at the end of the slideshow. "I got one more video that I know all of you will love!" Bruce boasted. "Especially for you, Karen… I haven't told you about this one. I left the best for last!"

After tapping the screen a few times, he opens one folder hidden deep within his iPad. The video plays on the big screen.

"So, what are we looking at?" Karen asked.

"The scene is one you have seen before of the park with people walking about and children playing on the swing sets.

One family is sitting on a blanket with a little girl, maybe three years old."

"So, what's so special about this?" Karen asked.

Bruce points to the family sitting on the blanket. "These people are out having a picnic. You can see the blue glows on the mother and father, but then there is nothing on the little girl. Watch what happens here."

"I wonder why the little kids don't have the blue glow?" Bill asked.

"Initially, I thought maybe they're too small to detect, but watch this," Bruce said.

As the video plays out, a small white dot floats across the park. "Look at this!" Bruce points to the screen.

"Looks like a firefly!" Karen said.

"Is it a bird?" Laura asked.

"That's what I thought by the way it was flying about," Bruce explained. "The one thing I did notice is no one else sees it. I could see it on the monitor, but nothing was there when I looked out the window."

The small white dot circles around the family while they are sitting on the blanket. Then it stops, almost hovering right in front of the man and woman.

"It has to be a hummingbird to do that," Laura said. "Maybe a big bumblebee!"

Bruce shakes his head. "No, there was nothing there."

"That's right, they're not reacting to it," Karen said, jumping up out of her chair to get a closer look. "They don't even see it!"

Bruce points to the screen. "Watch what happens!"

The small light slowly circles around the little girl. The girl is too busy playing with her doll and doesn't react to the light either. The light stopped, slowly approaching her, then went straight to her face. The little girl immediately responded, falling down.

"Oh, my God!" Laura shouted out. "It hit her right in the face!"

"Is she all right?" Karen asked, glancing over at Bruce.

Again, he points to the screen. "Watch!"

The little girl slowly sits up. She looks around and then starts laughing. Within a minute, a small blue glow shows up on the screen. The girl gets up and runs over, hugging her mother. Now, the screen shows three people with faint blue glows.

"What did we just witness?" Linda asked.

Bill Davis is so stunned, holding his hands over his mouth. "My God! It's the Well of Souls!"

Everyone is so shocked at what they have just witnessed.

"Play it back!" Jason shouted out. "I got to see it again. Slow it down, too!"

"You do know what this is, don't you?" Karen asked, looking over at Bruce.

"I think so… Maybe... You tell me what it is."

"You might have just recorded the first evidence of life after death! Reincarnation, a lost soul, coming back to live another life again," rushing over to hug Bruce.

"Do you have any more videos of these moving lights?" Bill asked.

"In the original videos, I saw a couple of things moving about, but it could have been a bird or bug in front of the lens. Back then, all I had was the ultraviolet recording. So, I didn't have the normal visual to compare it to."

"I don't understand?"

"All these images and videos you have seen today are from two cameras. The blue glow is from the new camera sensor. The other is from a regular video camera with a CCD sensor. I got both of them attached, so the images you see here are a composite of the two. In this way, we can see the normal video in addition to the blue, glowing things. Otherwise, you would only see a black screen with the blue lights moving about."

"Is that little floating light on the regular video?" Karen asked.

"No… At first, I thought it was a bird or something. I looked but didn't see a thing on the regular video. I was able to zoom in and look for shadows, but there was nothing. No one reacted to it either, like they didn't see it."

"We need to start some controlled tests," Laura said. "I can set things up in my office. No one will know what we're doing. I can mask it as part of my research if anyone gets suspicious. My office is down in the basement of this building, so it'll be perfect."

"I agree!" Karen said. "We need to get that camera in a secure location before someone finds out about it and takes it away."

"We need to do it fast," Bruce said. "They already got the military people doing inventory and watching everything we're doing. I have a feeling they're keeping an eye on us outside the job, too. We need to make sure we're not seen together when we leave here."

"Is it that bad?" Karen asked.

He nods his head. "Yeah! When you have someone escorting you to the men's room, it's getting bad. The security is now so tight. It's not a pleasant place to work anymore. They constantly ask us what our plans are for the evening or the weekend, like they're really interested. I have a feeling they are watching us all the time."

"When can we make the move?" Laura asked.

"Tonight would be good," Bruce said. "The sooner, the better, as far as I'm concerned. You have a safe?"

"Yes, it's a fireproof one. I keep all my documents in it. It's big enough to hold your camera and more. It's tucked away in the back corner, and most people don't even know it's there."

"Perfect!" Karen shouted. "Let's make plans to get this started. We need time schedules and equipment moved in, but mostly a cover story."

"I can handle that," Laura said. "It just so happens. I'm about to start this new research project. It'll blend in perfectly with what we're really doing. No one will suspect anything."

"What type of research?" Bruce asked, a little concerned, hearing that they wanted to go to the public with this.

"I'm going to need some test subjects for my reincarnation research. We'll bring in lots of people. Have them fill out a few questionnaires and take their photo so we can keep them on file. Being a college in California, we'll get plenty of willing participants!"

Bruce laughed. "That will work just fine. It's just what we need."

* * *

A few days later, Karen, Bruce, Laura, Bill, and Dr. Stewart have their first secret meeting in one of the library's study rooms. Their goal is to determine how to begin this research and decide the best use of the camera.

"Welcome, everyone!" Karen said as Dr. Stewart walked into the room. "Have a seat, Jack. We're about to begin."

"Sorry I'm late," Dr. Steward said. "It took me a while to find this place."

"Don't worry about it. Laura got a little carried away with all the spy stuff. She gave us all different instructions. She even made us park in various places on campus so no one would see us walking in together."

Laura laughed. "Don't blame me! I'm new at this spy game stuff," glancing over at Bruce.

"I thought you did a good job," Bruce replied, even though it took him a while to figure out the instructions as well.

Karen stands up. "Well, this is our first meeting. I guess I need to remind everyone this is a very sensitive situation we are dealing with here. If any of this gets out, it'll end this project real quick. Bruce will need to be kept anonymous for the entire project. There can be no emails or phone calls. Don't refer to him by name. There is a good chance that he is being watched. So that's why we need to be very careful not to be seen together."

"Do we give him a code name?" Laura asked.

Bruce just smiled. "Sure... How about Espionner?"

"That sounds like a good one!" Laura remarked. "We should all have code names," jotting it down in her notes.

Dr. Stewart laughs out loud. "Yep, nobody will be able to figure out that one. You got to call it as you see it, so I guess mine would be Hypnotiseur."

"Perfect!" Bruce said, trying not to laugh. "That really suits you!"

Karen is a little unsure about this, seeing the smirk on Bruce's face. "So, what's wrong with code names? That's what they do in the movies."

Bruce is trying not to laugh. "Using code names is just fine. We do it all the time at work."

"What's so funny?" Karen shouts out, seeing them both smiling.

"I guess you don't speak French," Dr. Stewart said. "Espionner is French for the word spy... I won't tell you what mine is. It's a secret."

Karen gives them a mean look. "You guys, stop playing around and get serious."

"Well, we got the camera locked away in a secure location," Bruce said, trying to get the meeting started on the right track. "So, where do we begin? What do we want to look for first?"

"I think we need to focus on one thing up front," Karen said. "We all have our own research, but we need to pick something that we can all use to get things rolling."

Bill raises his hand. "All of our research is somewhat similar. The one thing we need more than anything is people. Based on what we've seen so far with Bruce's recordings, we need to find out what this blue glow is. Bring as many people in as possible and start taking their photos with Bruce's new camera."

"I agree," Laura said. "The more, the better... We need a wide range of candidates. Male and female, different races, and all the age groups too."

"Bruce, so what do we need?" Karen asked. "Any special equipment?"

Bruce shakes his head. "All we need is the camera for that. Maybe a fake wall to hide the camera so no one will get suspicious. Just sit them down and get all the information. All we have to do is take their picture. We can analyze the data later."

"I need a 360-degree shot," Laura added. "Not just the front. We need to know all the parameters of this blue glow. Things like how big it is and where exactly it is located in the brain. Are all people one size, and what about the differences in the brightness?"

"Bruce, you said you were able to detect different levels in some of your recordings?" Laura asked.

"Yes, there are several levels of brightness. What it means, I have no clue. In the ones I have seen so far, I can't see any relationship. I thought the older you get, the brighter, but that's not the case. I saw an 18-year-old who was really bright, but then a 50-year-old man who was really dim. It has nothing to do with age, sex, or race. It's random. Recording people at the same distance and conditions will help out a lot."

"Let's go with that as our first order of business," Karen suggested. "We need to get as many people as possible to participate. Laura already has the cover story started. We'll need to put out an ad and put flyers all over campus."

"When we see the results, then we'll know how to proceed with the next phase," Bruce said. "We need to do as much as possible inside so we don't attract any attention. Later on, we'll have to risk going out in the field."

"After seeing the little girl in the park," Laura said. "I'd love to capture something like that! We need a before and after interviews, too."

"That's the difficult part..." Bruce said. "When do we know an event like that is going to happen?"

"It's the opposite one we need," Karen said. "Maybe we can get a terminal patient to sign up. We'll have the opportunity to see what happens after death. I know it sounds gruesome, but if we capture the image of a soul or spirit leaving the body. That's going to rewrite all the history books."

Dr. Stewart lets out a long sigh. "Damn, this is going to be big... If this is what we think it is, it will be groundbreaking."

Karen nods her head. "Yeah, if we can determine that this is the human soul and see it coming and going... The world will be beating on our door. We can't mess this up."

"Once we get some candidates in," Dr. Stewart added. "I can select a few to see how they do with regression. I like to know why some have different levels of brightness."

"Good idea," Karen said. "Once we get some people recorded, then we'll send them over to you. I guess you're going to get to check them out first."

"I think that's the best bet," Laura said. "Dr. Stewart can provide us with some valuable information without any risks. It'll also fit in with my cover story."

"Perfect!" Karen shouted. "Let's get things rolling!"

* * *

The Cover Story

Dr. Laura Scott's research is now in full swing. Postings for volunteers are all over campus and in the local newspapers. The cover story of her new 'Reincarnation, the story of human symbiosis' research is already bringing in curious volunteers.

All the meetings are held in various locations on campus. Research in reincarnation doesn't get much attention, but Bruce is still a security risk. To make sure no one gets suspicious of Bruce being on campus after work or on the weekends, he signs up for a few art classes. After working long hours in the lab, at least the art class is a refreshing break from the fast-paced technology world.

Dr. Scott's office on campus is so inconspicuous, tucked away in the basement of the science building. Since none of the administrators takes her work too seriously, it's not going to attract much attention. It makes for the perfect place to do research for Bruce Rollin's possible discovery of detecting the afterlife.

The test subjects are only told about the cover story. Each person is asked to fill out an extensive questionnaire to help filter out the prime candidates for the hypnosis sessions. The only odd request is for the full 360-degree scan, having to sit in a dark booth while the chair slowly rotates. No one has any idea that this is the real test. Hidden on the other side of the wall is the special camera that records the blue glow.

The real research is being done in the old storage room right next to Dr. Scott's office. A false wall was constructed in the room over the weekend while no one else was around. If someone walks in, they'll see nothing but obsolete computers, books, and junk that other departments have discarded. A huge bookcase is the secret entrance to the real research lab.

The location is perfect since not too many people go to the basement offices. During the day, if someone else is nearby, all one has to do is make it look as if they are storing away old junk. No one has suspected anything since most of the rooms in the basement are used for storage.

* * *

After a week, 20 candidates were selected for Dr. Jack Steward's hypnosis sessions. From the preliminary tests, the chosen candidates have very bright, prominent blue glow signatures. None of them had ever been through regression hypnosis, but all had experienced unusual vivid dreams of being in strange places they had never been to before.

"Well, you ready to see how it's all done?" Karen asked as Bruce walked into Dr. Steward's office.

Bruce is a little apprehensive. "I read quite a few of these regressions he has done. This is the first time I'm going to see one in person. It's going to be interesting."

"It's going to be downright boring! These things go on for weeks or even months."

"You're kidding? And this is the first one?" Bruce asked, a little surprised.

"No, this is her third… This is the one where he tries to get her to talk about her other lives if there are any. It's a difficult process. He has to get them comfortable. The first couple of sessions are easy and somewhat short. Getting into past lives can be extremely traumatic. Remember, their last thought or memory is when they died. Some recall drowning on a ship or in a fire. The worst are the ones that were murdered."

"That doesn't sound like a pleasant thing to listen to or to relive."

"That's why all the sessions are recorded, and they generally don't remember anything. Once it's all done, they'll have the option to listen to or watch the results after they've all been compiled. Depending on the subject, Dr. Steward carefully selects what he thinks they can handle."

"You would think so... I wouldn't want all that dumped on me. There might be some bad things I don't want to know."

"Exactly! This is not something to play with. We got to be careful with all this information we collect."

"Won't it bother these people with us staring at them while they're being hypnotized?"

"No, we'll be watching from the viewing room. Dr. Steward won't allow anyone else in the room while they're under hypnosis. He records the session and has monitors set up for us."

"So, where is Jack?" looking around for him.

Karen gives him a look. "You mean Dr. Steward? You know how he feels about that."

Bruce just shakes his head. "OK, Dr. Steward," not liking the idea of putting doctor in front of everyone's name.

"He's already with Frances. We can't go into the viewing room until she is under. When the light turns green, then he'll unlock the door. Then we can go in and watch the session on the monitors."

"Why?" Bruce asked.

"You don't want to be in the room while he is going through the induction process. Some people are a little too susceptible, so there is a risk of the viewer's getting hypnotized too."

"Really! I guess we'll wait out here then," becoming concerned about the power of this hypnosis process.

After a few minutes, the light above the door turns green. Karen opens the door motioning Bruce inside. The room is dark, with just a few chairs in front of a large monitor. Dr. Stewart is talking with the woman who is lying on a plush recliner.

"So, which one is this, and why is she so special?"

Karen pulls out the papers from her briefcase. "This is Frances Collins. She is a thirty-six-year-old mother of two who lives in San Francisco. She dropped out of high school at 15 and then got her GED. Went to college at 16, then dropped out four years later. She had no major. She just took classes she thought were interesting," handing the papers to Bruce.

He quickly reads the questionnaire that she had filled out. "How does one drop out of high school and then go straight to college at 16?"

"She had a 3.8 average. She dropped out of high school because she was bored. Then, she aced the college entrance exams. She never really finished most of her college classes, either. She got bored halfway through the semester and then took the final. She ended up with a 3.9 average. Never bothered to complete the last few classes to graduate."

"So, what does she do now?"

"She paints and plays the piano," handing Bruce a book containing copies of her artwork.

"Wow! This is impressive," flipping through the pages. "She took art classes in college?"

"Nope… She is self-taught in both art and piano. She has been painting since she was five. She sat down at a piano at thirteen and started playing like it was nothing."

"No wonder she is here… All her paintings are of country scenes. These don't look like San Francisco. Did she spend a lot of time in Europe? Looks like that is what she has been painting."

"Never left the country and doesn't even have a passport."

Bruce is so impressed with the details in the painting. "She must have used the Internet or other pictures as a guide."

"Nope… There was no Internet or any computers when she was five. She just started painting these country scenes of old farmhouses, horse-drawn carts, and plows. Look at the details in the clothing. The experts say these are from the 1860s."

"So, what does she use as a guide?"

"Get this… It's all from her dreams. She is one of those who have extremely detailed dreams. It's always from places she has never been to."

"She only dreams of these farm places--"

Karen interrupts him. "Sorry, but this is where he is trying to get access to her deep memories. Let's see how it goes."

"Is there someone else there I can talk to?" Dr. Steward asked. "Do you have a name?"

There is a long pause. Frances' demeanor appears to change. She seems somewhat agitated, jerking her head from side to side.

"May I talk with you?" the doctor asked again.

"Can you see the change?" Karen asked Bruce.

"Yeah, it's a little scary… Is it always like this? It kind of reminds me of that Exorcist movie."

Karen laughed. "I hope not… Oh, did you hear that?"

A strange voice is heard, almost like a harsh, grunting sound. Dr. Steward asks for a name and location, but the response is extremely hard to understand.

"My God! What was that?" Bruce asked.

"That's one strange dialect," Karen said. "That's definitely not English."

"What is your name? What do they call you?" Dr. Steward asked.

"Spurius!" she shouted out after a long pause.

"Where are you? What are you doing?" he asked.

Frances starts talking in a strange language. Even Dr. Steward is having a hard time trying to make sense of it. He tries to pick up some phrases he understands to continue with the session.

"I hear what sounds Italian, maybe some Latin?" Karen mumbled, entering her comments on the terminal.

Dr. Steward sees the comment flash on his computer screen. He just nods his head, indicating he agrees.

"What is the name of the place you live?" he asked, but there was no answer.

"What would we do without the Internet?" Karen mentioned to Bruce, typing in a few phrases on the computer.

Bruce looks over to see what she is doing. "Oh, Google translator… That will come in handy here."

"Yep, I can send in some translations. God knows how he is going to pronounce some of these words."

After several attempts, Dr. Steward finally gets his answer. "Alsium! Do you live in Alsium? What is it that you do there in Alsium?"

"I work the roads," she answered. "Supply stone for the roads," then continues talking in an ancient dialect.

Bruce is elated. "We did get something out of that! Sounds like a road worker. How do you make heads or tails of all this? I can barely make out what she is saying. It's strange how she goes from English to that weird language."

"Good thing for us there is a little English. We record it all and then get transcripts made. We have several language specialists to help. It's not easy, and it does take a long time. This is just one. We have 19 others to go."

"This is going to take forever."

"We're going to be doing four sessions a day, five days a week."

"She is going to be doing this every day?" he asked.

Karen shakes her head. "Oh, no... Only one session a week per person. We'll do all twenty in one week. That gives us time to do research, so we'll have more information to use for their next session. If the rest is like this one, we're going to be getting some interesting results. Because of your work, we're able to pick the very best of the best. As you can see, our very first candidate has already paid off."

Dr. Steward asks more and more questions, but Frances does not answer. She just lies there as if asleep.

"What happened?" Bruce asked after several minutes of silence. "I don't remember seeing anything like this in the videos."

"Sometimes they drift in and out... You have to be patient. The videos you saw are edited, leaving out these quiet periods, and were probably from several months of sessions."

Dr. Steward continues to ask questions and finally gets a response. The voice is entirely different, a very quiet, timid voice.

"What is your name?" he asked.

"Constance," she replied.

Bruce's mouth drops wide open, glancing over at Karen. "Listen to that accent. That's got to be old English or maybe Scottish."

She smiles, holding up two fingers. "That's two!"

"Two past lives! That's amazing!" Bruce replied.

"What are you doing, Constance?" Dr. Steward asked.

"Gathering the eggs," she replied.

"Where are you?" he asked.

"At the chicken roost."

"How old are you?"

"I don't know."

"Where is your family?"

"Momma in the house cooking… Father is in the field."

"What town are you in?"

There is a long pause. "I don't know."

"Do you know where you live?"

"Home…" she replied.

Karen types some questions on the computer.

Dr. Steward sees the message. "Do you have any animals at your home?"

She nods her head. "Got plenty… Lots of chickens. Some pigs and a horse."

"Do you grow things?"

"Father does the fields. He plows the dirt."

Karen typed in a few more questions to help him.

Dr. Steward nods his head. "Constance… Do you know what year it is?"

"No…"

"It sounds like a little girl," Bruce remarked. "How would someone that young know what year it is?"

"Ahh, there is always something that everyone knows no matter how young they are," typing in the message to Dr. Steward.

Dr. Steward smiled. "Constance… What's the name of the King?"

She laughed. "No King… We have Queen Victoria."

Bruce is surprised. "That narrows it down."

Karen is on the computer, looking it up. "Got it! Her reign is from 1837 to 1901. That's 64 years! That's a big window."

Dr. Steward continues with the questions. The answers are somewhat vague. So, he changes his tactics.

"Constance, you are much older now... What do you see around you?"

There is a long pause, and she doesn't reply. Dr. Steward repeats the question. Frances opens her eyes and then sits up.

Karen lets out a long sigh. "That's it... She is done. End of the session."

"What happened?" Bruce asked.

"Sometimes, they'll come out without any warning. The first few sessions are like that. After a while, they'll get more comfortable and will last a little longer."

Bruce feels a little letdown. "I was expecting a lot more. We did get two, but it seems somewhat limited."

"Oh no... That was one fantastic session. It's going to take us a while to decipher all this. We'll get the foreign language people to review this. Then, we'll have something to work with for the next session. We'll be more prepared."

"I didn't realize how long these things take," Bruce said.

"Be patient... We're off to a good start. We still have 19 more people. Frances is only the first, and she'll be back next week. Based on this session, it'll only get better."

* * *

The Blue Project

After several weeks of back-to-back hypnosis sessions, the results are phenomenal. Out of the 20 candidates, all had past lives, and most had multiple ones. With all the ancient dialects, translators have been brought in from all over the world to help. Many translators traveled at their own expense to attend the sessions, not wanting to wait for the recordings.

With so many new translators attending the sessions, Bruce had been warned to stay far away. Reluctantly, he has to keep his distance to make sure no one else finds out about his association with the project. To keep up with things, Bruce finds it best just to read the weekly status reports. After reading some of the more stressful transcripts of those recalling their own deaths, he is glad he wasn't present and finds it a little disturbing.

After reviewing the results of the initial candidates, additional people are brought in for testing. From the regressions they have done so far, a pattern has emerged. Most of the past lives were primarily in Asia, Europe, and India. Candidates are now selected based on their place of birth and race to see if they can discover those with past lives in other regions of the world.

The camera even got a few updates. With help from Bill and Jason, Bruce tweaks the software for the camera sensor. The sensor was designed to cover a broad electromagnetic spectrum, but it's only being used for an extremely narrow frequency. He can get a little more detail using the new software from the 299.704458 nanometers that they are only interested in monitoring.

With the regression sessions in full swing, the team will have more time to work on phase two of the Blue Project. The little orbs of light are now their primary concern. How and where to find them is the big question. The girl in the park video is always being analyzed. Several theories have suggested that these may be wandering souls or spirits. With all the people who have lived and died on Earth, everyone thought there would be many floating about, but it's the opposite. Only two orbs have been detected so far.

In addition to Bruce's own experience seeing these small lights, it seems to prove the theory, but more research is needed. The only way to find more evidence is to go out to various locations. That would mean taking the camera outside, and it would be a big risk.

* * *

"OK, I see we are all here," Karen said, looking around the room. "What's on top of the agenda for today's meeting?"

"We got to work on phase two," Bruce said.

"I agree... We got to get out of the lab," Dr. Stewart suggested. "We haven't seen one of those orbs since we've been here."

"I agree, as well!" Linda said. "Hiding in this basement is not going to get the results we need. We need to go out where they might be floating around. If those are spirits, maybe we should be in hospitals or graveyards?"

Dr. Stewart looks over at Bruce. "You said you saw some while you were in the hospital. You think we can set the camera up there?"

"The big question is, will they let us?" Bruce asked. "Security is pretty tight nowadays, especially in hospitals. Not many places will want someone coming in with a camera. Even if we give them a bogus reason for us being there, I can't see them letting us in. A waiting room will be filled with people who are there to deal with friends or family who have been in accidents like I was. I can tell you now those people will not be in the mood to be recorded. It's just not a happy place to be for anyone," remembering seeing his own family there.

"It sounds somewhat gruesome, but what about where people are terminal and close to death?" Bill asked. "There are some of those hospice places. We could get permission from some of the families."

Karen cringed. "You're right! That is gruesome but a good place to start. If this is what we think it is, capturing the moment of death and seeing one of these orbs fly away is the proof we need."

"It's like the old man Bruce saw," Dr. Stewart said. "He faded away into one of those glowing lights. Don't we have a time of death on him?"

"What was the time when the old man died and when Bruce was in the emergency room?" Linda asked.

Karen looks up the information. "The old man died at 5:35 a.m., then Bruce's heart stopped somewhere about 5:45. That's about ten minutes later, and they were trying to revive him for about six minutes."

"So that would put the event around 5:51," Linda said. "Would you say your out-of-body experience would have been about six minutes?" looking over at Bruce.

Bruce shakes his head. "Oh no… I remember it was a lot longer than that. I would say it was more like an hour."

"The out-of-body experiences always seem longer than they actually are," Karen explained. "Yours was about six minutes."

"It seemed like a lifetime for me," Bruce said. "Hard to believe it was only a few minutes."

"Bruce, you also saw a lot more of these lights floating about?" Jason asked, only hearing a few details of Bruce's experience.

"Yeah, I even had one pass right through me... That's the weird one. I guess that's why it seems so long. It was just like a dream switching over to another place. I remember standing in an old wooden shack, and everyone else was Japanese. It felt like I was there. I could smell the dust and even the food. Later, I was in the middle of a field. The cool breeze on my face was so real. I could even smell the soil. It was like I was standing out in the field."

"That's when you saw Mount Fuji?" Bill asked.

"The vision of that snowcapped mountain is one I won't forget. I remember looking around, and everything was old. No cars or electricity, just people standing about tilling the soil with wooden tools."

"What an experience!" Dr. Steward shouted out. "It's remarkable how you can recall it in such detail. Especially being able to smell the soil and the food being cooked. I have never heard of anyone being able to do that in the hundreds of regressions I have done."

"No one has done that?" Bruce asked.

"No, you are the first!" Dr. Steward replied.

Bruce glances over at Karen. "Why is my recollection so different from the others?" he asked.

"I have no clue," Karen said. "You weren't under hypnosis. You could actually remember the event. That's why we need to move on to the next phase. How do we do this? Where do we go that will give us the best results?"

"The hospice," Bill suggested again. "I know it's not the best place to be, but people go there when they don't have much time left. This whole research is about life after death. If there is something out there, that's the place we need to be."

There is a long silence. "I'll make some calls," Karen said. "We'll need to be discrete."

"All we need is one or two," Bill added.

Karen sees the scared look on Bruce's face. "Don't worry, Bruce... You are not going. We can't risk it."

He lets out a big sigh. "Yeah, that's going to be too much for me. It's way too soon."

"I'll see what I can come up with," Karen said, closing up her notebook. "Once we get someone signed up, then we'll move from there. That's it... I'll let you know."

* * *

Within a week, Karen finds a hospice that's willing to participate in the project. Luckily, the administrator of the hospice is familiar with Dr. Jack Stewart's work. Dr. Stewart always has a few copies of his latest book in his briefcase for such events. Personally signed copies of his book always opens a few doors.

Out of the 50 patients in the hospice, there are several terminal patients with only a few days to live. The administrator didn't want anyone to contact the families. He'll be the one to explain the situation and get permission from the families who are willing to participate.

* * *

After several days, Karen gets the call. One family agrees to participate. A woman only 45 years old with terminal cancer is their one and only hope. The sad part of it all is that their one and only patient knows that her last days are near.

There is a mad rush getting everything ready. It is the first time having to move all the cameras and equipment out of the secret lab. They all know it's a big risk setting everything up at the location, and it could be for days or weeks.

All the equipment is moved to the hospice late into the night. A small cleaning closet is the only place to set things up. The camera is inconspicuously placed on a bookshelf. It will record everything that goes on in the room 24 hours a day until the patient's last moments.

The patient, Barbra Williams, has already been moved to the adjoining room next to the closet, where all the monitors have been set up. One of the agreements is that only her family would be allowed in the room with her. No one on the team can go into the patient's room or even talk with the family.

* * *

What was supposed to be three days turned into two weeks. Barbra Williams had only a few days but is hanging in there. She has been suffering for a long time, and now the end is near.

Bruce reviews some of the daily recordings. Knowing that this woman is young and is going to be losing her life so soon, he is reluctant to be part of this. The memories of seeing his friends and family in the hospital waiting room on that fateful day are still painful. He feels for this family and especially her children. He is lucky to have a second chance in life but is now so depressed knowing her time is near.

Bruce receives the text message at 8:25 at night. Barbra Williams had passed away. It could be the groundbreaking evidence that they have been looking for, but no one can be elated. For two weeks, they have seen the family come and go. Now, it's all over.

Hours after the event, the team reviews the recordings. Seeing the room packed with friends and family all saying goodbye is painful to watch.

Moments after her death, only slight fluctuations can be seen. The blue glow is still present. To everyone's surprise, nothing had changed. The event never happened, and the orb is not there. This is not what they were expecting. An emergency meeting is called for everyone on the team to meet at Laura Scott's office to go over the results.

* * *

"So, what do you think we should do next?" Bruce asked.

"Not sure…" Karen said, closing her eyes. "This is not what we were expecting."

"This does throw everything off," Linda said. "Based on the other recordings, especially with the little girl, one would think it would happen right away."

"Are we still recording?" Bruce asked.

"Yes, everything is still running. Jason is still there watching the monitors. He'll call us if something happens."

Bill paces back and forth, so frustrated. "The big question I got, why is the glow still there? One would think it would have disappeared soon after her death. She shows no signs of life. The doctors have confirmed there is no brain activity."

"How much time do we have?" Laura asked. "It's been over four hours now… They can't keep her in that bed much longer."

"The family was ready to move her," Karen replied. "When I told them that we still see activity, they let us have until tomorrow, but not much more."

"If they let her stay in the room, we can still monitor things," Bill said.

"That's true," Karen said. "It's late, so we probably got until the morning. If it's any longer, the health department will be asking way too many questions. There could be some inquiries."

"Don't pressure the family," Bruce said. "Let them make the call."

"They are aware of what we are doing," Karen said. "I explained about the blue glow and what it could be. But you are right. We have to be very careful not to go over the line. They just lost a member of their family. We need to remember that."

"You said you saw some abnormalities?" Laura asked Bruce.

"Yes, there were definitely some fluctuations. Unfortunately, we lost the image right after she died. That was caused by her family standing up in front of the camera, blocking the view. Then they all got up and stood next to the bed, blocking everything."

"We didn't account for that when we set up the camera," Bill explained.

"Is there anything we could have missed?" Karen asked.

Bruce leans back in his chair, a little frustrated. "We could have missed everything! Normally, it takes days to process the images. We're still recording now and have lots to go over. Most of what we have seen is directly from the monitor. Once we process the data, then we'll know more."

"Can we just use what we have and start processing it?" Laura asked.

"We already have the data from when she died. It'll take a while just to go through that. I'm scared to interrupt the recording to change the flash drives. We could mess things up or corrupt what we have in the camera. It's programmed to swap to the secondary flashcard once the primary is full."

"When is the next scheduled change?" Bill asked.

"In about three hours," Bruce added. "That would be the safe thing to do."

Karen stands up. "Good... We can afford to wait for a couple of hours. You'll need to work fast. Start reviewing what we got now. When we get the next flashcard from the camera, you need to get that processed before sunrise. Once the administrator comes in, he'll probably put a stop to this. I know he has a meeting with the family first thing in the morning."

"OK, I'll go back and take a second look," Bruce said. "I might be able to enhance some of the images right after she died. There was so much going on, with everyone walking about and standing in the way. Maybe there's something we could use."

* * *

Bruce and Bill work through the night, reviewing all the videos. Processing hours of video is a massive undertaking. Just loading it into the computer takes hours. While waiting for the new video to load, Bruce reviews the old data. The most important part is the ten minutes before her death and ten minutes after. Everyone has studied it, and nothing is out of the ordinary. Right after the moment of death, the family is standing next to the bed, blocking most of the image. With the blue glow still there, it's a big mystery.

* * *

The latest data is ready to review after taking several hours to load the video into the computer. With not much time left, the only thing they can do is watch it all at four times the normal speed. With no processing done, the screen is completely black with just a small blue dot. The other camera will show the regular image, but there is no time to process both. It will take a week to combine both videos together.

Hours after her death, the faint blue glow is still showing up on the monitor. Once in a while, it brightens or dims slightly. On one occurrence, the blue glow gets brighter, and then it suddenly disappears.

Bruce and Bill look at each other, astonished. "Rewind it!" Bill shouts. "Play it back at normal speed."

"That was definitely the event!" Bruce said. "What's the time sync?"

"It's about 9:42... I'll pull up the regular video so we can see what else is going on in the room."

Bruce plays back the video. "There is definitely an advantage to playing it fast-forward. It's hard to see subtle changes in levels at the normal speed. We'll have to remember that. Oh, wait a minute. That's something getting in the way," seeing the blue glow disappearing.

Bill pulls up the regular video, matching it with the time sync. "Yeah, that's her husband walking into the room. He's blocking the view."

Bruce hits the fast-forward button again. The blue glow pops in and out of view while her husband is in the room. Then everything goes back to normal with a constant glow on the screen. Then, a noticeable change occurs when the glow suddenly gets dim.

Bruce hits the stop button. "Fast forward the normal video. Get ready to stop it at this mark," pointing to the time reference on the screen.

Bill plays the normal video fast forward. The image on the screen displays the husband with his wife. He is sitting right next to her, holding her hand, apparently saying goodbye. Bruce finds it painful to watch.

Bill hits the stop button. "OK, this is the same mark you have on your screen. He has left the room. What are we looking for?"

"I thought I saw some fluctuations in the levels. It got bright for a while, then went really dim."

"Oh my God!" Bill shouted out. "The blue glow lit up when he came into the room."

Bruce's mouth drops wide open. "You sure?"

"I think so... Let's see what the time is when he walked in and compare it to the time it started to brighten."

After playing it back and forth several times, it was evident that something did happen. The moment he walked into the room, the glow became more prominent, and after he left, it returned to a more diminished level.

"She reacted to his presence!" Bill shouted. "That is remarkable! Do you know what that means?"

Bruce just shakes his head. "At this point, I do not have a clue… I wasn't expecting this at all. But you are right! The glow did get brighter when he came into the room and got dim when he left. It's like she is still there. They say that after four minutes, your brain ceases to function. It's been hours since she passed away."

"I know… It's like she is still aware of everything around her."

Bruce lets out a long sigh. "Mark the time… We still have a lot to review. You go over the new recordings. I'll go back and look at what we got yesterday," glancing up at the clock.

With only a few hours to go, time is running out. With this new information, Bruce knows there has to be something at the moment of death or at least a few minutes later. He keeps thinking about his own experience and the confusion. He remembers how it all resembled a dream, not knowing that he had died.

Playing the video over and over again, he is so frustrated with the image continually being blocked. Having the camera set up high, they thought they would have an unobstructed view, not thinking about the family standing next to the bed. He sets the timeframe loop from ten minutes before her death to ten minutes after. With not much time left, he hits the fast-forward button.

After watching the same scene over and over, Bruce notices a small glitch. He stops the video, slowly stepping through it frame by frame. At precisely 08:31:47 time mark, a tiny white dot shows up on the screen. Adjusting the contrast, it becomes more apparent on the monitor. It is moving so slowly. A few seconds go by before someone walks in front of the small white dot obscuring the view. Resetting the timeframe, he plays the video in a loop.

"We got it!" Bruce shouts out. "I want to see the regular video of this part," pointing to the monitor.

"Wow! No wonder we missed it."

Playing the video at normal speed shows the family all standing around the bed. At the 8:31 time mark, there is a small gap between two people. Only for a few seconds the small white light can be seen. The event did happen, but it was being blocked.

"Let's get a composite of this from both recordings," Bruce said. "They'll want to see this. It's only a few seconds, but it's enough. We got what we wanted."

"Yeah, but we also have a lot more questions than answers."

"There are so many questions... The blue glow is still there. Why is it still there after all this time? Did you see anything else in the latest video?"

Bill shakes his head. "Nothing, but after seeing how tiny that light is, it'll take us forever to go through all of this. It'll be hard to distinguish that from the random noise."

"You are right... It'll take me weeks to reprogram everything. That light is small, but it's extremely bright."

"And probably months to go through all of this," Bill said. "We got a lot to learn, and this has taught us where to look. At least we got the evidence we needed. It's not much, but we did capture the event."

Bruce's iPhone beeps. "It's Karen... At least we got some good news for her."

Bruce answers his phone. "Hi, Karen... Bill and I have just gone through the video--"

Karen interrupts him. "Bruce, it's gone! The blue light slowly faded away. I'm sorry… We didn't detect anything else."

"What time?" Bruce asked.

"Just a few minutes ago… It was about 7:24 a.m."

"You still recording?"

"Yes, for how long, I don't know," Karen replied. "I think they are going to remove her from the room when the doctors get here."

"Keep recording until they take her away. You may have something but don't see it on the monitor. We also found a few things. We got the main event at 8:31 last night. It happened, but it was being blocked. We can see it move right between two people. It's only about a two-second window, but we think we got it. A small white light was slowly moving."

"How did we not see it before?" Karen asked.

"It's so tiny, almost like a pinpoint of light… We may have to rework some of the settings. Also, we got something else. Those fluctuations are more noticeable while playing it fast forward. Then we noticed one big event. When her husband walked in late last night, she reacted. It became brighter!"

"You saw this?" Karen asked. "It's all recorded?"

"Yes, we got a lot to go over… This is not as obvious as we first thought. There are subtle hints, but it's there."

"That's fantastic! OK, we'll keep going here until they take her out of the room. We'll have to review everything again once I get back. None of this is what we were expecting. Now we know what to look for, and at least I got good news for the family. They've been asking about it."

Bruce thought about the scenes of the grieving family he had just watched. "Yes, the family… When you see them, tell them that we are all so sorry. And thank them for letting us do this."

At 9:00 a.m., Barbra Williams is removed from the room. All the recording equipment, cameras, and computers are secretly stored back in the lab. With the first major test behind them, everyone feels lucky that the Blue Project is still going on undetected.

* * *

After several days of analyzing the data, the white orb was detected several times. The data is not what anyone was expecting. It was smaller and extremely faint compared to the one recorded in the park for reasons unknown.

The white orb had left the body minutes after death and then floated out of the room. To everyone's surprise, it returns later for a few minutes, only to leave again. At times, it can be seen hovering above the body. Why this is happening, no one knows.

With more analysis of the entire event, they discovered the blue glow is gradually fading at the moment of death until it eventually disappeared. With minor fluctuations, the blue glow could be clearly seen whenever a family member was in the room and would get slightly brighter.

The blue glow eventually faded away at 7:24 a.m. the following day. At that time, the small white orb could be seen slowly hovering above the body for a few seconds. After circling several times, it went up through the ceiling, never to be seen again.

The data they recorded will help them with the next test. With the first after-death experiment being a complete success, more families are ready to sign up. Another discovery at 7:24 a.m. is also the time of the sunrise. That made people start to wonder why the blue glow stayed so long after she passed away.

* * *

Three more families from the hospice signed up for the test. Learning from their mistakes, they place the camera up near the ceiling at the foot of the bed. That ensures that no one accidentally stands in front, blocking the view during the event.

In each case, shortly after death, the small white glowing orb can be clearly seen leaving the body. If the death occurs when no one else is in the room, the white orb slowly floats up through the ceiling. When the family is present, the white orb stays in the room, circling everyone, eventually leaving once the family is gone.

Secrecy is still extremely important. The results of the test have not been shown to any of the families. Once the information gets out, it will be in all the newspapers and on the 24-hour news channels. Questions will be asked about how these images were recorded, and that could lead to the confiscation of the camera.

There are still many tests to do, and with so much data to be analyzed, it could take years to publish the results. Everyone knows this is going to be extremely controversial. Scientists and religious theologians around the world will either question the results or call it an outright fraud. The information is so revolutionary and controversial, so it's important to get it right when it gets published.

* * *

CIA

With so much work to be done, additional people are brought in to help with the Blue Project. One particular person is an expert on remote viewing. That does have a lot of similarities to the out-of-body experiences. When Bruce finds out that this new guy is a retired CIA man, it immediately gets his attention. To make matters worse, they have already accepted him into the group. Bruce is so scared that this CIA guy might be a problem and could accidentally stumble on the true nature of the project.

Bruce, getting concerned, risks an unscheduled meeting with Karen Brown in a public place. Halfway through his art class, he leaves early. The meeting is in an isolated study room in the library. He arrives early, nervously waiting for Karen.

As she walks into the study room, she is concerned that something has gone wrong. "Hey, Bruce... So what's going on?" sitting down at the table.

"This new guy Chuck Wilson... I got a bad feeling about him."

"We checked him out. His background is extensive. He has published a lot of papers, plus about a dozen books. His work goes back more than 40 years."

He just stares at her. "I know... I read some of his papers. That's not the issue. He is CIA."

"Come on, Bruce! You're getting paranoid. He retired years ago."

He leans forward in his chair. "I know these people... I have been dealing with them for years. They never retire. They are always on the job. It's the old joke they have at the agency. The only time you know you're officially out of the CIA is when you're six feet under."

She laughed. "Chuck is just one of the second-string people on Laura's team. We got him working on the cover story. He does not know anything about the Blue Project and never will."

"You remember that movie 'Meet the Parents'? That guy who is future father-in-law was a retired CIA."

She nods her head. "Sure... That was a funny movie."

"Well, that's the way they are. You've seen the movie, and now you know what you are dealing with here. Remember, I'm working on their next spy satellite and have to deal with them all the time. They never tell you that they are CIA, but you can spot these guys as soon as they walk into the room. I can remember times when they would joke about that movie. The character that Robert De Niro played is their idol. I even know a few retired Naval Intelligence people who are just like him. Go to their homes and see how they live. They know you're coming the moment you step foot on their property. Their houses are filled with little cameras, passive detectors, and God knows what else."

Karen is getting concerned. "You never told me about this."

"I never thought you would actually bring one of them in! You know my business, and you see how cautious I am. You never trust these people. Never turn your back on them, either. Hell, they don't even trust each other. Wherever he goes, the CIA will be watching him, too. You may have pointed a big spotlight on us, and if they see me, the game is over."

"I'm sorry… I didn't think about that. So, what do we do now? We can't turn him away. I already got a few meetings scheduled with him in Laura's office."

"No, it's too late now. He will get suspicious. The fewer people he has access to, the better. How did you get mixed up with him in the first place?"

"He called me… He saw one of our advertisements and wanted to know if he could participate. When I found out who he was, I thought he would be a perfect fit for our research."

"He's going to do regressions with Dr. Stewart?"

"Oh, no! That's the one thing he said he would not do."

Right away, Bruce is concerned. "So, what good would he be for the cover story? For the Blue Project, yes, it would be great to get a recording of him with the camera during the remote viewing process."

"That's what I thought!"

"Without the regressions under hypnosis, how is it going to be of any use? He could just sit there and say anything about how he was wandering about with this remote viewing thing."

Karen sits in her chair, quietly mulling this over. She thought only about the Blue Project. Now, she is starting to wonder if she has been duped and has threatened the project.

"What do we do now?" she asked. "Did I just screw everything up?"

"No, just be careful what you say around him. Once he leaves Laura's office, we'll have to do a complete scan for bugs. Never let your guard down whenever he is around."

* * *

Karen's first meeting with Chuck Wilson had gone well. She explained the project to him and how his remote viewing would help with her research. With Bruce's suggestion, she really pushes the regression sessions with Dr. Stewart. That would give her a reason not to use him for the project. His response is always maybe, but he keeps insisting on demonstrating his methods of remote viewing to show her that it really works.

Once they see Chuck Wilson driving away, Bruce is in the office with a radio frequency scanner. Within a few minutes, he finds a bug. Right underneath the corner of the table is a small transmitter. He doesn't touch it, promptly leaving the office.

He enters the hidden lab where Karen, Laura, and Bill Davis are waiting. "Son of a bitch bugged the office!"

Karen is stunned. "Oh, God! What have I done? I'm so sorry."

"Maybe too soon to tell… Bill, let's watch the video."

With two cameras hidden up in Laura's office, it gives them a clear view from different angles. Fast-forwarding through the video, Bruce carefully watches Chuck's hands. The moment Chuck got up and started walking about the office as he spoke with Karen was a big warning sign.

"There it is!" Bruce shouted. "Play it back at normal speed."

"Yeah, that's the part I thought was odd," Karen said. "He just got up and started pacing back and forth."

"Stop it right there!" Bruce said. "Look how he does it so casually. He just leans back on that table, putting his hands on the edge. No one would ever think anything about it. Look at his left hand. He is using his index finger to put the bug there."

"Is that where it is?" Bill asked.

"Yeah, that's where it is!" Bruce replied. "Oh, he is good!"

Laura is so mad. "I can't believe this guy! We brought him right to our office, too. We should have kept him far away until we knew more about him. What the hell are we going to do now?"

Karen is so distraught. "It's all my fault… I wish I never returned his phone call."

"You had no control over that…" Bruce explained. "Normally, these people don't introduce themselves. I guess it's a good thing he was upfront with us. Usually, you don't see them coming and never know they've been around. If he had wanted to bug the place, he would have come in late at night, and we would never have known about it."

"The big question is why he is here?" Bill asked. "I have read about his work. He has been around for decades. This guy is legit. If it weren't for the Blue Project, there would be no reason for him to be here. He just does not fit in with the cover story."

"I guess we'll just play along and hope it works out," Karen said.

"So, what do we do with the bug?" Laura asked. "I can't have him listening to everything we say. Do we destroy it?"

"No, then he'll know we found it," Bruce said. "We need to mask it somehow."

"We can always whisper while we're in your office," Bill suggested.

"How about not even going in!" Laura said. "I'm not going to be able to work in my office again. What about our other candidates? I don't like the idea that he is listening in on all of our conversations."

Bruce thought about it for a while. "You always listen to the radio while in your office?"

"Yeah, so?" Laura replied.

"I got the answer… We'll set him up for some non-stop music! Even better, there is that horrible radio station that only plays the top ten hits. He'll love that!"

Bill laughed. "Good idea… How about some disco too!"

Quietly entering the office, Bruce takes the radio, placing it on a stool, right underneath the bug. To make it worse, he lays the radio on its side with the speakers facing up. After tuning to the worst radio station, he slowly turns up the volume and then leaves the room.

"How do we know if it's going to work?" Karen asked.

Bruce pulls out a small receiver. "With this… We can also hear what the bug is transmitting! I already got the frequency, so with a few adjustments, we'll see if it works."

Within a minute, the small receiver is playing the same music that's in the office. "This is what Chuck hears now. OK, let's test it out. You guys go in and have a normal conversation. I'll stay out here and see how much it blocks out the voices."

Right away, he knows the volume is way too high. He couldn't even hear their voices. Running back into the office, he motions for them to continue talking. He turns down the volume on the radio, running back to the hallway. After several more adjustments, he gets it just right. Now it's set, so muffled voices are in the background to let Chuck know people are talking, but there is no way he will hear what they are discussing.

* * *

Within a week, Chuck is back in Laura's office. Everything is being monitored in the next room. Again, he is very friendly, not giving any indication that anything is wrong. He never even glances over at the radio. Nor did he ask why it was always on while they were in the meeting. He did walk about the office, stopping once to admire one of the paintings on the wall.

Once Chuck leaves the building, Bruce rechecks the office. To no surprise, another bug is underneath the frame of the painting. Already expecting this, Bruce has another device ready to obscure the new bug. He sets up an old 'OPEN' neon sign on the bookcase right next to the bug. Once it's plugged in, the old sign still works, giving off a slight 60-Hertz hum.

"How is that old electric sign supposed to help us?" Laura asked.

Bruce holds up the receiver. "Listen to this," turning up the volume.

"What is that?" she asked, hearing nothing but an irritating humming and static sound.

"That's the sound of old technology," Bruce explained. "This one has a bad transformer, and it'll mess up any transmitter."

"We need to get this guy out of the way," Karen said. "Let's do this demonstration he has been pushing on us. We need to do it as soon as possible. We can use one of the empty offices and set up the camera like we did at the hospice and see what happens."

"I agree…" Bruce said. "He is a problem, and we got to be careful."

* * *

The Demonstration

The following week, Karen sets up Chuck Wilson's Remote Viewing demonstration. Everyone is attending except for Bruce and Bill, who will be monitoring the recordings in the secret lab.

Chuck asked Karen to place numerous objects in various predefined locations on campus. She also hides a few of her own signs to see whether Chuck is real or not.

The classroom is filled with curious onlookers. Karen asks several students to attend to help mask the team in an attempt to dissociate Chuck from her research. If anyone asks why the demonstration is on campus, she can tell people it's for the students and not for her and her research.

Bruce and Bill are watching the demonstration on the monitors. Bruce is getting worried about this guy.

"Something doesn't feel right about this," Bruce said.

"You can see how he comes off as a used car salesman," Bill commented. "It's nothing but a fast-talking sales pitch."

"I was thinking more of a con artist," Bruce said. "If he is for real, then why is he wasting his time promoting this? You would think he would be wealthy using it to his advantage."

"He is making lots of money writing books and going all around the world doing these shows. Actually, we're getting this one for free. He normally charges for this."

Bruce slowly looks over at Bill. "Why is he here? Why is he doing this for free? I don't like this at all."

"He knows Karen's research. It kind of fits into what we are doing. I read all his books and research. He has a lot of followers. He's been around for a long time and has been doing this since the Cold War days. He tends to prove his case more often than his critic's attempts to knock him down."

"If you could leave your body at will and travel anywhere in the world, what would you do?" Bruce asked.

Bill laughs. "The first place I would go is the girl's shower room at the gym!"

Bruce just smiled. "You must be thinking of the girl's volleyball team!"

"You got that right!"

That makes Bruce think about it. "Can you imagine what you can learn? You would have the inside track on the big corporate deals. You would think he would be playing the Stock Market after all these years."

"OK, here he goes!" Bill said, seeing Chuck lying on the couch in front of the classroom, preparing to go into his trance. "Starting the recording!" turning on the ultraviolet camera.

"Wow! Look how bright he is!" Bruce shouted, seeing the bright blue glow emitting from Chuck's head. "He must have a lot of past lives."

"I bet Dr. Stewart would love to put him through a few regression sessions."

"Nope, he will have nothing to do with Dr. Stewart," Bruce said. "That's the one thing he said that he will never ever do."

Bill laughed. "Yeah, I bet there are a lot of people who would pay big money to get into that guy's memories!"

Bruce sees a young woman always standing next to Chuck. "I have never seen her before."

"Oh, that's his assistant… I saw her in some of the videos. She watches over him like a hawk while he is in his trance. Otherwise, people would leave without paying or even pick his pocket. By the way, she is armed, too."

"Yeah, the old CIA people never change… They always watch over their shoulders. The poor thing probably has to stand outside the stall while he's in the men's room."

"Her nickname is the shadow," Bill said. "I was watching them come into the building. She is always a few feet behind him, no matter where they are."

The room is quiet. The assistant whispers to the audience, explaining the different stages of remote viewing. Chuck is now into his first phase. Monitors are displaying his heartbeat, respiration, blood pressure, and even his body temperature.

* * *

Twenty minutes have passed. The only signs of anything happening are reflected on the monitors. His pulse is slowing down, the temperature is dropping, and his breathing is slowing, too. To the untrained eye, this could be nothing more than watching a person taking a nap.

The assistant closely watches the monitor. Then she holds up her hand, indicating to everyone that the event is about to take place. The pulse rate starts to change.

"OK, let's see what happens," Bruce said, glancing over at the monitor displaying the blue glow.

"See anything?" Bill asked.

"Nothing… I hope we got this calibrated right."

Another ten minutes pass by. The assistant is quietly pointing out the deviations on the monitor to the audience. She acts as if something is happening and putting on a good show, but for Bruce, it's all for nothing.

"We got something here," Bill said, quickly pointing to the monitor. "Look at the luminance of the glow. It's dropped!

Look at the graph here. There is no doubt about it. Something strange is happening."

"OK, let the show begin!" Bruce added, trying not to laugh.

Now with additional software, any slight variation in the blue glow is charted on a separate monitor. Anything that moves will leave a track no matter how dim it is.

An alarm sounded. "Holy shit!" Bill yelled out. "That son of a bitch is for real!" seeing a small white dot floating across the screen, leaving a short trail behind.

"Wow! This new software really works," Bruce remarked, so glad they added more features to it. "Look at it go… The white dot is just circling above him."

Another alarm sounded. "OK, that's it," Bill said. "There is no more movement. The white dot went off the screen."

"That was fantastic! I wasn't expecting this at all. Karen will go nuts when she sees this!"

"I wonder how long he's going to be?" Bill asked.

Bruce shrugs his shoulders. "Karen said it could be an hour or more. No wonder his assistant is doing a song and dance to keep everyone amused. It looks like he's just sleeping. It's a shame they didn't see what we just did."

Bill starts to chuckle. "I wonder if he's going to stop at the girl's shower room at the gym?"

Bruce smiles, thinking about it. "Yeah, I bet that's where you'd be spending all of your time if you knew how to do this remote viewing thing."

"Damn right! I got to get into this. I'm going to take another look at his book. This is something I want to learn how to do."

* * *

After an hour, the small white orb returns for a few minutes, then it leaves the room again. The white orb comes and goes half a dozen times. Bruce keeps Karen informed with text messages. For those in the audience, watching someone who appears to be sleeping is an incredibly boring event.

"This tops anything we've done so far," Bill said. "He can come and go as he pleases. It looks like there is no limit to it, either. He can just wander about, and no one else knows where he has been."

That gets Bruce thinking. "You are right! He can go anywhere, and there's no limit to how far. Back in the CIA days, they were trained to go all the way over to Russia."

"Yeah, Chuck said they were trained to be assassins. Be interesting to know if it worked. Scary if you think about it."

"I wouldn't have believed any of it until now," Bruce remarked, glancing over at Bill. "If he can travel halfway across the world, then floating about the campus is nothing."

"Really! It's a shame we can't see where he has been. He could be going through all these buildings, trying to find all those hidden envelopes. Hell, he probably passed through here a few times."

Bruce starts beating his head on the table. "Son of a bitch! How stupid can we be?"

Bill is so shocked seeing his reaction. "What is it?"

"Bill! Think about it. He can go anywhere, and he has proved it. Look at the monitors. We've recorded him coming and going several times."

"This is what we wanted. We know Chuck is for real."

"Like you said, he might have been through here a few times. Bill, that's why he is here! He knows everything! The son of a bitch knows what we're doing. That answers the big question. Why is he even bothering with us!"

Bill just stares at the monitors. "Oh God! You're right. What do we do?"

"Nothing… I bet you he has been scoping us out as soon as he heard about Karen's research. Remember, he contacted her wanting to get involved. Who would be more interested in seeing our research than him?"

"It makes me think about that big question we had... What would you do if you could do this remote viewing thing?"

Bruce nods his head. "Yep, use it to spy and gather information that could be of use one day... Well, he's found us and knows what we are doing."

* * *

Without any warning, Chuck wakes up. The audience applauds. He slowly sits up, looking as if he has had a restless night with no sleep. The remote viewing looks like it's taking its toll on him.

Karen walks up to the front of the classroom, still applauding. "Well, Mr. Wilson... How are you feeling? You look exhausted."

He lets out a big yawn, stretching out his arms. "Oh yes... It really drains me. This is something that you don't want to do every day. You have a few questions?"

"Yes, we do... I have placed various signs all over the campus. You also had me place objects in sealed containers in public areas that you selected. We have people in those areas to make sure no one else peeks in to see what's in them. Mr. Wilson, where would you like to begin?"

"Well, Karen... The sign up on the shelf was an easy one," pointing over to the bookcase.

Karen walks over, pulling up a chair. "Well done... That's the first one," getting up on the chair, taking the sign off the top shelf, and showing it to the audience.

One by one, he can identify the objects placed in each box. Karen holds up a photo of each object to prove he is right. There is only one box that he could not find, but he can find most of Karen's signs placed on top of various bookcases and shelves. The only way anyone can see the signs is by standing up on a ladder or a chair.

The audience goes wild, applauding, and is so impressed with the demonstration. Chuck's assistant brings out boxes of his latest book to be purchased and personally signed. Karen is so thrilled with the results and glad it's over.

With only a few people left, Karen is shocked to see Bruce and Bill walking into the room. "Oh, I'm sorry, but the demonstration is over," wondering why they are here.

Bruce didn't say a word, pulling up a chair in front of Chuck Wilson. "So, did you get what you wanted?" so furious with Chuck.

Karen didn't know what to do. "I'm not sure I understand... We're done here. Maybe you can come back the next time," still trying to give the appearance that she doesn't know Bruce.

Bill stands next to Karen. "We hit a home run on the recordings," he whispers into her ear. "This guy has been on to us since the beginning. He knows everything."

Karen is shocked. "What? Is that true?" glancing over at Chuck.

Bruce is mad as hell. "Yeah, Chuck... Tell us why this demonstration is so important to our research. What did you really achieve here other than selling a few of your latest books?"

Chuck is getting a little concerned. "I'm not sure what you're referring to, Dr. Rollin. As you saw, it was a complete success. This can be useful in your past life research."

"I didn't see anything... I wasn't even here. You just saw me walk in, and I missed the show. Also, we've never met. So how do you know my name?"

Chuck slowly backs away, eyeing all the people in the room. His assistant quickly rushes over, standing behind him.

Her hand behind her back is a clear sign that she is armed, and the gun is already in her hand.

"What's going on here?" Laura asked.

Karen looks over at Bruce. "What happened? What went wrong?"

Bruce stares at Chuck. "Nothing went wrong… It was an absolute success. We got everything we wanted and more."

Chuck smiles. "Was it that good?"

"You tell me… Although, why don't you tell your pit bull to relax? I want to see her hands."

Chuck holds out his hands. "OK, let's all be friends. Gloria, take a seat and relax."

"You know all about us?" Karen asked, getting mad as well.

"He knows everything," Bill said. "That's why he is here."

"Yes, I heard about your research and checked things out. Then I discovered your Blue Project. The real project you guys are working on here. This is groundbreaking research you're doing here. It proves everything I have been working on for the last 40 years. Well, let's just say you need me, and I need you."

Bill is appalled. "That's great! That's really great. I have a good question for you. Did you use this for assassinations? How many people did you kill?"

Chuck laughed. "If we were able to, then we wouldn't need armies, would we? It was all propaganda we used against the Russians, and they did the same to us. We always kept them guessing. We ended up being nothing more than a special scouting party until we dropped out of favor with the big brass and the politicians. They'd rather have their billion-dollar planes and missiles than a bunch of wackos and drugged-up hippies. That made the defense contractors a lot happier, too."

"If it worked, then why aren't they still using it?" Bruce asked.

"Who says they're not? Why waste time and money on us? Remember, we're considered a joke. No one else believes in this anyway. All the big generals and politicians are only interested in their own jobs. None of them wants to be associated with this type of work. That will be bad for public relations and waste taxpayers' money. Besides, if they want to spy on someone, they just use the Internet or monitor cell phones. Hell, they can read all the information on any computer that's hooked to the Internet. It's all done using high-speed supercomputers that run 24 hours a day, seven days a week. Hell, you should know. You are in the business," pointing over at Bruce.

"Bruce is not a spy!" Karen said.

"Hell, he works for the worst ones of the bunch, the NSA. They're bankrolling the whole project. His new sensors are going to be in the next generation of spy satellites."

"So, what do you want?" Bruce asked. "What's your price?"

"Simple... I want in. This is going to be bigger than anything. You're going to rewrite the books with this one."

"Typical... It's all about the money!" Laura shouted out. "We do all the work, and you sit there with your hands out."

"No, it's exactly the opposite," Chuck said, waving his hands back and forth. "Bruce, you've been there. You've seen the other side. You're not here for the money. I have been doing this for over 40 years, and I want more than anything to prove it's all real. I don't want to end up being looked at as some sort of wacko. I have seen a lot of things I can't explain. I'm the one who wants you to succeed, and I'm here to help."

"How can you help us?" Karen asked.

"I can help you in more ways than one... Let's just say I have been in the business. I know how they work. There are people out there that will shut you down in a minute. They'll discredit you and your work. They'll plant false data, make up stories, feeding it all to the news media. You won't have a chance."

"So, you're going to provide us with protection?" Bruce asked.

"Precisely! When you have a major breakthrough, espionage is your worst fear. Not only will you have big corporations coming after you, but you will also have other countries. You've seen what they did to your place at work."

"Yeah, they've locked it down pretty tight."

"Does it feel like you're still in charge?" Chuck asked. "Do you like people always looking over your shoulder, watching your every move?"

"Not really," Bruce said, shaking his head. "It's getting worse."

"That's just the beginning. Don't be surprised to find out that you've been pushed out. They're just going to take whatever they want, and you'll be history. You've already done the job designing the sensors, so they really don't need you anymore."

"They wouldn't do that," Karen said. "He's the one who put it all together."

Chuck points his finger at Bruce's face. "Believe me... They already got the paperwork approved. You and your co-workers are history. They're just waiting for the right moment when they know they can go on without you. Just take the money and run. If you fight it, they'll bury you so fast. It just ain't worth it."

Bruce pauses to think about it. "Yeah, we've already got our suspicions. There is one person on our team that we're not trusting right now. He is a little too close and friendly with the suits and the military brass."

"You know I'm right… They already got their fangs into him. That's how they do it. They'll give him a big title and lots of money to make him look important. Make him feel like he's one of the boys. After a while, they'll convince him that the rest of you are not important and get him to sell you out."

"Yeah, it does feel like we signed a deal with the devil," Bruce said. "Unfortunately, they were the only ones with the money."

Chuck smiles. "You know I'm right!"

"What do you think, Karen?" Bruce asked, glancing over at her. "Is he in or out?"

"It sounds like we don't have much of a choice," Karen said. "Welcome to the team."

"Thank you… I can help by keeping an eye out to make sure no one gets too close. They're always snooping around. It's good that you're off the Internet. No more text messages or even phone calls. Always assume you are being monitored."

"Speaking of monitoring," Laura mentioned. "There are a few bugs in my office."

"Sorry about that… I'll remove them. At least you guys are on the ball, catching them fast. Nice job making it look like you didn't find them using the radio and the old sign."

"If you can float about with the remote viewing, why did you use the bugs?" Bill asked.

"Sometimes, I only see things but do not hear the sounds. I haven't figured that one out yet."

"So, are we done here?" Laura asked. "What's next?"

Chuck has a big smile on his face. "I can't wait to see the recordings. Are they that good?" glancing over at Bruce.

"Best we have so far," giving Karen a big smile.

They all got up, rushing over to the secret lab to view the results.

Walking out of the room, Chuck puts his arm around Bill's shoulder. "Oh, by the way... I did stop by the girl's shower room. I couldn't help myself. You would have loved it!" and starts laughing.

* * *

The Believer

On his first opportunity, Bruce couldn't wait to meet Chuck in private to discuss the remote viewing process. He was a skeptic at first, but after seeing the results and video, there are so many questions to be answered. With Chuck now part of the team, he will use the opportunity to pick his brain. At least with the security issues, Chuck could be a real asset.

"So Bruce," Chuck said, sitting down at the table. "I guess I made a believer out of you?"

Bruce nods his head. "In more ways than you can imagine. You clearly passed all of Karen's tests!"

"I know…" Chuck remarked, rubbing his hands together. "I hear that's how she found you. I have been reading her work for years. That's how I stumbled upon you. You had that big discovery, then that horrible car accident. You were in all the papers and on the news for weeks. When I read about how you died several times and were brought back, lucky for you, she works at the same hospital."

"Yeah, lucky for me, I saw all those signs too. Otherwise, I would have thought it was nothing but a bad dream."

Chuck laughed. "I spotted those signs as well. Clever to place them up high where no one else would know or even see them. So, you had the out-of-body experience. What do you think?"

"It was strange... More like a big dream where nothing really makes sense."

"So, what was your first impression of it?" Chuck asked.

"It was like being out snorkeling, floating on top of the water, and being pushed with the currents."

"How long did it take you to get in control of things?"

"Not long... When I saw my friends and family out in the waiting room, that's when I knew I had to do something. I quickly learned how to maneuver around. It's a good thing I did. I probably would have floated right out of the hospital."

"Everything felt like mush, didn't it?" Chuck asked.

"I'd say it was more like Jell-O that wasn't set properly. I could grasp onto things but had to be careful, or my hands just went right through. Is the remote viewing the same thing?"

Chuck pauses, thinking about the question. "I think so... I have always wondered if they were the same. I can get there by choice, but you had to die to get the experience. That's why I have been studying people like yourself. When some people die on the hospital table, they recall experiences like what you had. It's all the same, floating above their own body, seeing and hearing things when they are dead. In my experience, it's very similar. It takes a long time to learn to control where you want to go, but like you said, it's more like a weird dream."

"They taught you this in the Army? How do they select someone to do this?"

"There wasn't any random picking... They sent out questionnaires to everyone in the military. They stole the idea from the Russians, so they knew what they were looking for to make it work. Certain people have a gift, more like a higher level of consciousness. One of the key things they were looking for was people who had vivid dreams of places they had never been before. Anyone who had dreams of flying like

Superman was selected right away. That's how they got me. I signed up for the psych squad so fast without thinking twice about it because if I didn't, I would be shipped out to Vietnam."

Bruce laughed. "You signed up for this to get out of Vietnam?"

"I thought it was a good idea at the time… At first, I thought it was some sort of joke. I just played along for the first couple of years. After a while, I could see something was seriously wrong. Some of my buddies went from normal to basket cases. Most ended up in the mental wards. They were destroying people's minds, making them go nuts. Then, I had my first encounter. That really blew me away. Right after that, I was shipped out to another group. That's when things got really serious and downright scary."

"Where did they send you?"

"Have no clue… I had these strange people showing up in the middle of the night telling me to pack my gear. The next thing I knew, I was on a long flight to somewhere. When we landed, they put a hood over my head and walked me out of the plane. I remember it being extremely hot, dry, and dusty too. I was in an elevator going down deep underground. They walked me around for a while so that I couldn't backtrack. That was the psych squad's offices and the place where I lived for the next five years."

"Damn… Sounds like a prison. So this is where all the remote viewing took place?"

"Yep… It wasn't so bad. We got the best of everything. Food, entertainment, and they even brought in the ladies too. If we ever complained, they showed us some of the things going on in Vietnam, constantly threatening to ship us out there. After seeing that, we just did what we were told and didn't ask any questions."

"So, how does this work?" Bruce asked. "You go into a trance, and then you leave your body?"

"In a way… You have to prepare yourself first. You clear your mind and concentrate on your breathing. It's a lot to do with mind over body. That's why it takes a long time to master."

"How do you know when it's time to leave your body?"

"Once you're in the zone, you can feel this electrical tingling flowing down your body. That's when it's about to start."

"Then what do you do?" Bruce asked. "Is there a sign or something?"

Chuck shrugs his shoulders. "Not really… You just sit up like you would normally do when getting out of bed. When you look back and see yourself lying on the bed, at first, it really blows your mind. That's why a lot of people just go nuts. They can't handle it."

"Once you know you've gone over, what's the first thing you do?"

"Just look around, and try not to freak out… It's like the astronauts experiencing zero gravity for the first time. At first, you have no control. You do a little at a time, taking baby steps. After a while, you learn how to control where you want to go."

"You can go anywhere you want?" Bruce asked. "How do you go to other places that are far away?"

"That's the tricky part… Think of what you would do if you were Superman with no compass, maps, or anything. You almost have to know all the features like roads, towns, and mountains to use as a guide. Sometimes, you lose your way and have to go back."

"Yeah, how do you find your way back?" Bruce asked. "That would be the scary part, not finding your way back to your body!"

"Getting back is the easy part. It's like being on the end of a fishing line. When you are ready to return, it feels like you're being reeled back in and have no control over it."

"I vaguely remember that part... Yeah, it was like being pulled back."

"Precisely! See, you've already been there and done it. You just didn't have a choice in the matter, like I do."

Bruce stares at Chuck before asking the next big question. "So, can I learn how to do this?"

Chuck laughed. "I thought you would be interested... You are already halfway there. You've seen the other side. You know what you are up against here. That's the part most people can't handle. You seemed to have it under control and accepted it. Now, all you have to do is learn how to get there. But you have to be very careful. There are some strange things out there. Even I don't understand what the hell it is. I have seen some people go too far or to places they shouldn't be, and they never come back."

"You're telling me that people have died doing this?"

Chuck nods. "Yeah... You have to understand what we're dealing with here. If we're right to assume that these out-of-the-body experiences are the same as remote viewing, we're talking about our souls or spirits. These white orbs that you detected are probably the proof of it all."

"You think those white orbs are our souls?"

"Yes, I think so... I noticed how no one else around here wants to talk about that."

Bruce smiles. "I know... That's a forbidden subject, but they are all thinking about it. I guess everyone wants to collect all the data before coming to that conclusion."

"But the data you have so far does put it all together. Not only does this new sensor of yours detect the bluish glow in people, but you also see the orbs floating about. Now, you have recordings of people dying, and the blue glow disappears. Then the orb leaves their body. You got the same recordings of me during the remote viewing. In addition to that, there are all the regressions Dr. Steward has. Look at all those people who lived other lives hundreds of years ago. Bruce, do you really understand what we have here?"

There is a long pause. "That's what I'm so terrified with this shit. When we die, our soul leaves and eventually finds another host. That makes us a symbiotic species. Our bodies are just temporary hosts. Our thoughts, memories, and feelings are really part of something else."

"Exactly! That's the link I have been looking for after all these years. Remote viewing, reincarnation, and out-of-body experiences are all the same. It's all the proof that we are a symbiotic species. We just live on forever, going from one body to another. You even got that recorded, too, with the little girl in the park."

"Yeah, that was an eye-opener… We now basically got the whole round trip. A soul entering a new life, while others who died and saw their soul leaving. It makes you think, doesn't it? The question is the well of souls. There are more people alive today than ever lived before. What happens if there are not enough souls for the babies just being born?"

"I have been thinking about that for a long time," Chuck explained. "It's one of the things that you discovered. The little kids don't have a blue glow. That little girl didn't at first, but she did afterward when the white orb hit her. I think what happens is that if an old soul does not select them by a certain age, they'll develop a new soul. If you think about it, it does make sense."

"Yeah, I looked up the numbers. There are over seven billion people alive today. Back in 1800, there was only about one billion."

"Exactly! There are people with new souls. Then there are those who have old souls, coming back for more. That's the reincarnation part, the blue glow. Not everyone is the same. You can see differences in the brightness in certain people?"

"That's one of the first things we noticed," Bruce said. "We sent the bright ones over to Dr. Stewart. In the regression tests, we found the brighter the glow, the more past lives they had. That's how we were able to select the best of the best for Dr. Stewart. We went back and selected some of the others who had a base level. Not one of them had any past lives. So, if you are right, if people don't get selected for whatever reason, they develop a new soul. It does make sense."

Chuck laughs. "You know... This cover story you got for the project..."

"Oh, Laura's 'Reincarnation, the story of human symbiosis' theory."

"Yes, that's the one... It's almost funny how you hit the mark with that. It's basically what you got here."

Bruce pauses to think about it. "It seemed so... At first, we were trying to come up with something to bring in lots of people so we could use the camera on them. We also didn't want to get any attention from the boys back at work."

Chuck laughs again. "Out of the frying pan, into the fire! Leave that part to me. I'll wander over there a few times to see what's going on."

"That's a good question... When you're out wandering about on the other side, how do you see other people?"

"I see people like normal. It's not very clear at times. Although you had a different experience. You could see the blue glow and the white orbs. I have never seen that before."

"Yeah, nothing was really clear, almost like seeing things underwater. That blue glow people had is what got me onto this in the first place. It was like they had a small blue light bulb inside their heads. The other people I saw were even more bizarre. They had this blue glow around their entire body, just like I had. A couple of them were kind of spooky."

Chuck slowly leans forward, getting serious. "It sounds like you saw some of the lost souls. Those are people who died, and they don't know it."

"Yeah, I always wondered about that… One old man seemed to figure it out, but there was another. A woman, she was like me, not knowing what was happening."

"That old man was the one who dissolved into a point of light. Like one of the orbs we see now."

Bruce nods his head. "Almost the same, but the floating lights were blue. The ones we see in the recordings are white. That's the only difference I know."

"There was a time lag from when he died to when he turned into the orb. That must be the phase of acceptance. For some people, their deaths are so quick they don't know they're dead. They go about wandering the Earth, confused for an eternity. Those are the ones you have to watch out for while you are out there. There's a lot of anger in them."

"Now, we're talking about ghost stories!" Bruce said, starting to shudder.

"I told you there are things out there you don't want to get near. They are lost souls stuck between here and the other side. You were only out there for a few minutes. Can you imagine living out hundreds of years where it's nothing but total confusion? No one can hear or see you. You don't ever want to go near them."

"They still think they are alive?" Bruce asked.

"I believe so… It's so sad…"

Bruce laughed. "It sounds like you've been doing your homework."

"I have been doing research in this longer than you've been alive. Your discovery has put it all together. So, are you still willing to try it? Want to venture to the other side?"

Bruce pauses for a long time. "I have been there once… Now, I understand things a little better. Yes, I'm ready to go back."

"Good… I'll set everything up with Karen. We'll get you started up with some basic training with my assistant."

"Oh, your assistant... The scary one."

Chuck laughs. "She's harmless... But, when you're on the other side, you are vulnerable in the real world. She watches over me during the demos. She is very good at this stuff, too. She has been over to the other side many times. I taught her well. Best student I have seen in years."

"OK, let's get this scheduled," Bruce said excitedly, clapping his hands together. "I can't wait!"

"Don't expect things to happen overnight. It took me years to get there. Once you get near the threshold, then I'll take over. Remember, it's going to be baby steps all the way."

* * *

Replacement

With the camera constantly being used, the sensor is starting to give out. Designed to be in a cooled environment, it's shutting down because of overheating. The heat generated by all the circuitry and the battery is too much. Even after adding cooling fans, it's not helping at all. The end is near, and decisions are being made for the replacement.

The makeshift design Bruce slapped together will have to be reworked. A liquid nitrogen housing will be needed for the replacement. Now, with more people helping and with the additional funding, the new design will be a vast improvement.

The biggest obstacle is getting another sensor. The security is tighter than ever. Auditors are tracking everything that's going on in the lab. Getting caught would be the end of the project, and Bruce could lose his job and maybe get thrown in jail.

With all the additional security at his lab, Bruce thinks of ways to switch out the faulty sensor with a new one. He starts by going to work at odd hours to check out the security. Additional cameras have been placed throughout the lab. He knows someone out there could be watching, or worse, all of this is being recorded.

* * *

For weeks, Bruce plays it safe, waiting for the right opportunity. With help from Chuck, he taps into the security cameras and can see what the security people are monitoring. There are blank spots in the system. The surveillance cameras are watching all the exits. But mostly all the places where the sensors are being tested and stored.

Carlos, the security guard who watches the monitors, is the weakest link. After some small talk, Bruce found out that Carlos was a big 49ers fan. On Monday night, the 49ers are playing, and Carlos plans to watch the game at his desk. That gives Bruce the time and date to make the switch.

Bruce goes about his daily chores. Working odd hours is now so familiar no one even notices it anymore. With so much work to do, people are coming and going at all hours. With the Monday night game coming up, everything needs to be in place. If something goes wrong, it's over.

Since the sensor was too big to fit in his pocket, everyone pitched in to find ways to hide it. After seeing the fleece jacket Bruce always wears, it was the simplest solution. The hood on the back is the perfect place to hide it. Being chilly at night, no one would think twice about someone wearing a fleece jacket with a hood on it.

After a little experimenting, a small pocket is sewn into the hood to ensure the sensor doesn't drop out. Changing the jacket to an extra-large size and wearing the hood up, no one should notice.

* * *

"Are you sure you want to do this?" Karen asked. "We got plenty of data to work with."

Bruce nods his head. "We got lots to do. I still got some questions to be answered."

"At least get someone to help. You can't do all this yourself."

"No, it's my decision, and no one else is involved. If things go wrong, it's only me. Hopefully, they won't find a link between the project and me. Then you can continue with the data we got."

"When are you going to do this?"

"Monday night… Old Carlos is going to be watching the 49ers game. That will keep him busy for hours. It'll give me time to make the switch. I also need time to alter the logs."

"They won't know?" she asked.

"All they'll know is we got another sensor that didn't pass inspection. It happens, and some fail outright, while others are marginal. They are designed to run for years. That's why we go through a whole batch of tests that go on for hours. When they put these in the satellites, it's got to be perfect without any flaws."

"Why did the one we got fail so soon?"

"Probably because we always used it at room temperature. It wasn't designed to be used like that. Bill is going to help me design a liquid nitrogen mount. That will solve the problem and may get us better results, too."

Karen lets out a long sigh. "It's up to you, but I'm against it. I think you are spending too much time with Chuck."

He laughed. "He's a character, but he is helping us. Got some good intel at the place I work. I couldn't have done it without him."

"Good thing he is on our side."

"My thoughts exactly!"

* * *

On Monday night, Bruce drives to work, going over each step of the plan in his mind. He has been going through the same steps for weeks, hoping that nothing has changed. The only difference for today is swapping out the faulty sensor with a new one. He is just going to go through the test process and log it in as a defective sensor. The big risk is walking out with the new one without being detected.

Bruce parks his car in a special spot. With knowledge of the cameras, he knows just where to be. A little nervous, trying to act normal, he makes it look as if it's just another day at work.

Swiping his card in the reader, he hears the front door click. Walking into the main entrance, he is glad to see Carlos is already watching the game. Not wanting any attention, Bruce quietly walks past without even being noticed.

Entering his office, he needs to act as if it's just another day. There are new sensors to be tested that were assembled earlier. Also, there are numerous status reports and requisitions to approve. Too many people are watching his progress and always asking for endless paperwork. Whether he likes it or not, he still has a big job to do.

* * *

After several hours, Bruce finally completed the weekly status reports. The switch is the next thing on the list. He listens to the football game, making sure all the testing will be done during the fourth quarter. That will ensure the security guard will be glued to the TV watching the end of the game.

With a quick look around, he takes out the sensor from his hood. He quickly transfers it to another secret pocket on the inside of the jacket. With the sensor inside his jacket, he can inconspicuously take it out without being noticed by the security cameras right behind him.

Bruce goes through the logs to see what has been done and what new sensors need to be tested. Three have been assembled and are ready for testing. One of those three is going to be switched out. He goes over to the safe, unlocking it to get the first one. The testing process could take up to twenty minutes. Hearing the game is well into the fourth quarter. He knows there is only enough time to test two of them before the switch. Once the game is over, the security guard will surely be watching what's going on in the lab.

* * *

With only a few minutes left on the first sensor test, Bruce hears the door open. "Hey, Bruce! You not watching the game?" the security guard asked.

Bruce froze, not believing this. "Hi, Carlos! No, I'm too busy with all this work. Sounds like a good one."

"Like hell... They are losing big time. I got tired of watching it," pulling up a chair next to the table.

"And you call yourself a fan... You're supposed to be watching the game and rooting for them."

"The way they're playing, I don't know... Damn, the coach doesn't know what the hell he's doing. It's getting too frustrating to watch."

Bruce can't believe his luck. This is the last thing he needs. Not only is the security guard not watching the game, but he's in the lab sitting down at the testing table. Bruce continues as if nothing is out of the ordinary.

"What's all that stuff on those computer screens?" Carlos asked.

"Oh, it's all the results from the tests. We fire all sorts of different levels of light and colors to make sure it works."

"How many colors?" he asked.

Bruce cringes, not believing this is happening. "Millions... It'll take up to 20 minutes. All these screens do nothing but show graphs and charts," hoping Carlos will get bored and leave to watch the rest of the game.

"What's all that beeping noise?"

That is the one thing Bruce didn't want to see. "Damn... This one failed. It's a reject."

Things are going from bad to worse. He needs to load another sensor, and it might be a problem with the security guard in the room. The old sensor is still in the secret pocket inside his jacket and can be seen from the side. With his jacket open, Carlos might see it and start asking too many questions.

Bruce goes about the standard procedures for a failed sensor. He pulls out the logbook, recording all the numbers and the time. He ignores Carlos trying to make it look as if he is extremely busy, but it's not working. Carlos is now asking more questions than before.

The failed sensor has now created a new problem. The first test is over way too soon. The next sensor will have to be the one he is going to take back, but it has to be tested first to make sure it's a good one. That moves up the time to do the switch. With the football game not being the distraction he wanted, the whole plan might be a wash.

Bruce places the failed sensor back into the container. He is worried, trying to conceal the one under his jacket from not only the cameras but also Carlos, who is only five feet away. He grabs the logbook with his left hand, keeping it over his jacket pocket. Then he grabs the failed sensor container, making an awkward walk over to the safe.

Seeing how Carlos is also getting up, ready to follow him. "Oops... Can't do that. Top Secret stuff here. Oh, I can't open the safe with a non-approved person here. The big boys might be watching," glancing up at the camera.

Carlos quickly looks up. "Oh, that's right... Sorry, I better stay over here. I won't look."

Luckily, Bruce hears a loud roar from the TV back in his office. "Sounds like something happened in the game! Did someone score a touchdown?"

"I got to go!" Carlos yelled. "Talk with you later!" rushing out of the lab.

As soon as Carlos is gone, Bruce pulls out the next sensor to be tested, rushing back to the table. He quickly sets things up, then starts the test program. From the sounds of all the yelling and screaming, the 49ers must have scored. Luckily, the security guard may not be back for a while.

* * *

After an excruciatingly long 20 minutes, the program ended successfully. Now for the switch, hoping the security guard doesn't walk back in. After filling out the test log, he puts down the pen, slowly reaching into his jacket's hidden pocket. Carefully, he swaps the sensors, trying not to damage the good one.

He continues to record the information in the logbook once the swap is made and the new sensor is safely in his pocket. To cover their tracks, this will be the second failed sensor. The logs will match what's in the safe. So, when the auditors go through everything, no one will be the wiser.

Hearing the roar from the crowds on the TV, Bruce knows this is an excellent time to make the move. He returns the container to the safe, locking everything up. Keeping the logbook pressed against his left side, he has to make sure the cameras don't see anything under his jacket.

Back in his office, Bruce starts shutting everything down. With the two-minute warning in the game, he knows this is the best time to leave. With one last look around, he transfers the sensor from the side pocket to one within the hood. Making sure nothing looks out of the ordinary with his jacket, he casually walks out of the lab.

Bruce quietly walks out, keeping an eye on the security guard. Luckily, the game is nearing the end, and he can slip out of the building unnoticed. He is still not in the clear. No alarms have sounded, but there could be some silent ones.

Getting to his car is the next big step. This is when he will find out if it's been a successful operation or not. If several black Suburbans race into the parking lot, it is over.

Once in the car, he still keeps looking around. Everything is just too quiet. Slowly driving away, he is still suspicious.

This was just too easy. He keeps looking in the rearview mirror to make sure no one is following.

On the way home, he stops by the grocery store to get a few things. Then onto Wendy's to get something to eat. He has done this on most days to make sure nothing is out of the ordinary. Also, with Linda's little brother Tom working at the drive-through window at Wendy's, it's the best place to unload the goods.

* * *

Bruce pulls into the Wendy's drive-through lane. After giving them his order, he goes to the next window. Everything has been carefully planned out. Surrounded by walls and trees, this is the perfect place. No one can see anything behind the building, and luckily, he is the only one at the drive-through.

"Here's your order, sir!" Tom yelled out. "Thanks for stopping by," handing out the paper bag and drink.

Bruce places the empty bag on his lap. With one last look around, he puts the container into it.

"Excuse me," Bruce said. "I think I got someone else's order here," handing back the paper bag.

"Oh, I'm so sorry!" Tom said. "Let me double-check this," taking the bag away.

"No problem…" Bruce replied.

After a few seconds, he hands Bruce another paper bag. "Sorry about that… This is your correct order."

"Thank you!" Bruce replied, slowly driving away.

Bruce is so relieved to unload the sensor. He keeps watching behind him to make sure nothing is going on at Wendy's. He wants to make sure Linda is not going to have any problems leaving the restaurant and getting the new sensor back to the college lab.

With the aroma of the French fries filling the car, Bruce can't resist it. He hasn't eaten anything since lunchtime and is starving. After eating a few fries, he can't hold back and starts munching on the hamburger.

A few blocks from the Wendy's restaurant, he notices a huge black suburban following right behind his car. The two men in the front seats are wearing suits. That is not a good sign.

Having to make a right turn at the next intersection will tell him if he has a problem. His heart starts beating hard, seeing the suburban is still right behind him. Within a few seconds, another black suburban rushes past and then pulls right in front of his car. With all the red and blue lights flashing, Bruce knows this is the security detail. Stuck between the two huge suburban trucks, several men in dark suits rush out, surrounding his car.

Bruce unrolls the window. "Was I speeding or something?" he asked, then took another bite from his hamburger.

"Would you mind stepping out of the vehicle, sir?" the burly man asked.

"Don't you want to see my driver's license?" Bruce asked, still eating his hamburger.

"Dr. Rollin, I don't think that's necessary. Please step out," opening the car door.

Bruce grabs his drink and hamburger before getting out of the car. "You know you're interrupting my supper here."

The other man rushes over, searching the car for something. Pulling out the grocery bags, it's all laid out on the top of the car, carefully inspecting every item. One man uses a small black wand waving it back and forth over everything.

"Can I see some identification, please?" Bruce asked.

The man reaches under his coat, pulling out his identification card, 'Stan Taylor, Senior Security Officer.'

"So, what's up?" Bruce asked after checking the identification. "What's the problem?"

"The magnetometer detected a device when you left the building."

"That's odd... I didn't hear anything. You sure it's not a false reading?"

"That's why we are here," motioning to the other security men to come over.

Bruce stands next to his car. Two of the men run what looks like a small metal detector over his body. One of the detectors starts beeping when it comes close to his right pocket.

"Please remove the items from your pocket," the security officer asked.

"No problem," reaching in and pulling out his car keys.

Again, they wave the detector over the keys. "What exactly is that?" the man asked, examining the keychain.

"Oh, this is a gift I got for my birthday the other day," Bruce explained. "That might be the problem. It's titanium, with gold inlays. It has some nice red rubies and diamonds on it too. A little gaudy, but it was an expensive gift, so I kind of have to use it."

"Check his other pockets just in case," one of the other men suggested.

Bruce obliges, pulling all his pockets inside out. "Come to think about it... My keychain may have set off the alarm when I left. You may want to check to see if it did the same when I got to work."

The look on the security officer's face said it all. He quickly turns to talk on his radio. After a minute, the security officer shakes his head. Bruce knows the answer. They did detect something when he walked into the building. These security people are going to have some explaining to do when they get back.

The security officer returns. "I'm sorry, Dr. Rollin... You were correct. The magnetometer did detect something when you entered the building as well. May I suggest you start using a different keychain to ensure this incident won't happen again?"

"Oh, no problem... You're just doing your job. I'll remember to leave this at home next time," holding up his keys.

The security detail quickly repacks all the groceries placing everything back into the car. Like clockwork, they rush back into their vehicles, quickly speeding away. Bruce knows they are going to be in trouble for stopping him for nothing. These security people are a bunch of ex-military nuts, always looking for action, constantly overreacting when they think there is a problem.

Bruce is so grateful to have Chuck on their side. Because of Chuck's knowledge of the security contractors, they were ready for the hidden metal detectors on all the exits. The titanium keychain Chuck gave him was designed to set off the alarms intentionally.

The plan was perfect, and he was able to walk out with the sensor from the lab even though it did set off the alarms. The security team thinks it's the keychain, and that's the end of that. The mission was a complete success. Now, they can continue with their research with a brand-new sensor.

* * *

The camera is redesigned from scratch. No more duct tape and loose cables dangling from the camera. A new sensor mount has been designed to utilize liquid nitrogen. That will prevent it from overheating but mostly keep it running at its designed operating temperature. Once it's completed, the results are even better than before.

Having to deal with liquid nitrogen, Bill had to modify a backpack, filling it with insulation to keep in the cold. With the camera stored inside the backpack, it can be carried about in public without anyone seeing it. With several solid-state drives and the latest iPad, there is enough computer power to process all the images in real time and store hours of data while out in the field.

* * *

The Next Phase

The next phase of the project is to discover why young children do not have a blue glow. Secretly recording children in the park will be a problem and could be illegal. This has to be done in a controlled environment, and detailed information about the age, place of birth, and ethnicity is needed.

Karen sets up meetings with a few preschools to study children under six. Her research in child psychology opens a few doors. A cover story has been created on how children interact with each other while at school. It will help explain why the children need to be recorded and will be asked a few simple questions. A standard video camera will be used as a decoy, while the real camera is hidden in the backpack.

The sessions with the children are simple. Nothing more than having them all sit down in a row while Karen and Jason ask a few questions. While all this is happening, Bill operates the cameras. With the regular video camera on a tripod in clear view, the camera concealed in the backpack won't be noticed. With both cameras having WIFI, he can monitor everything remotely with his iPad and not have to touch either camera to make adjustments.

* * *

"Good morning, Dr. Brown!" Principal Whitney said. "We're glad you picked our little school for your research."

"Thank you for letting us be here today. These are my associates, Dr. Jason Lee and Bill Davis. This is Principal Barbra Whitney."

"Nice to meet you!" Jason said, reaching out to shake her hand.

"Hello…" Bill said, stepping over to shake her hand as well.

Barbra motions them to follow. "We have an empty classroom that you can use. When you are ready, we can bring in a few children, about a dozen at a time. Is that OK?"

"That's perfect… That will give us enough time to interview each one until lunchtime."

"So, you want to record them playing in the yard?"

"Yes, that's correct… Just to see how they interact with each other. There will be no contact with us."

"We'll have the camera on the tripod in the far corner, and hopefully, they won't notice we're there," Jason added.

"I'll have Ms. Evans monitor the children while you're here," Barbra said as they entered the room. "We don't want them getting into mischief. They can get a little unruly when we have guests."

"That will be fine," Karen said, knowing that someone would always be escorting them while at the school.

Bill looks over the room, trying to find the best place to put the cameras. "Let's put the chairs over by that corner so the windows are behind us," grabbing several chairs.

"What about the cameras?" Jason asked.

"We'll set it up between you and Karen," Bill replied. "I'll put the backpack right underneath the tripod. We'll get a good view from here. It'll be out of the way, so we don't have to worry about anyone accidentally kicking it," knowing it'll be an excellent location for a clear shot of the entire group.

* * *

With a dozen little chairs set in a row, the first group of five-year-olds slowly enters the room, escorted by Ms. Evans. Karen and Jason sit in front with the video camera perched up on the tripod right between them.

Bill sits out of the way next to the wall. Using his iPad, he sets up both cameras, switching between one and the other.

With all the children in their seats, Ms. Evens walks over, standing next to Bill. "I see you got one of those fancy iPads."

"Oh, yes! I use it for the camera. I can operate it remotely with my iPad. It makes it a lot easier not having to stand up all the time," showing her the view that the camera is recording.

Karen quickly notices the problem. Bill won't be able to monitor both cameras, with Ms. Evens looking over his shoulder.

"Ms. Evans… Please, have a seat next to me," pulling up another chair.

"It's all right… I don't want to interfere with your work. I'll stay back here."

"It might be better not to have the children glancing over at you during the sessions. We need to have their full attention. Come and sit next to us," seeing the concerned look on Bill's face.

"Oh, sorry… I didn't think about that," promptly sitting down next to Karen.

The session begins with Karen asking each one of the children to say their names and age. The entire interview was provided by one of her colleagues. The questions were valid, but the answers were irrelevant. The most challenging part is keeping a dozen five-year-olds amused for 15 minutes. Once the session is over, Jason hands out all the gifts, ranging from boxes of crayons to stickers.

With the first session over, within a few minutes, the next group of children is marching into the room. When they see the other children walking out with toys, the new group gets a little rambunctious. Karen asks the same questions repeatedly. Within 15 minutes, it is over, and another group of children is brought in. This goes on all morning long.

* * *

As the morning draws on, the younger children are getting more difficult to handle. The questions were designed for each age group, but it's not enough to keep them in their seats for long.

Bill only needs a few minutes to get the recording. At times, when things are out of control, he just nods at Karen to let her know that he got what they needed and to end the session early.

The two-year-olds are handled differently. Little toys and teddy bears are used instead of questions. Their reaction, if they smiled or cried, was enough. Even the babies still in the carry seats are tested in a similar way. Karen acted the part, telling Jason to note positive or negative reactions to what the babies were doing. With Ms. Evens always in the room, Karen has to keep to the script to make it look real.

* * *

With all the sessions completed, the team regroups, setting up the cameras outside next to the playground. Bill selects the best location in the shade under a tree. Already getting hot, he is concerned about the camera, making sure it's never in the direct sunlight. The video camera is set up on the tripod while the backpack is hanging on the chain-link fence facing the playground.

Jason walks over with three lunches from the cafeteria. "This is far better than what I got at school!" handing out the lunch sacks.

"How much time do we have?" Bill asked.

"About ten minutes... Then they'll let the little buggers out for recess!" Jason said, pointing to the main door.

"Will have to thank Principal Whitney for all this," Karen said, seeing what was in the lunch sack.

Bill laughed. "Don't forget about Ms. Evens... Poor thing. Having to listen to those same questions being asked over and over. It must have driven her nuts."

"Yeah, she is one of the new teachers here," Karen explained. "She got stuck having to watch us."

"I was hoping she wouldn't get up and see what's on my iPad screen," Bill added. "I'm so glad she sat down next to you guys!"

"Speaking of iPads... How did we do?" Karen asked.

"We got some good images," Bill said. "Not what we were expecting. The older kids were mostly blue. We got a couple that had really bright readings. But, there were a few that had no readings at all."

"What? On the five-year-old kids?" Karen quickly asked. "No readings at all?"

"That's right... On the iPad screen, it's hard to tell. When we review it back at the lab, we may see something. We might have to tweak the software again."

"Damn... Yeah, we'll check the data when we get back. I wonder what age it's going to be when we get 100 percent?"

"That means we need to go to the six-year-olds or older," Bill added.

"Elementary school, here we come!" Jason said jokingly.

"That might be a problem," Karen said, shaking her head. "It's going to be hard trying to pull this off in a public school."

The bell rings, and the door slams open. All the children run out yelling and screaming. Bill is on the iPad, turning on all the cameras. Standing in front of the children is Principal Whitney. She is also standing right in front of the camera, blocking the view.

"You think you can move her out of the way?" Bill asked.

"No problem," Karen said, slowly walking to the left, away from the camera, waving at Principal Whitney.

While Karen talks with Principal Whitney, Bill and Jason monitor the recordings. This is the first time being able to record this many children at once. With no one looking over their shoulders, they eagerly watch the composite view from the backpack camera.

"This is just remarkable," Jason said, seeing the iPad image from the camera.

"Check out these guys," Bill whispered, pointing to the screen. "Look at it… No readings at all."

"They are the older kids too! I thought at that age they would have a reading?"

"Me too… My God, the bright ones really stand out from the rest," Bill said, pointing them out on the screen.

"There are only a few of them."

"Yeah, it's funny how they are all standing together in a group."

"How many kids we got out there?"

"I counted 210," Bill answered, glancing down at his notes.

"Damn… There are about two or three of the five-year-olds that don't have the glow. You know what that means."

"Yep, that means elementary schools are next. That's going to be a lot tougher to get in."

* * *

Later that night, the team is going over the recordings from the school. Bill was right. This is not what they were expecting. Karen thought all the five-year-old children would have a blue glow, but a few didn't. Out of the 210 children recorded, only five had higher levels than the rest. The one thing that surprised them was discovering that the blue glow starts showing up as early as three years old.

"Those two five-year-olds are still a mystery," Karen said, going over the list. "Is it a mistake? Why don't they have a blue glow? These are the ones we need to go back and interview again."

"We got them recorded out on the playground too. No readings at all."

"What was different about them during the interviews?" Bruce asked.

"One of them was really quiet and didn't respond much," Jason explained. "The other always fidgeted, not paying attention. Out on the playground, it was a different matter. They came off as bullies, constantly pushing the other kids around."

"That makes sense now I think about it," Bill remarked. "When I was in elementary school, we had this horrible kid always picking on everyone. I bet you he didn't have a blue glow, either. He probably had no soul, the sick bastard!"

"Interesting," Karen mumbled, ignoring Bill's comment. "The five kids that were higher levels… How did they react to the other kids?"

"I got them tagged on the video," Bill said. "I didn't notice it at first, but if you play it fast forward, you can see how they tend to stick together out on the playground. They're also more relaxed, not running about screaming and yelling like the others."

"How did they respond in the interview?" Bruce asked. "Are they any different than the rest?"

"Absolutely!" Jason said. "You can easily pick them out. They're more articulate. At times, you can tell they're really deep in thought. The other kids just shouted out the first thing that popped into their heads."

"Only five," Bruce said, still trying to comprehend it all. "I would have thought it would be more."

"It's the two I'm concerned about," Karen added. "I didn't expect that. I'm going to talk with the principal again and see if we can focus on the ones we got issues with."

"Just the two bullies?" Bill asked. "You want to risk taking the camera out there again?"

"We don't need the cameras," Karen explained. "We need a real interview with the two that show no readings and the five bright ones. I'm going to ask Dr. Martha Campbell to come along on this one. She's the one who gave me the questions we used. I want her to talk with these seven kids."

"I have a feeling when you tell that principal the names of those kids you want to see, she will know something is up," Bruce added.

"Yeah, they definitely stand out from the crowd," Karen said.

"How are we going to handle the elementary schools?" Jason asked.

"I'll talk with Martha about that first. They don't let just anyone in nowadays. There could be a full investigation of who we are and what we are researching."

"That will be some red flags right there," Bruce said.

"What are our other options?"

"Public places," Jason said. "There are no laws against it. We're not going to publish anyone's image or name."

"Why don't we just record the elementary school playground from a distance?" Bill asked.

"No way!" Karen said. "Not for a public school or any school! All it'll take is one phone call to the police, and they'll be on us in a minute. Remember, we had to get permission just to do the preschools, and they're all private ones. The public schools are a different matter."

"Yeah, there are too many perverts out there," Jason added. "We need to be out in the open with the camera in full view with several of us around. Maybe we can make it look like we're doing a documentary on parks and things."

"There are a lot of students doing video projects," Bruce said. "We should be able to blend in that way. Bill has one of those little remote-controlled drones with a GoPro attached. Bring that along, and no one should bother us."

"That's a good idea!" Bill shouted out. "I have been wanting to take my drone out and get some flying time."

"That will work even better," Karen said. "All we need to do is find a good time and place where there are plenty of kids out playing and set up the cameras. The biggest problem we have is not knowing any of the details. We still need to know their age to determine when the blue glow hits 100 percent."

"There are lots of soccer games going on," Bill added. "The kids are all about the same age for each team."

"That might work!" Karen said. "My niece is in one of those. They group them all by age, too. Even better, there are about eight kids for each team."

"We can record a few games and do some group shots. We just give them some photos and videos to make it legit."

"What if they ask why we are doing this?" Karen asked.

"Simple, we tell them we are testing out some new cameras," Bill explained. "And are thinking about starting a business doing videos of kids playing soccer. We can even set up a web page too. It's all to help promote getting kids into soccer."

"That might work!" Karen said with a big smile.

"What about the schools?" Jason asked. "Are we still going to pursue that?"

"I'll talk with Martha first… There might be a chance of tagging along while she's on one of her studies. But we still need to go back to the preschool to do a follow-up. We have two more to do. We'll know if there is a pattern when we get more data."

* * *

Days later, Karen and Dr. Martha Campbell visited the preschool to interview the seven selected students. Bruce was right about the principal's reaction when hearing the names of the children Karen wants to re-interview. The two children with no readings were not the best of students, always getting into trouble.

Dr. Martha Campbell's assessment of the seven children did not discover anything out of the ordinary. The two that had no readings were definitely troubled students who were well-known as bullies. Out of the five that had brighter readings, three were somewhat above normal and very articulate. The other two were not interested in most activities, always bored, and fell asleep most of the time while in school.

Based on what they learned from the first preschool, Karen asked Dr. Campbell to attend the next two sessions. Assuming they might get similar results, Bill will signal Karen the level of readings of each child during the sessions. In this way, she will know the results immediately and be able to use the information without having to schedule a second interview.

Bill sets up another iPad so Karen can use it during the sessions. The program he wrote displays twelve squares in a row that matches the children's seats. Each square will be assigned a number to match what level Bill reads off his monitor. So Karen will instantly know the results and be able to adjust the questions for each child.

With Dr. Campbell in charge, the meetings run a little smoother. A dozen children are brought in to be interviewed using the same configuration. Bill can send Karen information on each of the children within a few minutes.

After the initial questions, Dr. Campbell can concentrate on the selected children before the interview is over.

After completing the final two preschools, the data is even more confusing. With 105 new children added to the database, only two were at the brighter level, indicating old souls. In the five-year-old group, seven of the children didn't have any readings at all.

Now more than ever, Karen is determined to expand the testing. Now, the big question. What is the age when everyone has the blue glow reading? With Dr. Campbell's help, work is already in progress to try to get into some of the elementary schools.

* * *

Karen makes plans for another group to test. With the number of test subjects showing no readings, she has so many questions about how the criminal element will do. With Karen's numerous friends in the industry, it is easy for her to get permission to do interviews in several prisons.

"I'm not sure about this," Jason said, reading all the restrictions.

"It's the standard precaution they use," Karen said. "I talked with my friend who's been doing this for years. There is going to be plenty of security for us while we're in there."

"Yeah, but how are we going to get past the security with all our gear? That's what I'm worried about with this group. Look at the list of all the things that we'll have to go through to get in. It's worse than the security at the airport. They are going to be doing pat-downs and using metal detectors on us. They'll even inspect everything we bring in. How the hell are we going to get all our equipment in?"

"Yes, the security at the prison is extremely tight," she explained. "All people and equipment will be inspected. There will be no one sneaking in anything hidden in a backpack. Everything has to be out in the open. The camera looks like a normal Hasselblad, so it's no big deal."

"No big deal?" Jason asked. "Have you told Bruce about this?"

Karen nods her head. "Yes, I have... They're more worried about weapons and drugs. We're just bringing in cameras to record the interviews. It's nothing they haven't seen before."

"The processing is done on the iPad and stored on external hard drives," Bill added. "So, there is nothing unusual being brought in."

"He is right," Karen said. "All they're going to see is a camera, iPad, and some external hard drives. No different than a normal video interview."

"Sure, we're just more high-tech than the news people," Bill said. "I have seen people do interviews with just an iPhone. Don't worry about it."

Jason is not too happy about this. "Easy for you to say... You won't be getting frisked by prison guards and be in a room with a bunch of murderers."

"We survived the preschool interviews," Karen said. "So this should be a piece of cake. I have arranged to have a variety of criminals tested. We're going to talk with people who are in for murder down to petty crimes. Also, we need an equal number for each race. We'll get the men first, and then the women's prison is next."

"We got to make this look real," Jason said. "What do we say to these people? They'll be expecting something from us."

"Yeah, we can't go in asking a bunch of bogus questions," Bill added. "We can get away with it with the school kids, but not this bunch."

"Unlike the schools, these people are willing participants eager to tell their story," Karen said. "All we have to do is ask them why they are in prison. I got Dr. Purcell to help with some of the basic questions. Most will use this as an opportunity to promote their case to get out early or to get on some reality TV show."

"So, who is this Dr. Purcell?" Bill asked.

"I have known him for years," Karen explained. "He agreed to join the interview sessions. His work with rehabilitating convicts brings some validation to our being there. He already has a few questions for his own research. So, we'll be helping each other out with these interviews."

"I'm still concerned sitting in a room with some of these people," Jason remarked. "What protection do we have?"

"Only six prisoners will be allowed in the room during the sessions. Four armed guards will be present at all times. Don't worry… Dr. Purcell will probably do all the talking. We're just there to assist him but mostly record all the candidates."

Bill can see that Jason is still too nervous. "I'll go in your place. You can go when we do the women's prison. That will be a lot of fun."

"I hear that's even worse," Jason said, slowly shaking his head.

Karen closes up her notebook. "Make up your mind on which one you want to attend. We need to be there at nine o'clock tomorrow morning."

* * *

The prison interviews are nonstop. There is no end of candidates, and all want to be interviewed. Many are there just to vent their frustration with the conditions or the food.

To help motivate more people to come in, Dr. Purcell brings in several cases of cigarettes, handing out a pack to everyone who attends the meeting. Initially, they estimated getting a couple of dozen people. After several days of handing out free cigarettes, the entire prison population was interviewed.

After visiting numerous prisons from Federal, State, and Juvenile facilities, the results are shocking. Initially, they thought everyone would have a blue glow. After seeing the data from the prisons, many do not. Only a few young children didn't, and it was assumed that they would at a later age. The new data has proven that their initial theories were wrong.

Once all the data has been compiled, a pattern quickly emerges. Most of the hardened criminals who took a life always resulted in no readings at all. The results were the same, no matter of sex, race, or creed. Those who indicated multiple lives were always in Federal prison, convicted of espionage, ethics violations, bank robberies, bribery, and always having to deal with money.

Now the big question did any of these convicts ever have the blue glow. A lot more research is needed for people under eighteen. All the information they have now brings up a lot of questions. When people reach 18 years old and don't have the blue glow, are they destined for a life of crime?

* * *

Remote Viewing Study

Bruce has been studying remote viewing techniques for months. He finds it very similar to meditation, a process of closing your eyes and clearing the mind to the world. With a full-time job during the day and working on secret research at night, it helps to deal with the constant pressure of working over 80 hours a week.

After his art class is over, Bruce sneaks down to the secret lab. Having this extra meeting with Chuck, he wonders if he can keep this up much longer. Not getting home until after ten at night is getting old.

Walking through the dark, empty halls, Bruce slips into the lab. "Hey, Chuck... Ready for another late night?"

"Sure, these are my best working hours. I get more done at night than at any other time of the day. Well, you ready for the big jump?"

Bruce drops his backpack on the floor, collapsing on the recliner. "I think I'm ready for a nap more than anything else. I am so tired!"

"That means you're already halfway there," Chuck said, dragging over a chair. "Pull up that handle so you can lie back. This is your big night!"

Bruce laughs. "You've been saying that for the last couple of weeks!" he then reaches down, pulling on the chair handle. "It'll be like the last time. I'll probably fall asleep."

The old Lazy Boy recliner stretches out almost flat. Bill was smart to bring in the old chair. Too many times, someone works late into the night and sleeps in the old chair instead of driving home.

"Don't worry, Bruce… Just do what you've been practicing. Close your eyes and clear your mind of all the day's hassles. Once you get into the zone, concentrate on your breathing. I'll get everything ready here just in case," hooking Bruce up to the monitors and turns on the camera.

"Looks like you're already halfway there with that pulse rate of yours," Chuck jokingly said.

Bruce laughs. "Yeah, halfway asleep."

"No talking… Concentrate on every breath you take," Chuck whispers.

After several minutes, Bruce's vital signs are slowing down. "OK, start imagining this electrical energy is in your mind. It's like a tingling sensation on your forehead. On every breath, push it down through the rest of your body. Down through your arms and then your legs. Let it flow with your breathing."

Bruce fights hard to stay awake. His mind is clear of everything but his breathing. With every breath, he is pushing the energy down to his arms and legs. Once in a while, he can feel himself dozing off. He concentrates on Chuck's voice to stay awake.

After a while, he peeks over at the clock on the far wall, seeing 45 minutes have passed. He must have fallen asleep. Taking in deep breaths, he concentrates on his breathing again. The last thing he wants to do is fall asleep and wake up the next morning in the chair.

He notices a weird tingling sensation in his hands as if they had fallen asleep. Then, every time he exhales, it feels like a pulse of electricity moving throughout his body. He feels as if he is half-asleep and not much in control of things.

Opening his eyes, Chuck is still sitting next to him. Unable to move his arms and legs, it feels like he is paralyzed. Fighting to sit up, but nothing is working. Feeling like being in a drunken stupor, he is not in control of his own body. He doesn't like this at all and is fighting like mad to wake up.

Finally, Bruce is able to sit up. Feeling exhausted, he rests for a few seconds, unable to move his legs. An odd buzzing sound is blocking out everything, and his vision is also blurry. He sees Chuck facing the other way, looking at the monitors. Feeling somewhat nauseous, he yells out. Chuck is ignoring him and doesn't even react to his voice.

So frustrated, Bruce tries to push himself off the chair. His legs feel numb, and he is unable to move them. He leans over, using his hands, trying to push himself off the side of the chair. Expecting to fall on the floor, he starts drifting as if in a weightless environment.

He is confused about what is happening. It gets worse when the room starts spinning around. It is the same type of experience after having way too much to drink. The last thing he needs is to end up getting sick all over the floor.

Constantly yelling at Chuck, but he is too busy watching the monitors. Bruce doesn't understand what the hell is going on. He keeps yelling out, but that buzzing sound is drowning out everything.

Slowly drifting across the room, Bruce is in a daze and is so confused. As the room rotates, he sees something very odd. The old chair he was sitting on now has someone else on it. Then it dawns on him. He is looking at his own body, still lying on the chair.

Bruce's whole body jolts as if being hit by a Taser. He opens his eyes, seeing the ceiling above. He is back on the chair again.

Chuck screams out loud. "Bruce! Way to go!" clapping his hands.

"Holy shit!" Bruce yells out. "What the hell was that?"

"You did it! You son of a bitch! Damn, you don't waste any time either. You went straight for it."

Bruce tries to sit up but is utterly exhausted. "That was absolutely horrible!"

"Don't try to get up… It really drains you at first. So, tell me everything you experienced."

"Oh, it was weird… It's like when you wake up in the morning, and you're half-asleep and can't move your body. I also felt like I was about to get sick."

"Yeah, you do get a little motion sickness at times. Then what happened?"

"I tried to get out of the chair, but all I could do was sit up. My legs didn't move at all. I kept yelling at you, but you had your back to me, and you wouldn't turn around. That was really pissing me off. Then there was that damn buzzing sound!"

Chuck laughed. "Yeah, it goes away after a while… What else?"

"I pushed myself off the chair, expecting to fall, but ended up floating. When the room started spinning, it was horrible. I thought I was going to lose my lunch. I noticed you didn't tell me about all the side effects."

"If I told you about the motion sickness, it would have been worse. You'd be expecting it. Everyone is different. You have to see what happens when you get there. The same thing happens to the astronauts when they are in zero gravity for the first time. Some are OK, while others just puke their guts out. Don't worry. You'll get used to it. So, how did you get back?"

"I don't know… When I saw someone else sitting in the chair, I couldn't figure out what was going on. Then I realized it was me! Talk about weird. Next thing I knew, I was back in the chair looking up at the ceiling!"

"Classic case! Damn! You did good for your first time. It took me years to get there."

"It was like being in a bad dream. I had no control. The strange thing about it all is that it was over so quickly."

"Remember the last thing you saw?"

Bruce shrugs his shoulders. "Me lying in the chair?"

"That's right… Think about it. The best way to explain it is you're five years old and out in the park with your mother. You go for a walk all by yourself, but your mother has you on a long leash. She is always watching over you. She sees what you see. At any time, she can punch the button and drag you back in. So, when you saw yourself on that chair, your mind knows your fear, sees through your eyes. Without warning, you're quickly dragged back in!"

Bruce laughs. "Oh, great! A doubting mother is always watching over me."

"Remember, part of you is leaving your body. There is always some sort of link between the two. No matter how far you travel, at any time, you can be sucked back in. After some experience, you learn to control it."

"So, you can come back when you are ready?" Bruce asked.

"That's the hard part. You still have to learn how to control your fears. Otherwise, it'll just drag you back without any warning."

"So, did we get any of this recorded?" Bruce asked, glancing over at the monitors.

"Yep, got it all. I saw the fluctuations and knew you were in the zone."

"Oh, did you see that I went right by you?"

"Yeah, I saw the white light go across the monitor. It was over real quick, but we got it!"

Bruce has a hard time keeping his eyes open. "Can't wait to see that… Although, it feels like I have been up for days. I need to go home and take a nap."

"You're in no shape to drive home. Get some sleep. I'll monitor you for a while, so don't worry about it."

Bruce lays back, closes his eyes, and quickly falls asleep. Chuck grabs a blanket, pulling it over him. He knows the first jump is the most exhausting, but with Bruce being so tired after working all day, it'll be worse.

Chuck decides to continue working the rest of the night and to watch over him. It will take a while to process the data, even though it was a short jump. He knows everyone will want to see the video of Bruce's first jump to the other side.

* * *

Utterly exhausted, Bruce calls in sick for a couple of days. His first successful remote viewing was not only frightening but brought back too many bad memories of when he had his accident. The similarities are there, the lack of control over his body and the total confusion. Now, he understands why some people go nuts after doing this remote viewing thing.

Chuck and Karen are at Bruce's apartment to talk with him about his experience. They want to be there while he watches the video of his first remote viewing session. Bruce is the only person who has had an out-of-body experience and successfully accomplished remote viewing. There are theories that the two are similar or even the same. Now, they can actually talk with someone who has done both.

Seeing the recording of the event is breathtaking. The tiny white light hovers over Bruce's body and then slowly moves right behind Chuck. What is more astounding is seeing how the path of the light is the same as the vision he remembers.

Seeing his blue glow on the monitor for the first time is a little unnerving. The blue glow is extremely bright. He now knows that he has been around the block a few times.

"How do you feel about the experience?" Karen asked after watching the video of the event.

"Real spooky," Bruce said. "It's very similar to when you're not fully awake. You can open your eyes, but you can't move your arms and legs. Your whole body is paralyzed."

"Similar to your other experiences in the hospital?" she asked.

"In a way, with the floating about and no control. Everything was really murky and not that clear. Before, I was able to see the bluish glow in other people, but not this time. I didn't see any blue glow on Chuck."

"Why is that?" she asked, glancing over at Chuck.

He shrugs his shoulders. "I have no clue... I have never seen it either in all my experiences. It could be at a different level. In remote viewing, maybe a smaller portion can transcend. In a near-death experience, that's a whole different thing. We think it might be a greater portion of the soul that leaves. There is a big difference in the recordings in when someone dies, and someone leaves voluntarily."

Bruce laughed. "Oh, it's another one of those mothership analogies."

"Exactly!" Chuck shouted out. "In the remote viewing, a scout plane is sent out to explore. It's also on a long tether line so that it can be drawn back at any time. You don't have to worry about getting lost. It'll always pull you back home."

"And when someone dies?" Karen asked.

"That's different... It's more like the opposite. The main entity leaves the body, but it leaves a marker so it can get back. That marker is temporary. When the brain ceases to function, the marker fades away."

"This marker..." she said, glancing over her notes. "Chuck, you think it's some sort of claim or a territorial thing?"

He nods his head. "I think so... What would happen if another lost soul is wandering around? It sees this fine human specimen with no caretaker and moves on in. Then the original soul comes back only to find out someone else has taken over."

"That would lead to a big change in personality," Bruce suggested.

"How about multiple personalities?" Chuck asked. "Think what would happen if more than one soul occupies a person."

"We've been looking at that, too," Karen said. "There are some people we'd like to interview. Their families claimed that they were possessed or had an evil spirit. We are wondering if that could be the case."

"You mean like an evil soul just comes in and takes over?" Bruce asked.

She nods. "Yeah, it could be."

"How would we be able to detect it?" Bruce asked.

"Would that show up as a brighter level like some of the others?" Chuck asked. "Would we see two glowing blue lights?"

"That's a good question," Karen said. "What happens when two souls occupy one body? These evil spirits or souls, there are plenty of documented reports of that. I love to be able to bring in one of those to study."

"I remember that Exorcist movie," Bruce said, starting to shutter. "I don't think I'd want to get near one of those."

"I wouldn't either," Chuck said. "You got to watch yourself with those people."

She laughs at them. "There is another theory... Maybe not so evil. Dr. Stewart and Jason have reason to believe that these people who are possessed or have multiple personalities might be having issues with other past lives. Think about it. If you lived many times and could recall all those memories, what would happen if you could switch from one life's memories to another?"

"Interesting…" Bruce said, thinking about it. "A lot less spooky than the evil spirit thing."

"Dr. Stewart has two patients who may fall into this category," Karen said. "He's already completed the first stages of regression. He said it was a wild ride with those two. Normally, it takes a long time trying to pull up old memories, but with these two people, the past lives are all in there together."

"So, it could be any of those," Bruce said. "Evil spirits or those who can recall all their past lives. It's scary to think about it. In either case, it's not a good thing."

Karen lets out a long sigh. "We got so many unanswered questions. We'll just have to put that on the to-do list."

Chuck leans back in his chair. "OK, it's getting late and off-subject. So, how do you want to proceed? You ready for another go?" glancing over at Bruce.

Bruce hesitates, thinking about it. "Well, not too eager after that first one. You didn't tell me about all the side effects."

"I didn't want to scare you. Most people experience the same side effects, motion sickness, general weakness, and that awful buzzing sound. That goes away over time. It does drain your body, though. You have to prepare for it. You can't be working a twelve-hour day then go into a remote viewing session."

"He is right… You are working way too many hours. If you are going to start dabbling into this, you better cut back."

"Karen is right… Start taking vacation time or call in sick more often. Sunday afternoon might be the best time if you are ready for another go. Just sleep in and take it easy for the whole day. Get plenty of sleep the night before."

Karen is still wary about all this. "You got to be sure you want to be part of this. Like Chuck said, many have ended up in the mental ward."

"He'll be all right," Chuck added. "If you have someone monitoring you, it's a lot safer. That's why I always have my assistant with me. If things get out of control, you can be brought back. The ones who get into trouble are always the ones going out on their own. It's just like scuba diving. You always need a buddy with you at all times."

"I think I may try it one more time," Bruce said. "If I can get past the phase where the room is circling around, then I might do OK."

She laughs. "I can't believe your first remote viewing experience felt like being drunk and nauseated with the room circling around you."

Bruce smiles. "I didn't realize in my college days I was prepping myself for remote viewing with all those heavy drinking parties."

"OK, we're going to let you get some sleep," Karen said, motioning to Chuck it's time to leave. "Make sure to call in sick for a few more days. You need the rest."

"Well, thanks for stopping by to visit. I'm going back to bed."

"I'll check back with you in a day or two," Chuck said as he walked out the door.

* * *

Walking out to the parking lot, Karen grabs Chuck's arm. "I'm not sure we're doing the right thing with this. He is still recovering from his accident. I think this remote viewing is too much for him."

"He knows what he is doing… I have never seen anyone jump over so quickly. It was like it was no effort at all for him."

"That's my point… It's all going too fast. Bruce needs time to adjust. Since his accident, he has changed a lot."

"He seems normal to me."

"After talking with his family, even they noticed how much he has changed. He doesn't see his friends anymore. His girlfriend left him, or he left her. All he does is work seven days a week. Now he is jumping into the remote viewing."

"Don't forget you are part of the problem as well. All the work Bruce has been doing to help your research and mine. When you decide to publish, you'll be doing the talk show circuit, book deals, and all those paid lectures."

"And you're not?" she asked.

"I'll be there as well, but I'm not doing it for the money. This is big! You have to admit it. Nothing is going to come close to this, and we are going to rewrite the history books. Bruce has already been in the news all over the world with his new camera design. His work is so revolutionary."

"Your point?" she asked.

"Has he done any interviews? No, he hasn't done one. Yeah, he was in the hospital at the time but still refuses to talk with any news media to this day. All of his colleagues are the ones getting all the glory. He doesn't care at all."

"That's what I'm worried about."

"You and I are talking book deals and the like. All Bruce talks about is getting a log cabin out by the lake in Wyoming after all this is done. Where there is nothing around but trees, and he can go out fishing every day. That's what he's planning."

"Damn… He is going into the deep end. I need to talk to him about that."

"Karen, you deal with these people all the time. When they go over to the other side, it changes them. They see life a lot different when they have experienced that. He doesn't care about money or fame. He's looking for answers and nothing more."

"I think it's time for him to take a little vacation. I'll see about cutting his hours with us, too."

"Good…" Chuck said. "I'll talk to you later," knowing it's going to be difficult to get Bruce to cut back on the remote viewing sessions.

* * *

Days later, Bruce is so bored staying at home. Karen bans him from the meetings and access to the lab. He made a mistake calling in sick at work. Now, he has nothing to do or anywhere to go.

He gets tired of watching the junk on daytime TV, so he goes back to bed for an afternoon nap. The only thing still on the plate is the meeting with Chuck on Sunday afternoon, and that's a couple of days away. With nothing else to occupy his mind, he keeps thinking about his first remote viewing session.

Lying on the bed, Bruce stares up at the ceiling, mentally going through the process. Deep breathing and clearing the mind is something he has been practicing for months. He expected a lot more to it. The electrical energy thing was a strange experience. All the aftereffects surprised him the most, but the rest was rather easy.

Feeling so tired, Bruce closed his eyes, concentrating on his breathing. A few times, it feels as if he has dozed off. Fighting to stay awake, he notices a tingling sensation going down his body every time he exhales. Right away, he realizes this is similar to the electrical energy experience from the first session with Chuck. The sensation gets stronger, moving down to his legs.

Hearing a loud bang, Bruce is jolted awake. He is wondering what fell off the wall or if someone is beating on the door. Slowly getting up, he feels a little dizzy. For some reason, his vision is blurred. He keeps blinking his eyes, hoping it clears up.

He struggles, trying to walk down the hallway to see what caused that loud bang. Everything is hazy as if there is smoke in the room. Again, he blinks, wondering what is wrong with his eyes. At least the smoke alarm is not going off. Nothing is on the floor, and he doesn't hear anyone knocking at the door. Now he is wondering if it was an earthquake he heard.

Walking into the living room, he starts feeling nauseous. He tries to stop, but it feels as if he is walking on ice, slowly moving forward. Eventually, he stops and slowly turns around. For some reason, he doesn't have control over his body. It feels more like a bad dream, where he is totally confused.

Feeling so dizzy, he is starting to wonder if there is carbon monoxide in his apartment. He doesn't remember using the stove, or is there a fire somewhere filling his apartment with fumes? Desperate to get some fresh air in his apartment, he rushes over to the sliding glass door before it's too late.

Reaching the door, he lunges for the door handle. To his surprise, he misses it. His vision is so poor that he is having a bad time judging how far away things are. Again, he tries to grab onto the door handle, but this time, his hand goes right through it.

To make the situation worse, after failing to grab onto the door handle, now he is slowly spinning in a circle. Unable to stop, Bruce moves right for the glass door. He knows this is going to hurt, hoping not to break the glass. Waiting for the big collision, it ends up being nothing. He goes right through the glass door as if it's wide open. So confused, he thought the door was closed.

Once outside, he slowly moves across the patio. Again, it feels as if he is on ice, unable to stop or even slow down. Coming to the edge of the patio, he frantically reaches out for the railings. Just like the door handle, his hands go right through as if it's not there.

Passing through the patio railings, he panics. Seeing the two-story drop, he waits for the fall, but nothing happens. Far below, the grass and the small bushes move slowly beneath him. He turns to look behind, only to see the strange sight of his apartment slowly drifting away.

There is no falling at all, just floating along above the ground. It's another strange dream where he is flying around. Seeing some neighbors walking, he calls out to them. They don't even notice he is there. Birds fly right by, almost colliding with him. Feathers are floating everywhere as the flock of birds scatters around him.

Slowly floating across the apartment grounds, he feels a sense of euphoria. Then, it dawns on him what is happening. This is no dream. He has inadvertently gone to the other side without knowing it. The first thought in his mind is how to get back. Glancing over at his apartment, he panics, seeing how far away it is.

Bruce's whole body jolts as if struck by lightning, hearing a loud bang. Everything goes dark. Taking in a deep breath, he is trying not to panic. Slowly opening his eyes, he is back in his bedroom, still lying in bed. Feeling extremely weak, he struggles to get to the living room to call for help.

"Hey, Chuck…" Bruce mumbles on the phone. "I think I got a problem here."

"What is it? You sound awful."

"I was taking a nap… Practicing my breathing. I think I might have accidentally gone over."

"Oh no… Are you sure?"

"Not too sure of anything right now… Was it a dream? I don't know. So tired…"

"Stay right there! I'm coming over!" Chuck shouted on the phone.

So exhausted, Bruce can just manage a few steps before collapsing on the couch. As soon as his eyes are closed, his mind starts drifting. Then he starts feeling a sensation of falling. Everything is spinning again, almost like getting vertigo.

Again, he is confused. His vision is still blurry, and he is trying to focus his eyes. Everything is green with these brilliant lights dotted about the place. Strange music is coming from a distance.

His vision slowly starts to clear. He then recognizes far below him is a park filled with people. Everything is dark, but the whole park is illuminated with lights. A small symphony is playing music, surrounded by a huge crowd.

Slowly, he descends, floating just above the trees. Feeling like a bird, he is enjoying every minute of this. Flying about, he swoops down, just a few feet above the ground. Hundreds of people, all sitting on blankets listening to the music, and not one person notices him.

Flying above one of the sidewalks, Bruce sees this one woman standing all alone. Right away, he can tell she is watching him. Everyone else is ignoring him except for her. His curiosity is getting the better of him. He circles around, going back, slowing down as he approaches the woman.

Her face is full of rage. "Why are they doing this to me!" she screams out with such anger. "I know you see me! You can see me! Tell me why this is happening!"

She starts moving closer, constantly screaming out in a rage. Bruce doesn't know what to do at first. Seeing the look on her face, he has never seen such anger before. Moving straight past the woman, he gets as far away from her as possible.

Hearing her screaming, he looks back, so shocked. She is right behind him, only a few feet away. He quickly turns, racing for the trees. At times, she is so close that he can feel her trying to grab onto his foot.

Once he is within the trees, he turns left, then right, trying to lose this madwoman. No matter how fast he turns, weaving through the branches, she is still right behind him.

As a last resort, he turns, going straight up to the clouds. With all of his might, he pushes to go faster and faster. The sound of her screaming gets fainter. Looking down, he sees the woman far behind. Eventually, she stops following him, returning to the park.

He is familiar with the city lights after all those night flights out of Los Angeles airport. He is trying to figure out how high up he is, recognizing some of the highways and shopping malls far below.

In a flash, everything turns gray. Inside the cloud, it's cold and damp. He quickly changes direction, moving deep within the cloud in case the madwoman decides to follow him.

The gray mist is soon replaced by blackness as Bruce emerges from the far side of the cloud. The view of the stars is astounding. Everything is so clear. The glow of the Milky Way Galaxy is so bright, and he has never seen such brilliant colors before.

Glancing down, he sees the city lights far below. He panics, realizing he must be miles high. He starts to lose control of things, and he feels himself beginning to fall. His arms and legs are flailing with the wind as he goes into a spin. His speed picks up as the ground gets closer and closer.

The vision startles him so much that it jolts him awake, gasping for air. Taking in a deep breath, he focuses on what looks like a ceiling. For some strange reason, he is in another room, somewhat dark with beeping sounds and a horrible rumbling noise.

The beeping sound is coming from a monitor with a green strobe dancing across the screen. More instruments with flashing lights and various numbers are displayed on the digital readout. He knows he is back in a hospital again, seeing railings on the bed and all the tubes sticking out of his arms.

"How are you feeling, Mr. Rollin?" the nurse asked, walking into the room.

"Not sure…" Bruce mumbled. "Why am I here?"

"You apparently collapsed from exhaustion. Your friend called the ambulance," turning on the lights, pointing over at the corner.

Bruce laughed. "So that's what that horrible noise is!" seeing Chuck slumped in a chair, sound asleep and snoring away.

"Yes, we need to wake him up. His snoring is bellowing down the halls," nudging Chuck's arm.

Chuck coughs a few times. "Oh, Bruce… I see you are up," letting out a long yawn. "So, how is he doing?" he asks the nurse.

"I was just about to check on him," she answered, looking over at the readings and jotting them all down on the chart.

"So, what's the verdict?" Bruce asked.

"You have lost a lot of weight since you were here last. You're extremely dehydrated and malnourished. Basically, you are working way too many hours and not eating properly or drinking enough fluids. We got you on vitamins and saline for now. You'll be in here for a few days. I'll be back in a few hours. If you need anything, just press the call button," promptly leaving the room.

Chuck pulls the chair up close to the bed, looking very serious. "We got to talk."

"What happened?" Bruce asked.

"Looks like you're going over to the other side… I told you that you need to have someone with you at all times.

You're playing a dangerous game doing this on your own. That's how people get hurt, physically and mentally."

"Believe me... It wasn't intentional. I was drained and ready to go to sleep. I was just practicing my breathing. That's when I started thinking about the process we were doing back in the lab. Then I heard this loud bang and got up to see what it was."

"What? You didn't go in on purpose?"

"No, I didn't even know. At first, I thought it was another weird dream. It wasn't until I floated outside that I figured it out."

"Damn... This is not good. You weren't even trying?"

Bruce shakes his head. "No... I remember thinking about the process that we went through before. I hadn't a clue what was happening."

"You managed to get back. That's good."

"Yeah, once I was outside floating about, it was OK. Seeing how far I was from my apartment, that was when I got so scared. I wondered how I was supposed to get back then, bang! I'm back in bed. That loud noise. Is that an indicator that you have moved over?"

Chuck nods his head. "Yep, sometimes it's not a smooth jump. When you hear that loud bang, you know you're there. It works both ways."

"Yeah, I remember hearing it both times, once going in and the other coming back. It's like a big explosion. It really wakes you up. I was really exhausted. I barely made it out of bed."

"That was way too soon for another jump. I couldn't even revive you. Ended up calling 911."

"How long have I been here? What time is it?" trying to look out the window.

"It's about nine... You have been asleep for six hours. Everyone's been coming in all day long, checking up on you."

Bruce cringed. "Anyone from my office?"

"A few... I got my assistant to watch the main entrance. She warns me when they come in. I think your days are numbered at your work."

"I kind of figured that... I ain't worried. I'll drag it out a little longer. I don't like the games they are playing there. Fortunately, they need me more than I need them."

Chuck laughs. "Good for you! Like I said before, take the money and run."

Bruce is deep in thought, trying to make sense of everything. "You know... I'm still having a hard time figuring out what's real and what's a dream. When I was floating outside my apartment, I knew I was on the other side. After I called you, I had another weird dream, or was it a dream? I can't tell the two apart anymore. It was all so real!"

"You think you had another experience after the first one?"

He stares at the wall. "I don't know... In that second dream, or whatever it was, I was flying about in the dark. It was at a park that was all lit up with lights and filled with people. There was a small band with a few violins and cellos. It was like being a bird flying around the trees in total control. That was a great experience, but the weird thing about it all. I think I have had a similar dream in the same park. At least in that dream, it was during the day, but that last one was at night. That was a spooky one."

"It's not uncommon to have recurring dreams. Why was it spooky? I thought you said you were flying about having a good time?"

"Flying about was the good part... No one else noticed me, but this one woman did. I got up close to her, and then she started screaming. She really scared the hell out of me. That look on her face. I'll never forget that look. It was like absolute rage!"

"Holy shit!" Chuck shouted, putting his hands over his mouth. "What happened?"

"I tried to get away, but she kept chasing after me. No matter what I did, I couldn't shake her. I could even feel her grabbing my feet. She was that close. I was zipping in and out of the trees, and then I made a beeline for the clouds. I remember seeing that in those old war movies. The airplanes would go for the clouds to hide. It really worked, too."

"This woman was actually chasing you? You could hear her and feel her touching you?"

"Yeah... That screaming was horrible. She sounded like she was mad as hell about something, or worse, insane."

"But, you were able to get away?" Chuck asked.

"I shot straight up, going real high, and finally got some distance from her. Once I hit the clouds, I changed course, hoping to lose her."

"You got lucky... Wait a minute! You went all the way up to the clouds?"

"Yeah, with that madwoman chasing after me, I had to do something. Why? What's wrong with being up in the clouds?"

Chuck just shakes his head. "So, what happened next?"

"After a while, I popped out of the clouds, and the view was spectacular. It was so real. The stars were so clear and bright, and I could even see the Milky Way. Then I remember looking down. That was one scary moment. I could see the city far below. That's when I got so scared and started falling. That's one hell of a drop. It felt like falling out of an airplane with no parachute!"

Chuck just stares at Bruce, not saying a word.

"What is it?" Bruce asked.

There is a long pause. "I don't think that was a dream... You slipped over without knowing it. That woman you saw. That's one thing you don't want to meet up with while you are out there. You're not ready for that."

"What? That was real?"

He slowly nods his head. "You have to stay far away from those people."

"What was she?" Bruce asked, getting concerned.

"She is a lost soul, stuck between the worlds. She doesn't know she died. You described it very accurately. They all eventually go insane. No one can see or hear them, and they don't know why. They just wander the earth, and it could be for hundreds of years or more. If she had caught you, she would have never let you go and could prevent you from getting back."

"Thanks for warning me about this in advance," Bruce said, getting scared.

"That's the dark side of this... And I did warn you."

"So, I guess when they talk about heaven and hell, that was definitely the hell part. Can you imagine having to live like that for eternity? That's really scary!"

"No shit... You said you've been to this park before. If so, that probably wasn't a dream either."

"It could have been in the same park. I remember doing the same, flying about like a bird. There were lots of people sitting about watching the sunset. Wait a minute! There was this one woman. It was the same situation where no one else knew I was there, but she did."

"When did this happen?" Chuck asked, getting concerned.

"I'm not sure... Maybe a long time ago, just after my accident. It was like the same dream, where I was flying around in the park. The only thing different about her is that she was the only one who had the blue glow all over her. That's why I remembered how she stood out from the rest. It's all coming back to me now."

"So... That was during the day, and you saw the blue glow around the woman?"

"Yes... I remember it from a dream I had a long time ago."

"And the recent one, you were in the park at night. You didn't see any blue glows?"

"No, I didn't... I have never seen any of these blue glows at all while out on these remote viewing things."

"So, Bruce, this first dream, when you were at the park during the day... Was that when you were in the emergency room?"

"It's hard to place the time... No, I think it was later. The first time, I was wandering about in the waiting area. When I came back, I was on the operating table. I'll never forget that one. The dream in the park, I remember waking up in bed in the hospital room."

"Damn! If that's the case, you are going over to the other side, and you don't even know it."

"So these weird dreams I have been having are not even dreams," Bruce said, getting nervous. "You mean to tell me that I've been jumping over to the other side all this time!"

"Yeah... I have been wondering how you were able to jump over so quickly. You better be careful from here on out. You need to stay away from that park. She is probably out there waiting for you."

"I don't even remember how I got there. I have no clue where it is."

"Wait a minute," Chuck said, pulling out his iPhone. "There may be a way to find out where it is. Music in a park at night. There should be something listed out there on the Internet."

In less than a minute, he finds it. "There it is! MacArthur Park Concert under the stars. That's tonight! It's from eight to ten o'clock. Son of a bitch! What the hell were you doing way out there?"

"Where is that? It doesn't sound familiar."

"Oh, it's that small park with a lake, about twelve miles from here."

Bruce is shocked. "Twelve miles! That far away?"

"That's way too far for you... For a first-timer, you need to keep close by."

"How do you keep close? I never intended to go anywhere."

Chuck thinks about it. "That's the big mystery... It took me years to get where you are today. I wonder if it's got something to do with your accident."

"I haven't a clue... From the sounds of things, I'm not really in control. It's like a weird dream where you don't have a say in what happens. Damn, I'm so glad this day is over so I can get some rest."

"Well, you're not going to get much rest when Karen gets here to give you the riot act. Remember, your boss was here earlier as well. I think you may have to deal with them too."

"Oh, hell! Maybe it's time to take a long vacation?"

Chuck laughs. "I think they mentioned that... You need a break from it all. No more experiments, no more tests, or work. Go fishing at that place in Wyoming you've been talking about."

"Good idea... I need to get away for a while. Too much work and no play..." slowly falling asleep.

* * *

The Second Attempt

Weeks later, Bruce has fully recovered from his ordeal. Spending a few weeks out fishing, he has been able to concentrate on his new goals in life. Work is now a thing of the past after being put on medical leave. The only thing he has on his mind is another remote viewing attempt.

With Karen's blessing, Bruce is scheduled for another session with Chuck. Karen and Jason will be present to make sure nothing goes wrong. New rules are in place. There will be a complete physical before and after each session. After the remote viewing session, Bruce cannot be left alone for 48 hours and will be constantly monitored.

"Bruce, are you sure you want to do this?" Karen asked. "You know all the problems you had last time."

"I was just tired back then," Bruce replied. "I got plenty of rest, and now I'm ready for whatever is out there."

"We are going to keep it simple," Chuck explains. "Nothing elaborate. You need to practice the jump and learn some control. It's like learning how to fly an airplane. You just do a little at a time."

"You going to bring a parachute?" Jason asked jokingly.

Karen kicks Jason's leg. "You need to get serious! We're not playing games here."

"Sorry… I was just trying to lighten up the mood."

"OK, Bruce, we got everything set up," Chuck said. "Just relax and get in the recliner. Start with the breathing exercises."

Bruce leans back, resting on the heavy leather chair, trying to relax. It is not going to be comfortable with everyone watching. He is covered with sensors and wires leading up to various medical instruments. They even make him wear a special helmet covered with sensors to record his brain activity. Karen is going to make sure nothing goes wrong, monitoring all his vital signs during this session.

"I'm ready to go," Bruce said. "Hold on to your hats. It's going to be a bumpy ride!"

Karen just stares at him. "Be serious about this."

"Relax and breathe slowly," Chuck said, seeing the pulse rate was still way too high.

"How long does it normally take?" Jason whispers.

"Sometimes up to an hour for beginners," Chuck explains. "With him, I'm not sure. He went over really fast last time. Maybe it was a fluke. We'll see how it goes today."

"Jason, I want to make sure we record everything," Karen whispers, trying not to disturb Bruce. "Once he goes over, I don't want to miss anything. Let us know when he jumps."

"OK, get to your stations," Chuck said quietly. "Keep your voices down. We got to let him relax. Be best not to talk from here on out," seeing how Bruce is still not ready and getting irritated.

Ten minutes go by, and nothing is happening. The monitors are already indicating a slower respiratory rate and lower blood pressure. Karen and Jason are both wondering if Bruce has just fallen asleep and all this is for nothing.

Within a minute, an alert starts flashing on the screen. The computer detected a small fluctuation in the blue glow, so Chuck motioned to Karen and Jason to begin recording.

Without any warnings, Bruce has crossed over. A small white light appears on the monitor, slowly rising above Bruce's head.

"Damn!" Chuck shouts out so loud. "This is unbelievable!"

Jason is startled by all the yelling. "Are we allowed to talk?"

"Sure, he already crossed over," Chuck replied.

"Already!" Jason shouts. "How can that be? You said it could take an hour?"

Chuck laughs. "Well, he ain't one of the normal ones. I have never seen anything like this," glancing over at Karen.

"Can he hear us?" Karen asked.

"Not sure... We'll know when he gets back."

"Why don't we ask him?" Jason said, looking over at Bruce. "Hey, buddy! Can you hear us?" waving his hands back and forth.

"Bruce, if you can hear us," Chuck added. "Just move about a little. Can you do that?"

They all look over to the monitors. The white light doesn't move at all. All it's doing is floating right above Bruce's head.

"He might be trying to get his bearings. We'll know more afterward."

The white light starts circling and then disappears through the wall. Karen panics, frantically going over Bruce's vital signs. She is so wary of the remote viewing. It is so dangerous, both mentally and physically, to the body.

"Well, he is out exploring," Chuck said. "Son of a bitch makes it look so easy. How are all the readings?"

"Everything looks good," Karen replied. "From what I see here, he could be asleep."

"If he gets into trouble, can we tell from here?" Jason asked.

Chuck nods. "I think so... There is always a link between the two. His body should react. If his mind doesn't like what it's seeing, or he panics, then it'll drag him back in a flash."

* * *

Bruce has no idea that he has crossed over. Everything went so smoothly this time. As he sits up, he notices everyone is staring at him. The loud humming sound is blocking out all their voices. They are trying to talk, but for some reason, he does not hear anything.

With Jason waving and pointing to the monitor, it gets his attention. Seeing the small white light on the monitor, he is so shocked. For Bruce, it feels as if he is sitting up on the chair. On the monitor, he can see himself lying down, and the white light is hovering a couple of feet over his head.

Now, he knows this is all for real and not a dream. The first thing he has to do is perform a few tests. The control experiment is the first on the list. When he had done this before, he was always out of control, like drifting with the wind.

Remembering what Chuck had taught him, he has to concentrate on what he wants to do. Just being able to stay in place is the first thing on the list. He thinks about slowly rising a few feet above the chair. Immediately, he feels the sensation of moving up. Again, he thinks about stopping, and it all works like a charm.

For the next test on the list, he imagines himself moving in a circle. Without any warning, he is flying in circles exactly as he did in those dreams. You just think about what you want to do, and you are there.

Bruce is so thrilled with the experience. It is just like flying about like a bird. Now, he wants to explore, wanting to go outside and see the world. In a flash, he shoots right through the walls. Nothing is slowing him down.

Within a few seconds, Bruce is outside, flying about in total control. Flying is not so difficult. He starts to experiment, going through the various buildings on campus, going down one hallway and into another.

Turning down one hallway, hundreds of people quickly spill out of the classrooms. The hall is packed with people. Without any warning, someone runs right in front of his path. Unable to slow down, Bruce accidentally travels right through him. That was an incredibly bizarre experience. Not one that he'll want to do ever again.

Roaming through the old college buildings is getting a little boring. Back outside, Bruce decides to check out the beach. The moment he thought about it, he was traveling so fast over all the houses and streets, going straight for the ocean.

In a matter of seconds, Bruce is on the beach. Flying a few feet above the sand, he goes all the way down to the shoreline. He sees the waves breaking nearby, wondering how this works while in the water. Again, without any warning, he plunges into the ocean.

He is a little nervous being underwater like this. Although, it is noticeably more sluggish than traveling through the air. A small school of fish is swimming nearby, so he decides to join them. In a flash, he is surrounded by all the fish as if he is one of them.

Right then, he realizes that he needs to watch what he thinks because it becomes reality. His thoughts are controlling his destiny. He cannot let his mind wander and needs to focus on what's around him.

The school of fish is swimming around erratically, darting from one side to the other. Bruce has a hard time keeping up with them. Then he sees why they are frantically swimming about so fast. Huge dark shadows emerge from the distance. Looking as if it's lunchtime for the bigger fish, he decides this is not the best place to be. Slowing down to get a little distance from the school of fish, he does not want to be part of this massacre.

As he slowly wanders off, going farther out into the ocean, one of the bigger fish quickly turns to make a beeline for him. The last thing he sees is the huge mouth opening up. Everything goes dark for a second, and then he is back in the ocean again. He went right through the fish. Another fish darts for him, and again, the same thing happens. Somehow, these fish can see him and think he is some kind of meal.

Getting a little flustered by these fish trying to have him for lunch, Bruce slowly rises out of the ocean. The fish follow him up to the surface but swim away once he is out of the water. He wonders if he looks like a shiny fishing lure with the fish going after him like that. This is something that he needs to discuss with Chuck later.

Returning to the beach, he thinks about the fish being able to see him and wonders if it works with other animals. Seeing a dog running about on the beach, chasing after a tennis ball, Bruce flies over in that direction for a little experiment.

Floating above the woman, Bruce waits to see whether the dog will react to him. She tosses a tennis ball down the beach, and the dog quickly chases after it. When the dog is halfway back, Bruce slowly drops down, getting between the woman and the dog. Immediately, the dog drops the ball and starts barking. The woman calls out to him and waves, but the dog does not want to get any closer.

The woman runs over, picking up the ball, wondering why her dog is acting so odd. Bruce slowly approaches, not wanting to scare the dog. Right away, he can see the dog is looking right at him. He circles around the woman. The dog is watching his every move and is constantly barking.

Bruce stops, hovering about a foot above the sand. It is the first time he realizes that he can hear the barking. He calls out to the dog. The dog's ears pop up, reacting to his voice. The dog is frightened and starts whimpering with its tail between its legs, trying to hide behind the woman.

That's all Bruce needed to see. Not wanting to scare the dog anymore, he slowly rises up and continues down the beach. The entire time, the dog is still watching him.

Noticing some seagulls standing on the beach right next to the water, Bruce swoops down to see what happens. As he moves through the birds, they scatter away, flying in all directions. That answers that question. At least the birds aren't chasing after him like the fish did.

Seeing a group of preschool kids out on the beach, he wonders if they can see him as well. He slows down, running right through the middle of all the kids. Not one reacted. He even gets right in front of one girl, only a few inches from her face, but there is no reaction at all.

The only reaction is from a small Chihuahua dog. The dog is not scared at all, always chasing after him. All the kids are laughing, seeing how the dog reacts, and chases after something that is not there.

Getting tired, Bruce slowly rises up. Seeing the huge cumulus clouds gets his attention. The view is spectacular, and for some reason, he is drawn to the clouds. As he rises higher and higher, the sky turns dark blue. The curvature of the horizon can clearly be seen. Looking down, he is surprised at how high up he is. The massive city of Los Angeles is far below, looking so small.

Reaching the base of the clouds, he can feel the rising warm, moist air. He lets himself go, allowing the warm air currents to push him up through the clouds. Within a few minutes, he pops out of the top of the cloud. The air is freezing. He can feel the turbulence and is being sucked back down with the air currents.

Floating with the wind, he is pulled back up through the base of the cloud again. The turbulence is more dramatic, feeling the surge pushing him up faster and faster.

A brilliant flash of light blinds him. Everything lights up as a lightning bolt surges through the cloud. Small coronal discharges resembling St. Elmo's fire are shooting up all around. Strands of blue and purple light dissipate throughout the cloud.

Thrust up through the top of the cloud, the sky is now dark blue. Flashes of light come from far below. More cloud-to-cloud lightning is stirring things up. Bruce feels a powerful surge pushing him up even faster than before. A faint glowing blue, purple, and red plasma surrounds him.

Looking down, he can see the city lights between the clouds. Moving straight up at a high rate of speed, he tries to get in control, but nothing is working. Seeing another cloud in the distance, he tries to move in that direction but feels something is holding him back. It feels like being in some sort of rip current going straight up, well above the clouds.

He panics, realizing he can't do anything to get out of this mess. He wishes he were back in the lab at the college. No matter what he does, nothing is working. Everything goes dark, and then a loud bang startles him. His ears are hurting with this awful buzzing sound. The buzzing noise slowly dissipates, replaced by a voice.

"Bruce! Wake up!"

He opens his eyes, seeing Karen right above him. She slaps his face hard.

"I'm OK!" reaching up to block the next blow coming his way.

"Oh, thank God!" Karen said, sitting back down in her chair. "I don't like this at all," glancing over at Chuck.

"What happened?" Chuck asked. "You had a hard time getting back?"

"Yeah, I'd say so... I was so scared there for a while!"

"Your vital signs went off the chart!" Karen shouted. "What the hell happened?"

"Did that crazy woman chase after you again?" Jason asked.

Bruce shakes his head. "Oh no... Nothing like that. It was going pretty good, and I was in total control, having a good time. It was a blast. Then, I made the mistake of getting up into a cloud. At first, it was no big deal, but then there was some lightning. After that, it was pushing me straight up, and I had no control over anything."

Chuck is stunned to hear that. "Holy shit! You got mixed up in a lightning storm. I always keep near the ground, and you may want to do the same. There are a lot of things we still don't know. A lot of energy is in those clouds. It's best if you keep far away from them."

"I think so too... It felt like I was in some sort of plasma energy field high above the clouds."

"What! It sounds like you might have been in one of those sprite lightning events," Jason explained. "It occurs high above thunderstorms. More like a large-scale electrical discharge. That's the last place you want to be!"

Karen glares at Chuck. "You didn't warn him about that?"

"Hell no! I always keep near the ground," Chuck said, a little embarrassed. "He's going to places I have never been to!"

Bruce lets out a long yawn. "I got some great research done while I was out there. The cloud thing was a little too much, but as for the rest. It'll blow your socks off. I'll give you all the details after I get a short nap. I am so tired now. Need to get some sleep."

* * *

Bruce wakes up, still feeling tired. His whole body aches. The room is dark, with a small light on in the corner. Karen is sitting in a chair reading a book.

"So, how long have I been asleep?" he asked.

"Not long enough... It's been ten hours, but you need more after going through that mess. I have been monitoring you since you fell asleep. You're right on the edge of total exhaustion. I even did some blood work on you, and it's not looking good."

"It kind of explains the tubes sticking in my arms."

"I got you on vitamins and a saline solution. We need to talk about these little experiments Chuck got you mixed up in."

"It's not so bad... I had a blast out there. So, how long was I gone?"

"About ten minutes."

Bruce is shocked. "What? That's all! I thought it was more like a couple of hours."

"It's not worth it! Your body can't take the strain. After only ten minutes, it's going to cost you a day or two in bed to recover from it."

"Wait till you hear what I got! Turn on the recorder. I want to make sure we get it all before I forget some of it."

"It can wait... Get some sleep first."

"No... You got to hear this."

Bruce tells his story in detail. He goes through every event, making sure not to leave anything out. He wished he could record the event to show everyone how spectacular it was.

Late into the night, Bruce is asleep again. Karen is still up frantically translating everything from the audiotape to her word processor. She had no idea that this session would bring back so much new information. She now knows it's going to be impossible to prevent Bruce from experimenting with this remote viewing after today's event.

* * *

Early in the morning, everyone on the team is expected to show up for the status meeting. All are curious to hear about Bruce's big adventure on the other side. Chuck is the first one in, bringing in a load of breakfast tacos. He knows Bruce will be tired from the ordeal, but a good hot spicy breakfast taco will do him a world of good.

"How are you doing, my friend?" Chuck bellowed out.

"Not too bad… Got a lot of sleep even with all this crap on my arms."

"You'd be in bad shape without it!" Karen said. "You're going to be taking it easy for the next week or more."

Bruce smells the aroma of cooked eggs and chorizo. "I see you got what I need," holding out his hand.

"Plenty to go around," handing out the tacos. "Where is the rest of the gang?"

"They should be here soon," Karen answered. "I'll make the coffee. Make sure he doesn't eat more than one," then leaves the room.

Chuck pulls up a chair. "So Bruce… I have been thinking about what you said. Give me all the details."

"I told Karen all about it last night. She has it all down on paper. I wanted to make sure she got it all. That was one hell of a ride," pointing to the stack of papers on the desk.

"This is from the transcripts?" Chuck asked, flipping through the pages. "Looks like she's got it all!"

Within a few minutes, the room is filled with people. Everyone is grabbing a taco and a copy of the transcript. The room is quiet as Karen reads aloud the events from Bruce's latest remote viewing session.

Jason is shocked, hearing all the details. "Damn, I wish we had a sync between what you were experiencing and the data we recorded."

"You got two big spikes here," Karen said. "One about halfway through and the other at the end. I know the one at the end of the session is probably the cloud situation. But, what the hell got you fired up at the five-minute mark?"

Bruce had to think about it. "It could be from the fish?"

Jason laughed. "That's one scary nightmare! You had fish trying to eat you?"

"Yeah, it was kind of scary seeing those things coming right at me with their mouths wide open."

"I have never gone into the water," Chuck said. "You said it was more of the same, but it just slows you down?"

Bruce nods. "You know that feeling when you go through a solid surface? The water is not as bad, but it's always there. You go through a wall, and once you're out, that's it. There is a little hesitation or slowing down, but in the water, it's constant. The only odd thing was the relative size of things. I had never noticed it before because I was always at a distance from other people or objects. Maybe because I was in the water, that made things look different."

"How was it different?" Chuck asked.

"I had seen this type of fish before when I was out snorkeling. They're about the size of your hand. When I was in the middle of that school of fish, they were huge. It was like I was right next to them. It was the same when the bigger fish came at me. All I could see was this huge mouth coming right at me."

"If you had to guess, what size would you say you were in relation to the fish?" Jason asked.

"I think it's more like the size of a dime."

Jason turns to Karen. "That's a lot bigger than what we see on the monitor."

"Yeah, it would be great to get the actual dimensions," Karen said. "We need to figure out a way to measure it."

Bruce shutters, thinking about those fish coming at him. "That was the first time I have ever seen anything up close like that. Chuck, have you ever gotten up real close to something?"

"Not like that," Chuck replied. "I have always seen things from a distance. Never that close!"

"This is really fascinating!" Jack shouted out. "Chuck, in all the years doing this remote viewing, have you ever experienced anything like this?"

Chuck laughs. "I have been doing this since the 1960s. I have never come close to what Bruce did in that last session. All my training was for espionage. Going to remote places trying to see what the enemy was doing. It never occurred to me to do experiments like that."

"This is some groundbreaking research here!" Karen said. "It's also dangerous as hell."

"She is right," Chuck added. "Bruce, you need to be careful. You're going to places I don't think anyone has ever gone before. What gave you the idea to go up through a cloud like that? Especially when there's lightning going on."

"At the time, there was no lightning. I just saw some big white clouds."

Laura quickly flips through a few pages. "You mentioned here that you let the air currents push you up through the clouds."

"Can you elaborate on that?" Chuck asked. "That's a new one on me."

"I didn't think much of it at the time… I was surprised that I could actually feel the flow of air. So, I just relaxed and let the wind carry me along. It's surprising to feel all the turbulence and how fast it's going. I popped up out of the top of the clouds and then back down again. I could even feel the temperature change. It was freezing at the top, but once I got down to a lower altitude, I really noticed the moisture and the humidity. Going up and down through that cloud was a lot of fun."

Jason is snickering. "Yeah, until the lightning hit. In the future, you might want to stay away from cumulus clouds!"

The questions went on for hours until Bruce fell asleep. The amount of information obtained from that one remote viewing session is enough material to publish a groundbreaking research paper. The team is already setting up more experiments for the next session, but Chuck will be the next test subject.

For reasons unknown, Bruce comes out of these remote viewing sessions so exhausted. Rules are being set in place. There are not going to be any more freelancing experiments from here on out. Everything is going to be planned in advance, and the remote viewing is going to be under five minutes.

* * *

Published

Dr. Jack Stewart is the first from the group to publish his latest research. Everyone on the team is outraged, not being warned about the book release. News media from all over the world are showing up and asking way too many questions. With Dr. Stewart already doing the talk shows and book signings, it is making everyone else on the team so nervous.

With help from Bruce's camera, Dr. Jack Stewart was able to select the best candidates, which resulted in the most astounding research he had ever done. The highest number of past lives they discovered for one person is now up to seven. Some are recalling lives as far back as 1,500 years. The separation between past lives is from a few years to up to several hundred.

With all the varieties of ancient languages and dialects, audio transcripts were sent to universities around the world to help with the translations. All the past lives discovered so far are from Europe, Asia, India, and the Mediterranean. Teams are now being created to handle the four primary groups. No one has yet discovered why these four regions are so prominent in the regressions.

Because of the new regressions, historians now have glimpses of significant events in history. Getting a person to describe in detail the times during the Roman Empire, the

Dark Ages, the Tang Dynasty, and the Renaissance period is rewriting the history books.

Since Dr. Stewart published his work early, all research and tests have been put on hold. Karen and Jason are now racing to publish their work and submit it for review. Chuck is now pushing to get his new book published. The only person not publishing anything is Bruce. He is on medical leave in Wyoming, living in a log cabin next to a lake.

Being the first to publish, Dr. Stewart constantly has to defend his research. The news media is now fixated on how he was able to obtain such brilliant results. Many are claiming this is all fabricated since it sounds too good to be true. No one has been able to find that many people who possess multiple past lives. Even his previous book doesn't even come close to what he recently discovered.

Always having to defend himself, Dr. Stewart makes the mistake of hinting about a secret method of detecting people who had past lives. After hearing that, the media turns into a frenzy, trying to speculate what this new mystery device could be.

With so much attention from the news media, the camera is placed in a safety deposit box. Three keys are required to get access to the camera. Karen has one, and Jason has the other. The third key is sent to Bruce, who is oblivious to it all. He has no phone or television. All he does is go out fishing and hiking the many trails.

* * *

Karen, Laura, and Jason publish their book 'The Human Species, a Symbiotic Host.' The book describes in detail how the human body is just a host for a spirit or soul. This soul is our mind and our thoughts, the essence of our being. The fact that we live a life, and in the end, our soul moves on to drift in the heavens, eventually finding another host to live again.

Their book is even more controversial than Jack Stewart's. With the church demanding that it should be immediately banned and pulled off the shelves, it's now the top subject of every news program. Within a week, it's on the top ten best sellers list.

The most controversial part of the book is the subject of the creation of new souls. Their theory suggests a soul can return by entering a child by the age of three or four years old. Once a child passes the age of four, a new soul is created if one is not present.

Even more controversial is the claim that not everyone has a soul. For reasons unknown, a new soul is not always created. With all the research done on convicted prisoners, many of the extremely violent ones have no sign of the blue glow. That was no surprise to many people.

Also, one of the things they have discovered, these out-of-body experiences don't only happen in near-death situations. Certain people unknowingly can have an out-of-body experience during the stage five-sleep cycle. Anyone who has constant dreams of flying, and detailed visions of places they have never been before, is a good sign they are probably one of these candidates. Most of those who have this ability are generally old souls.

* * *

Karen, Laura, and Jason are now big celebrities, promoting their book on all the talk shows. They are on the front page of every newspaper and all the magazines. The subject matter is so controversial, with people having extreme views on both sides. Some call it groundbreaking proof of heaven and God, while others call it outright blasphemy.

To make matters worse, Chuck publishes his book. His work on remote viewing is well known. In his new book, he is also linking remote viewing to the human soul. His new theory is that part of the soul can leave the body for a short time to wander the Earth.

Chuck's new book is starting to sound too familiar. At first, people were questioning whether he was jumping on the bandwagon, trying to associate his work with the other best-selling books of Karen, Jason, Laura, and Dr. Stewart. In an interview, he made the mistake of mentioning his association with them.

With the news media looking for a scandal or an exclusive, it didn't take much to discover the truth. The news media has stumbled upon the fact that Dr. Jack Stewart, Dr. Karen Brown, and Chuck Wilson have been working together for a long time.

After reading the three books, people can now see the similarities. These are not three separate books being published by different individuals, but three different subjects from the same research.

* * *

In a matter of weeks, the entire team has been exposed, except for Bruce. He has been mistaken for a test subject because of his almost fatal accident. Anyone related to the project is now talking to the news media. The families of the hospice research are also talking. Anyone who's been a test subject is running to the news media to talk about their experiences.

With the release of a few videos showing the blue glow and one from the hospice of the soul leaving the body, the news media turns into a frenzy. With knowledge of the camera, referred to as the device that can detect the human soul, is now the main subject of every conversation. Everyone wants to see it, but mostly, they all want to be able to see their own soul.

The world's news media has descended on the small college. With everyone being monitored, no one can go anywhere without being followed by the press. With so many people snooping around the college, everything has been removed and placed in various non-disclosed locations.

Rumors are flying everywhere about the location of the device. Mostly, people want to know what this secret device is that can detect a person's soul. Many are speculating that this device is from an alien spaceship, an advanced ancient civilization, or even a tool used by God.

The religious extremists are demanding that the device should be returned to the church so it can be kept out of the hands of the non-faithful. The politicians have also jumped on the bandwagon. They are also demanding the device be turned over to the government for safekeeping. Many had hired lawyers to take legal action against the team to force them to release the device.

The situation gets worse when an employee at the bank tells the news media about Karen and Jason getting a safety deposit box. Once Karen hears that, she sends the two other keys to Bruce so that he can remove the camera. The news people are getting too close and may discover the camera.

Since Bruce is still in the clear, he is not being bothered by the news media. He has no TV or telephone and is surprised to learn about all their research being published. Hearing how the news media has pounced on the team and is looking for the camera, now he is worried about being linked with the others.

* * *

After reading all the news stories about their research, Bruce reluctantly returns home. Being away for several months, the hustle and bustle of the big city is already too much. Living in the country with no one else around for miles, he feels out of place being back in California.

Bruce drives by the college, surprised to see all the news vans parked all over campus. Camera crews are in front of the building doing live interviews. There is no way that anyone can get near the building without being spotted by the press.

He can't even meet with anyone on the team or risk calling them on the phone. Their research is now blown out of control. Luckily, no one has linked him to the team. The last thing he needs is for the security people at his work to start asking questions. They could discover that the secret device everyone is looking for is actually one of the sensors he designed.

The discovery of the camera is now a possibility. The news media are now scoping out the bank. Since Bruce still has not been linked to the team, he is the only one that can retrieve the camera without being noticed. He has to do this alone without any help.

* * *

Bruce rides the bus in case someone is recording license plate numbers. Even with a rental car, it can still be traced back to him. Parking near the bank is going to be a problem anyway. After seeing some of the newscasts about the bank, he knows there are going to be a lot of people, as well as the news media.

Walking up to the bank, he is so shocked to see the massive crowd. Right away, he knows it will be impossible to get near it. With all the rumors about the device being hidden in the vault, the entire building has become a shrine to the religious fanatics. There are hundreds of people camped out in front of the building. Now, the news media are here in force.

Anyone who enters or leaves the bank is having their photo taken by curious onlookers. The news media is also on the prowl, always interviewing anyone with an opinion.

The police are preventing anyone from entering the bank unless they have proper identification. The bank is not happy with the situation, and most of the customers are complaining.

Walking around the block, Bruce notices the employee parking lot at the back of the building. There are no religious nuts camped out here, but the bank security is here in force.

Bruce follows behind two other people as they walk through the parking lot. He quickly notices how the security guards are eyeing everyone, always talking on their radios. A woman hands over an identification card. The security guard promptly enters the information on his tablet while the others look on.

"Sorry for the inconvenience, Mrs. Wheeler," the security guard said. "Go right up to the back door, and they'll let you in."

The woman is not happy. "When is this madness going to end?"

The security guard shakes his head. "Don't know, mam… Hopefully, soon!" motioning her to pass.

This is the break Bruce is looking for, pulling out his wallet. He is so glad he didn't toss the bank card and the fake ID Chuck gave him.

"Hi, I got some business with the bank today," Bruce said, holding up the card to the security guard.

Again, the security guard taps his finger on the tablet. Apparently, they are making sure no one gets past without a valid bank account.

"Go right ahead, Mr. Smith," he said with a smile.

"Thank you!" Bruce said, promptly walking past.

Glancing around the back of the building, he notices all the security cameras. He knows he is being recorded, but at least it's not the news media. The first thing he has to do is to walk through a metal detector. He was ready for this, having a small tin box filled with mint lozenges. That set off the metal detector. He quickly reaches into his pocket, pulling out the mint lozenges. Once the security guard sees it, he just lets him pass.

Another security guard is at the rear entrance. He smiles, trying to be pleasant, opening the door.

"Thanks," Bruce said, so glad to get into the bank without a mob of people watching his every move.

Usually, the back entrance is primarily for the employees. With all the customers using the rear door, most of the rooms and hallways have been taped off. Armed security guards line the hall to make sure no one walks into the wrong place. A bank teller stands at the end of the hallway to help the customers.

"Hello... I need to get to my safe deposit box, please," Bruce quietly said, not wanting to be overheard.

"Yes, sir... May I see your account?" holding out her hand.

Bruce hands over the card. The teller turns and then starts entering the information on the keyboard. He is beginning to wonder if the bank is monitoring anyone getting access to the safe deposit boxes. With all the religious nuts camped out in front of the building, they are probably getting scared of what might be stored in one of these safe deposit boxes.

"Mr. Smith, I'll escort you to the room," motioning him to follow. "I apologize for the inconvenience. We have no control over this fiasco out in front of the building. Will you be closing your account?"

"No, not today... I just need to get some papers."

"Thank you!" she said, so relieved. "Many of our customers are getting scared with all this nonsense."

"It's OK... It doesn't bother me."

"Our procedures have changed since you opened the account. We'll have to be present to unlock the box and remove it from the vault. We will place the container on the table, and then we'll leave the room. When you are ready to exit, just push the red button on the door."

"No problem…"

"Oh, you have one of the high-security boxes," she said after looking at the form. "You do know that this requires three key access?"

"Yeah, I got all three," Bruce said, holding up the keys. "My friends got scared, not wanting to get close to this place. They think the Ark of the Covenant is hidden in here."

"I assure you it's not!" she said, looking a little awkward. "There are no religious artifacts here, so don't worry about it."

After signing the forms and getting a thumbprint, he follows the teller and a security guard into the vault. The fake thumbprint Chuck gave him still works, and luckily, no one noticed it on the end of his thumb.

The security guard unlocks the first door, getting access to the safe deposit boxes. Bruce pulls out the three keys, unlocking each one. The teller promptly pulled out the container and placed it on the table in the center of the room.

"The guard will be outside the vault door," the teller said. "Close the container when you're ready to exit. Press this button to leave, and we'll return the container to the vault and lock it up in your presence."

"OK, thanks…"

Once everyone is out of the vault, Bruce slowly opens the safe deposit box. The old camera is still here. Along with some folders filled with useless paperwork to make it look like the contents are important.

Pulling out the camera, he carefully removes the sensor mounted on the back. He couldn't help but admire the years of hard work that had been put into producing this small device. What was supposed to be a replacement sensor for the space telescope to view the wonders of the universe is now the secret device everyone is trying to find. If they only knew that dozens of these are already in orbit spying on people throughout the world.

He dumps the mint lozenges into his pocket, placing the sensor into the tin box. Luckily, they put in the original digital back that came with the camera. Even if someone finds it, it's nothing more than a regular Hasselblad digital camera that you can find in most camera stores. He takes one of the folders to give the appearance that this is the reason for being at the bank. Closing the safe deposit box, he pushes the exit button.

Waiting next to the table, Bruce watches as the teller picks up the box, placing it back in the wall. He takes the three keys, securing the safe deposit box. It's almost over. Now, he has to get out of the bank without being searched or caught by the news media.

With no fanfare or fuss, Bruce slowly walks out of the bank. Holding the folder to his side, he makes sure everyone can see it. If someone is reviewing the security cameras, they'll see him walking in with nothing but leaving with just a few papers.

Bruce catches the bus a few blocks away. He always keeps an eye out just in case someone is following. His next designation is a friend's metalwork shop. He made the arrangement as soon as he got into town. He was there late at night, back in the days when they used to fabricate their own tools, so no one should think anything of it.

* * *

After riding the bus for several hours, making sure no one is following, Bruce stops off at the metal shop. With everyone who works in the shop at home, he has the place to himself. He thinks about the good old days when he used to come here late at night to create things from scratch because they didn't have any money. Life was simpler back then.

With so many people trying to get hold of the device, he knows there is only one solution. He has not told anyone on the team about his plan. He dares not risk contacting any of them. With so many people monitoring their every move, he knows it is best not even to try.

Removing the sensor from the container, he places it on the worktable. He puts on protective eyeglasses. Reaching over, he grabs the biggest sledgehammer on the table. After a long pause, he brings down the massive weight of the hammer, smashing the sensor. Again and again, he pulverizes the sensor until it is nothing more than a pile of debris.

Bruce sweeps up the remains, placing them all in a small crucible. Then tosses in a few fragments of Zink and Copper. Reaching into his pocket, he pulls out a dollar gold coin, tossing it in as well. Lighting the acetylene torch, he slowly melts it all together.

Once everything in the crucible has liquefied, he turns off the torch. After waiting several minutes for it to solidify, he tosses it all into the water tank. The tank almost explodes, with the water coming to a boil. The steam rises high above. Waiting for a few minutes, Bruce grabs the tongs, pulling out only the metal since the crucible had shattered upon hitting the water.

He grabs another hammer, walks over to the huge anvil, and starts pounding away at the metal. The metal shop class he took in high school is coming in handy. It will be one of the most expensive metal bowls that he has ever made.

Late into the night, Bruce returns to his apartment. He places his new metal bowl on his bookcase for all to admire. The entire world is looking for the mystery device. Little do they know, it's now sitting out on display in plain view in its new form, a candy bowl.

* * *

The next day, Bruce decides to go back to work. After being gone for months and with no contact with anyone, he is curious to see how things are going. The last thing the management told him was that he was on extended medical leave and to come back whenever he felt ready. No one said anything about how long it was supposed to be.

Once he drives into the parking lot, right away, he can see the change. There is a new sign on the front of the building. He wonders if they have moved to another location.

Walking into the main lobby, it's all different. Everything is extremely plush, looking more like an expensive corporate lobby filled with plants and lots of people in suits. He feels awkward walking in wearing a tee shirt, shorts, and sneakers.

Bruce walks up to the extremely attractive and well-dressed receptionist. "Excuse me... What happened to the Banyan Research Labs? Didn't they use to be here?"

"Oh, yes! They were bought out by US Systems a while back," she answered. "May I help you with something?"

"What happened to the people working here? Where is everyone?"

"Well, there are some still here, but many have left. Do you have an appointment?"

Bruce is getting agitated. "No, I don't have an appointment. Is Paul Anderson still here?"

She looks the name up on the screen. "Yes, Mr. Anderson is here but currently unavailable. I can set you up for a meeting, maybe next week. Just leave your name and number, and we'll get back to you."

"I don't think so... Get Paul on the phone and tell him Bruce Rollin is here. Get his lazy ass down here right now!" getting rather loud.

The security guard slowly walks over. "May I help you, sir?"

"Yes, you can! I want to see Paul, and I want to see him right now! Not tomorrow or any other day!"

"Excuse me…" the receptionist said. "The vice-president of the company just doesn't drop everything because someone comes walking in off the street."

"Oh, he does now! You want to see my ID?" pulling out his wallet.

"Ahh, yes, we would," the security guard said, motioning for the other guard to come over.

"Does that name sound familiar to you?" holding up his old ID card.

"No, it doesn't, sir… Maybe we can walk outside to discuss this."

Bruce can't believe this. "Why don't you turn around and look at the picture on the wall back there? Also, look at the name on the plaque. See any resemblance?" noticing his old portrait is still hanging on the wall.

The security guard slowly turns. "Oh, I'm so sorry, Dr. Rollin. I didn't know it was you."

"You still want to go outside and discuss this?"

"No, sir… I'm very sorry," starting to get scared, realizing he had just insulted one of the founders of the company.

The receptionist quickly grabs the phone after hearing who this man is. She calls up Mr. Anderson informing him that Dr. Rollin is waiting for him in the lobby.

"I'm sorry for the delay, Dr. Rollin," the receptionist said, being extremely polite. "Mr. Anderson will be here shortly."

"That's good to hear," Bruce replied.

Within a minute, Paul Anderson rushes into the lobby. "My God! Bruce, how are you doing?"

"Still breathing so far… What the hell did you do to the place? You are now the vice president?"

"A lot has changed!" reaching over to shake Bruce's hand. "We got a lot of catching up to do. We've been trying to get in touch with you, but you just disappeared off the face of the earth. Where the hell did you go?"

"Not far... Just went out to do a little fishing."

"Hell, it must have been some good fishing!" Paul said. "You have been gone for months... Well, it's good that you're back. Let me fill you in on the latest scoop," ushering him to the back offices.

* * *

Bruce is appalled that his company has been taken over. All his friends and coworkers are gone. All the government contracts they were awarded have been canceled. US Systems bought out the company, but the military satellite sensor was all they wanted. Everything else was tossed out. Having only a twenty percent stake in the company, Bruce could not have stopped it or had a say in any of this.

The Banyan Research Lab was started by Bruce, Peter Smith, Sarah Evans, Tom Harris, and Paul Anderson. With Paul's thirty percent investment, he ruled everything. He was the project manager who dealt with the customers. Everyone else did all the work.

Eventually, all the founding members were driven out. They took the money and left the company. Bruce was absent for months after his accident, and no one knew what to do with his position. Since Bruce designed the sensor, he is now the most valued partner and the only one that matters in the eyes of the big corporation.

* * *

Corporate Greed

Word spread fast throughout the building that Bruce has returned. Everyone runs down to meet the famous Dr. Bruce Rollin. Since most of the employees are new or were transferred in, many have never met him.

Executives from US Systems are racing over from across town to talk with him as well. Paul has already mentioned the possibility of a vice president's position in the new company. Right away, Bruce knows something is wrong with the way people are acting. They are almost relieved to see him here.

Walking around the new facilities, Bruce can see the company they created is long gone. Everything is now automated inside huge, clean rooms. What really surprises him is all this fancy and expensive equipment. But something is wrong. After hearing some of the numbers, he knew right away that these people were not producing the same quality sensors. The error ratios are way too high.

After the tour is over, Bruce is escorted back to the executive meeting room. This is very different from what he used to have back in the old days. The room is filled with expensive furniture, and the walls are covered with original artwork. What's worse, everyone is wearing expensive suits.

"Let me be the first to welcome you back," a man walks up, shaking his hand. "I'm John O'Neil, Executive President of US Systems."

"Nice to meet you," Bruce said.

Paul is at his best, kissing up to the brass. "Bruce and I go way back... We've been together on this project from the beginning. He's the most valued person on the entire team. He's the one that made it all happen."

Bruce just nods while he is introduced to all the people in the room. Everyone is either a president or vice-president. He feels funny with everyone wearing $10,000 tailor-made Italian suits, and he is wearing nothing more than shorts and sneakers.

Sitting down at the table with all these executives, Bruce can see right through them. They are all scared. They have taken over the company, bringing in all this expensive equipment and failing to achieve the quality control required to keep the contract. After kicking out all the people who did all the work, they kept the one who was the most worthless, and that's Paul. Now, they are paying the price.

"Bruce, let's cut to the chase here," John said. "We want you back... I know you had some issues after your accident. I think we can find you a position here that's not too stressful. Basically, it'll be one that's right up your alley."

"And what would that be?" Bruce asked.

"Vice-president of Public Relations... There will be a great salary to go with it, too."

Bruce is trying not to laugh out loud. "So, what would I be doing in a PR job? I'm a techie type of guy. More like the hands-on, getting my fingers dirty type of thing."

Paul leans forward. "Well, Bruce... You'll go out and talk with the prospective clients, telling them how it all works. You are really famous for the new sensor that you designed. You missed all the interviews while you were in the hospital and after the accident. We can change all that. You'll now get all the publicity and notoriety that you deserve."

"Yes, I agree!" John added. "We already got a few people interested in doing some interviews with you."

"If this is such a big success, why the PR push?" Bruce asked. "The images from the space telescope will sell the product. Can't get better PR than that, and it doesn't cost anything."

"Well, we've had some issues in production," John reluctantly said. "The contract is under review."

"So, with me doing the PR, how would that help with the production problems?" Bruce asked.

"You could highlight what we did in the past," Paul added. "With you back in the company, they would see that we are changing things for the better."

Bruce busted out laughing. "So basically, you bought us out. Then you kicked out the people who did all the work. You're telling me that you can't reproduce what we did with all that fancy equipment you brought in. Now, you want me to go out and do a song and dance, telling everyone that we're going to bring back the good old days!"

Everyone in the room looks awkward and is very quiet.

"Not exactly…" John said, not used to being talked to in that way. "We are a team, and we work together for the good of the company. Are you part of the team?"

Paul reaches over, putting his hand on Bruce's arm. "We can offer you $250,000 per year. That includes a company car and access to the company jet to take you wherever you want. All you have to do is attend a few conferences and do some interviews. We're not asking too much of you. Just a little of your time."

"All we are asking is for you to make us look good," John said. "This is all your work. Don't you want to see it succeed?"

"How much did you buy us out for?" Bruce asked.

There is a long pause. "It was about 450 million," Paul answered. "But that is not the issue here."

Bruce is shocked by the number. "Is that all! I guess you got a good deal out of it," staring at Paul.

"It was the best we could do under the circumstances."

Bruce smiles, leaning back in his chair. "Let's do the numbers... You are going to pay me $250,000 to do nothing more than boast about how good things used to be before you showed up. Then, on the other hand, twenty percent of the company minus taxes ends up being what?" glancing over at John.

Another long, quiet spell fills the room. "Excuse me, Dr. Rollin," a man mumbled, sitting across the table. "Your portion, if you decide to sell... That would be approximately $36,000,000 after taxes."

Bruce rocks back and forth in his chair. "That's a difficult decision... I can work here for $250,000 per year, working with a bunch of clowns. The alternative is to take the $36,000,000 in cash. Considering how you screwed up everything so quickly after only a few months, my twenty percent would be down to nothing within a year. I think I would rather cash out now. I have a feeling you guys won't be around much longer."

Bruce stands up. "I take it that you are the accountant here?" pointing to the man who told him how much his portion of the company is.

The man looks scared. "Ahh, yes sir..." glancing over at John O'Neil for guidance.

"I'd like to sell all my shares in the company. I'll let you know where to send the check," then promptly leaves the room.

On his way out to the lobby, he stops, looking at his portrait hanging on the wall. Right next to his picture is Paul's. There is a long row of executive pictures, including

John's, at the far end. He pulls his portrait from the wall, ripping out the photo, tearing it into tiny pieces. Then he pulls off the plaque bearing his name, bending it in half.

Everyone in the lobby is shocked. The security guards do nothing. Bruce walks up to the nearest trash can, dumping the remnants of his portrait into it.

Walking out of the building, he turns to the security guard. "You may want to start looking for a new job. I don't think this company is going to be around much longer," promptly leaving the building.

On his way home, he feels sad knowing that he can't talk with anyone. With the news media always hounding everyone on the team, there can be no phone calls or emails. At least he doesn't have to worry about the security breaches from his old job. Now that the sensor has been destroyed, the evidence linking him to Karen's group is gone. The secret device will always be a mystery.

Stuck in traffic for over an hour, Bruce knows what he is going to do next. The big city is not for him anymore. He is going to pack up everything and move back to Wyoming. Once he gets the money from his stocks, he'll never have to work again. He is already thinking about buying that big plot of land where he has been staying by the lake up in Wyoming, making it his permanent home.

* * *

Sensations

Bruce leaves the world behind, enjoying the solitude of the Grand Teton National Park. Selling all his shares in the company means not having to work another day. The years of working late into the night are over. All of his research is done. Now, all he wants to do is live an easy life, being one with nature in his small cabin at Jackson Lake.

His days are filled with doing nothing but hiking the many trails. With just a backpack, he wanders through the wilderness. The area surrounding Jackson Lake is vast. No matter how many times he tries to get away from the civilized world, there are always some tourists or fellow hikers who are never far away. Even the distant roads and various buildings can still be seen.

Walking through the dense forest, he is always thinking of how things were years ago when the early settlers first arrived. Knowing that no other person is around for hundreds of miles is an intriguing thought. The idea of being isolated from the rest of the civilized world is always on his mind.

With his cabin miles away from any other building, he never sees anyone for weeks on end. For some reason, being around other people is starting to irritate him. His food is delivered to the cabin, and he always makes sure not to be around when the UPS guy shows up. Rarely going to town, he is turning into a hermit. With no phone, radio, or television, he enjoys the solitude.

* * *

Tramping through the dense trees on unmarked trails, Bruce enjoys the challenge of finding his way back home. One of the strange things he soon discovered was that he could never get lost. Even deep within the forest, he can always find his way back home. For some reason, he notices how he can tell which way is north, south, east, and west even with no visible landmarks. Many times, he tests himself by closing his eyes, turning around in circles to get disoriented. Coming to a stop, he points north and then checks the compass. He gets it right every time.

He never uses the trail maps anymore. He wanders about for hours, trying to get lost. Even deep within the trees, with an overcast sky, he can always find his way back home. At times, he can make a beeline straight back to his cabin. He attributed this new skill to experience and being one with nature.

* * *

One day, when out hiking the trails, he notices something odd. He feels this strange sensation come over him. Sitting on a fallen tree, he rests for a few minutes, drinking some water. This weird feeling in his head doesn't go away. Closing his eyes makes it worse, and he starts to feel a little light-headed, wondering if he is dehydrated.

After a few minutes, he notices this strange sensation on his right temple. As he moves his head around, it changes position, feeling as if something is pulling on him like a magnet. Closing his eyes and keeping his head still, he can feel it slowly moving. This weird feeling is almost like there is something in his head pointing at an object that is slowly moving in the distance.

When he opens his eyes, he can see a lone hiker walking way off in the distance. This slight pull is in the same direction to where the man is. As he moves his head about, the strange sensation always points to the hiker.

Bruce sits down for an hour, realizing he can track where the man is. He can literally feel him walking along. Once the man is over a hundred feet away, he finally loses the feeling and cannot detect him anymore.

Walking back to the cabin, it happens again. Bruce doesn't hear or see anyone but knows other people are nearby. Now, there is more than one person, and he can sense a difference between them. Even from a distance, he notices the subtle differences between the local hikers and the tourists. In addition to knowing where they are, he can also sense their emotions. The local people give off an essence of harmony, while the tourist has more of a sense of fear or nervousness about being out in the wilderness.

* * *

For days, Bruce is experimenting with the new senses he has somehow acquired. Out in the wilderness, he can detect other people almost a hundred yards away. Going into town is a big mistake. Being around so many people, he is overwhelmed. It's like being in the middle of a crowd, and everyone is talking at once.

After all those years of living in a big city in California, he now realizes that his sense of smell and hearing has also been enhanced. Without all the noise and pollution, the smell of pine trees or a field of flowers is really noticeable. Seeing all the stars at night is still something he can't get used to after living in the big city.

Living in the wilderness has cleansed his body. He wonders if this is why he can detect the magnetic North as the birds do. That would explain being able to walk about in the forests and never get lost. Detecting other people is another matter. He has no clue why this is happening and is scared to discuss it with anyone else. There is only one thing that could be causing this, and that is the aftereffects of remote viewing. Chuck is the only person who could answer that question.

* * *

The Dream

For a change of pace, Bruce decides to explore part of the forest where he has never been before. Now that the weather is clearing up, he can do a long multi-day hike, camping out for a few days. Since most of the tourists are up at sunrise and back in their cabins or hotels by sunset, that will guarantee him some solitude at night.

After a whole day wandering off the beaten path, he finds a small outcropping on the side of one of the mountains. The small flat ledge is only about 100 square feet, but it gives a spectacular view of all the lakes and hills far below. Facing east also means a great view of the sunrise in the morning.

Setting up the tent, he knows this is the perfect spot to camp out for a few days. At least here, no one else will unexpectedly be walking in on him. The last thing he wants is for some tourist to set up camp right next to his. That has happened way too many times. For some reason, when a tourist sees a tent, they automatically assume it's a public camping area, always setting up their tents nearby.

* * *

With the sun long gone and with the clear skies, the stars are incredibly bright. Looking up at the stars is the one thing he loves the most. Lying outside in his sleeping bag, Bruce stares up at the sky. Using his binoculars, he scans the heavens, searching for obscure galaxies or the occasional meteors shooting by.

With the cold air running down the mountain, Bruce gets deep into his sleeping bag. With just his face sticking out from the small opening, he stares up at the stars while still comfortably warm. The skies are exceptionally clear, and there are plenty of meteors to keep him occupied.

Getting late into the night and feeling so tired, Bruce closed his eyes. He thinks about his day tracking through the forest. Mentally taking inventory of his food supplies to ensure there is enough for the next few days. In his mind, he sees the trail maps, planning out a scenic path back to his cabin. He slowly drifts off, sound asleep. In his dreams, he is walking on the many trails through the mountains.

* * *

The day is perfect for hiking, with a cool breeze and clear blue skies. Bruce stumbles upon an old path, overgrown with grass and shrubs, looking as if it hadn't been used in years. Seeing how this trail is not on any map, his curiosity gets the best of him. There is nothing better to a good day of hiking than an uncharted path.

Struggling for hours, Bruce is having a difficult time. The old trail gradually fades away. Many times he has to walk in circles trying to find where it picks up again. Rockslides and years of rain had erased most of the trail away.

The trail comes to an end as he emerges through the dense trees. There is nothing ahead but grassland and a small creek leading up the hill. The gray color of the gravel indicates this might be the remains of an old glacier.

At the bottom of a vast valley, the trail can't go left or right. In the distance, a massive gray snowcapped mountain range with almost a vertical cliff face. The beautiful sight is enough to give him the energy to keep on going.

He trudges on, curious to see where this all ends up. With no trail in sight and having gone this far, it makes no sense to go back. To the left, there is a dense forest leading high up a steep hill. On his right, a vertical cliff face goes straight up. A few hundred feet ahead up on the hill is a ridge. He is getting curious to see what is on the other side.

Once he reaches the ridge, the view is spectacular. In front of him is a huge lake surrounded by a tall pine tree forest. The lake is enclosed by snowcapped mountains. These mountains reach almost a mile high. Some of the cliffs are nearly vertical, going straight into the water.

The trip was well worth it. The spectacular sight gives Bruce a second wind, running down to the lake. In no time, he finds the trail again. He can't help looking up at the tall mountains far above. He wouldn't be surprised to find this is uncharted territory. Not many people would have hiked up that thousand-foot climb without knowing what was up there. This is indeed a hidden gem in the middle of nowhere.

Once he reaches the lake, it's one of the most pristine scenes he has ever witnessed. The water is like glass with no ripples at all. To no surprise, there are a few nice-sized trout slowly meandering near the water's edge.

The water looks so nice. He is thinking about taking a little swim after that long hike. Kneeling down, Bruce runs his hand through the water. The pain shoots through his hand, feeling the ice-cold water. He quickly changes his mind about swimming here.

Walking along the pebble beach, Bruce can't think of a better place to be. His mood quickly changes, when he sees a small cabin just within the trees. Getting closer to the cabin, it gets worse. There are about a dozen more dotted about, all hidden by the tall trees. These cabins are a little strange. They all have this oriental look to them, not like the typical rustic log cabins of the area.

"Hello, friend!" A voice bellowed out to his left. "Welcome to our little world."

Bruce is startled, having no clue that anyone is nearby. He turns to see a man, almost seven feet tall, standing a few feet away. The man is very pale, looking as if he has never been in the sunlight. His clothes are odd as well, and this is not the sort of thing one wears at such high altitudes. To make it worse, he is wearing sandals.

"I'm sorry," Bruce said. "I didn't know anyone was staying up here."

"Not many people do… We don't really encourage guests. This is our little world, and we like the solitude. It is our way."

Bruce's first impression is that he is a Tibetan Monk and a very tall one at that. The light skin and very poised mannerisms are a dead giveaway. He is not Asian at all but most likely European with bright blue eyes. The accent is a little strange, too, maybe German or Swedish.

"Sorry to intrude," Bruce replied, ready to make a fast exit.

"We've been watching your progress. You have achieved a level that most have not yet reached. It is very impressive. I commend you on that. Would you like to join us for tea?" motioning him to the cabin.

Bruce is a little wary. "It would be my pleasure... Maybe a short visit, then I'll be on my way back. Oh, sorry I didn't introduce myself. My name is Bruce," holding out his hand.

"I am Kayden," clasping his hands together, then bows. "It is not our way," awkwardly glancing down at Bruce's hand.

"Of course," Bruce replied, quickly following suit, bowing in return.

He cautiously follows this strange man to the cabin. A woman appears on the small porch. She too, is exceptionally tall, wearing similar clothes. Her fair skin is also odd for someone living in the mountains. People who live up at these high altitudes always have a tan. The dense trees do block out most of the sunlight. That could be why they are so pale. Maybe they are Monks, never going out in the direct sunlight.

Again, he is getting worried. These people are a little odd. The little sixth sense he has acquired was a nuisance, but now, he has become accustomed to knowing when other people are nearby. Unable to sense anything from these people, he wonders why things are so different up here.

"This is my mate, Petra," Kayden said as they walked up the steps to the cabin.

"Welcome to our home, Bruce," she said, bowing her head. "It would be our pleasure for you to join us for tea," opening the door.

"Thank you," Bruce said, noticing the other sandals outside the door.

He was expecting this, reaching down to untie his boots. The sandals were a dead giveaway. They make it a lot easier when going in and out of the house.

Entering the small cabin, Bruce is surprised. This is not the rustic cabin he was expecting and resembles a traditional Japanese home. The floor looks like it's made of bamboo or tatami. The walls and doors are paper screens, and the rooms are very sparse with not much furniture.

Bruce is led to the dining room. The only thing in the room is a small table about a foot off the ground. Four small cushions surround the table. Luckily, he has been to one of these places before, so he won't be embarrassing himself with no knowledge of their customs.

Sitting on the cushion and crossing his legs, Bruce is already in pain. The long walk is taking its toll. Kayden sits on the opposite side, merely smiling, not saying a word. Petra leaves the room to prepare the tea. It could not get any more awkward with the silence.

The first thing Bruce notices that's really odd is the ceiling. The entire ceiling is illuminated. The other room is the same. He has seen these light panels before in big corporate offices but never in someone's home, especially in a cabin out in the middle of nowhere. This is a very modern little cabin.

Even the pictures on the walls are impressive. There are plenty of flower pictures with huge wooden frames. When one of the flowers slowly changes, Bruce realizes these are not photographs but flat-screen monitors displaying images. The entire room is a cross between traditional Japanese and modern technology.

"I see you have electricity out here," Bruce mentioned, getting a little awkward with the silence. "You run a line all the way up here from town?"

"No, we have our own energy source," Kayden replied.

"So, what exactly do you do up here?"

"We tend the gardens… Maintain the flowers and such."

"You have gardens up here?" Bruce asked, wondering if this place was some sort of commune.

"We have gardens in many locations. We make sure all the flowers grow and flourish."

"What type of flowers do you grow up here?" Bruce asked, wondering how they could grow anything in this climate. "It must be a short growing season up here with this altitude."

"Our flowers have been selected especially for this region. They have been crossed with other flowers from distant locations to ensure their survival."

"More like survival of the fittest," Bruce mentioned, thinking about his own little flower garden next to his cabin.

The comment caught Kayden off guard. "In a way, yes… Sometimes imperfections arise, but they do not survive the changing climates."

"How do you deal with the pests or weeds?" Bruce asked, curious if they use pesticides up here.

"We tend to keep them distant… We do not want undesirables crossing with our flowers, bringing in imperfections."

"So, what do you do when the weeds get into your gardens? I have been having a lot of problems with that lately. Sometimes it's difficult to keep them out," remembering how his vegetable garden was overrun with weeds.

"We reluctantly have to eradicate them."

"Interesting," Bruce said, finding the comment a little odd for someone who grows flowers. "After seeing how remote this place is, I don't see how you can grow much of anything up here."

"Our gardens are spread all over the region here. We tend many gardens."

Bruce finds this conversation is getting really bizarre. "So, it sounds like this is the headquarters of your little gardening world?" he asked, wondering if this guy was for real.

He nods. "In a way, yes…"

"Why such a remote place?"

"There are other gardeners in distant locations. We all have the same goal. Unfortunately, some of their flowers did not prosper and were abandoned. Now, those flowers spread to other regions and are a threat to our gardens. We must keep our gardens free of imperfections."

The responses are vague and unusual. More and more, Bruce thinks that this guy is from the sixties. He is an old hippie living in a commune with a traditional Japanese taste in their homes.

Petra walks in, carrying the tea. Her grace is uncanny. Not the type of thing he expected to see for people living up in the mountains. Most people that live in this area are extremely rugged. They have to be to live off the land. These people are coming off as somewhat wealthy, living a pampered lifestyle.

Before she sits down, another man enters the cabin. "My apologies for being late… I see our weary traveler is already here."

"Yes, we're about to start tea," Petra said. "Julian, please join us."

Bruce is about to get up to greet him, but his legs are going numb. "Please to meet you… My name is Bruce."

"Stay seated, my friend… You have endured a long journey," sitting down next to him.

"May I introduce Julian," Kayden said. "He is what you would call an administrator."

"Oh, so you are the manager here?" Bruce asked.

"I would not say that… More of a lead caretaker. So, Bruce, what do you think of our little world here?"

"From what I have seen so far, it's beautiful. You have a nice little place up here. It must be challenging during the winter. Do you stay up here just for the summers?"

"Oh, no… We are always here. This is our home."

Bruce is shocked. "Really! How long have you been up here?" glancing over at all three of them.

They appear to be somewhat awkward hearing the question. "This has been our home for many seasons," Julian answered after a long pause. "We have learned to adapt to the changing environment."

"So, you grow your food up here?" Bruce asked, finding their responses so odd and vague.

"Yes, we have growing rooms for our fruit and vegetables," Petra explained. "With the abundance of sunlight, we can grow our food year-round."

"It's not that difficult," Kayden added. "There are those who live in the Polar Regions doing the same. Their climate is more extreme. Once you learn to adapt to the change, it becomes part of your routine."

"These flowers you grow... They must be very special for all this attention," Bruce remarked.

"They are a very special species," Julian said. "We found them in an isolated region very far from here. They have the ability to adapt to their environment more than any flower we have ever seen."

"We discovered that this flower has another extraordinary trait," Kayden added. "They have the ability to pass their knowledge to the next generation. Once they have learned to survive a drastic climate change, the next generation will also obtain this knowledge."

"That makes this flower very special and most desired," Julian said with a smile.

"Sounds like you have something everyone else would want," Bruce replied, wondering what type of flowers they were growing up here. "Is that the reason for being isolated up here from the rest of the world?"

"The isolation is to preserve our gardens," Julian said. "We openly trade with other gardeners. They, too, have special flowers that might be useful."

"We cross our flowers with the others to introduce new traits," Kayden explained. "In that way, we can grow a stronger flower that will always flourish."

"So, tell us about your journey here," Julian said. "I hope it was not too stressful."

Right away, Bruce is leery of giving out details. This is a beautiful little paradise they have up here in the mountains. They probably don't want any tourist or anyone else stumbling into their little world.

"It was a difficult hike… I tend to wander about through the hills, going off the marked trails. I stumbled on this by accident. I had no clue you guys were up here," making sure not to mention the old trail.

"You enjoy the mountains and the solitude?" Petra asked.

"Oh yes," Bruce replied. "Can't get enough of all the clear skies and the clean air. The best part is walking on the many trails through the forest, and the views are just spectacular."

"I take it that you did not like the place you came from?" Julian asked.

"No," Bruce said, slowly shaking his head. "After years of living in California with all the people, smog, and violence, it was a little too much. I now prefer a simple life. Maybe I should take up gardening as well."

The gardening comment brought smiles to their faces. "You would make an excellent gardener," Julian suggested.

Again, Bruce is surprised by the comment. "I don't know about growing things up at this altitude. That would be a challenge."

"Indeed, but the stars are much brighter, viewing them from up here," Kayden said.

"I have noticed that," Bruce remarked. "I remember doing that the other night, or was that last night? I was in my sleeping bag, staring up at the stars. It was so clear. I could see everything!" trying to recall when that was.

Bruce realizes something is wrong. He remembers being up on that ledge watching the stars but doesn't remember getting up in the morning. He has been walking for most of the day but feels like there's a big chunk of time missing.

"That's really odd," Bruce said, trying to think back. "Was that last night? Something is not right…"

Sweat starts running down his face. He is getting light-headed and feels exhausted. His whole body feels weak. Now, he is beginning to wonder if he will be able to make the long hike back to his cabin.

"I see your journey has made you tired," Julian said.

"I may have to rest up a little before heading back. It's a long way from here."

"Do not worry, my friend," Julian said. "We will help you with your journey back home," reaching up with his finger then touches Bruce's forehead.

Bruce feels a surge of energy hearing a loud bang. Everything goes dark. He feels a numbing cold on his face, and every breath is bringing in the ice-cold air. Opening his eyes, he sees nothing but darkness. He can't move his body, feeling as if he has something wrapped around him.

His eyes start to focus on a faint glow. Slowly, things are getting brighter. Able to sit up, he realizes the thing tightly wrapped around him is his sleeping bag. The faint light in the distance is the sun coming up.

Unzipping the sleeping bag, Bruce reaches over to his backpack pulling out the flashlight. Shining the light around the area, to his surprise, he is back in the camp. Everything is still here. Checking his watch, it's almost six in the morning. He has been asleep for at least seven hours.

As the morning draws on, Bruce is confused about the dream. He goes over it again and again. The big question is, did he actually go to that lake, or was it just a really bizarre dream? He wonders if he accidentally went over to the other side.

* * *

Month after month, Bruce can't stop thinking about those strange people and the lake. He retraces his path, going back to the same location where he camped out on the ledge, scouring the area, looking for the path up to the lake. He even asks many of the locals, but no one has ever heard of such a place.

Going over the maps, he looks for the lake hidden up in the mountains. There are so many in the area, but none look anything like the one in his dream. He is trying to recall the path he took. Everything is still clear in his mind. The only thing that's missing is the place where he stumbled upon the old unmarked trail.

Spending hours each day, he searches Google Earth for that elusive mountain lake. There are lots of lakes in the area, but none of them look like the one in his dream. With nothing around in the area, he is starting to wonder if he did cross over. There are thousands of mountain lakes around the world. Many are nothing more than barren rocky areas with a small lake in the center. Some are remnants of old volcanoes, while others are man-made to capture water for some nearby town or city.

He focuses on Japan for a long time because of the Japanese-style cabins. Even though the people were obviously European, the Asian cabin design is something that wouldn't be found anywhere in Europe.

With not much luck, he looks over Nepal and Bhutan with Google Earth. The entire area is covered with mountains, but there are not many lakes like the one in his dream. The tall gray mountain features that surrounded the lake were so unique. He can still see those three massive gray peaks at the end of the long valley.

Remembering the vision of the snowcapped mountains, the lake, and all those trees, it could be anywhere in the world. More and more, Bruce is coming to the conclusion that maybe it was just a dream.

* * *

The Bookstore

One day, Bruce ventures out to the local bookstore. To his surprise, the front window display is filled with Chuck Wilson's new bestselling book. Even better, Chuck is here for a book signing event. He can't believe his luck. He was looking for something good to read, and now he has found it.

The bookstore is packed with people. Many are lined up to get their copy signed. Bruce sneaks around the back of the store to surprise Chuck, trying to blend in with the other customers. He had read some of Chuck's preliminary notes, but that was long ago. He can't wait to get his hands on the book to see the results of all their research.

There are so many people getting their books signed. The line goes all the way around the store. Bruce decides to join the crowd, grabbing a copy. That will give him time to browse through the book before surprising his old buddy.

Flipping through the pages, he knows right away that this is indeed groundbreaking research. He can't wait to get back to his cabin to read it. Chuck was very thorough. Just from glancing over a few pages, this information is going to be extremely helpful in explaining a few things.

More and more people are coming in. In no time, the line is all the way out on the street, all here to meet the famous Chuck Wilson. Bruce is amused by some of the conversations going on around him. There are many believers, but worse, some want to dwell in the remote viewing experience.

After a lengthy wait, Bruce is moving to the front of the line. So far, he has been lucky that Chuck hasn't seen him. He makes sure to keep his face down, looking into the book, hiding behind the people in front of him.

The two people in front are having a good time talking with Chuck as he signs their books. As they walk away, Chuck is still looking in their direction. Bruce slowly walks up, tossing the book on the table. The book slams on the table, making a loud bang.

"What a load of crap!" Bruce yelled. "I can't believe you are charging $24 for this garbage."

The look on Chuck's face is priceless. Everyone heard the comment, and all the attention is on the man standing in front of the table. Chuck's two assistants are ready to pounce. Even the bookstore manager is rushing over to prevent the situation from escalating into a brawl.

Chuck jumps up from his chair. "Bruce! My God! It's good to see you! What the hell are you doing here?" reaching out to shake his hand.

"I live here... I came here looking for something to read, and here you are! So, this is the book? You finished it. Congratulations!"

"Thanks! Don't tell me you haven't seen it yet. It's been out for a while."

"No, this is all news to me... I heard a while back that everyone is rushing to get their books published. I didn't think it'd be this quick."

"Oh, it's been a madhouse. I have been on the road for a month now."

"A month? I figured it would be a year or more before it gets in the bookstores. I can't believe you're here doing a book signing."

"It's all part of the game... I'll be traveling the country for most of the year doing these book signings and speaking tours. Are you aware of what's been going on?"

Bruce shakes his head. "Nope... All I know is the big mess that started right before I left California. I have been on vacation ever since. I kind of lost track of the civilized world since I don't have a TV or radio."

"I need to fill you in on all the latest gossip... Oh, I better finish up here first. I'm staying at the Amangani Hotel down the road. We'll go out to dinner tonight. I'll get you caught up," noticing all the people in line are getting impatient.

"Good idea... It'll give me time to start on this," handing the book to Chuck. "I want mine signed!"

He flips the book open, writing a personal inscription to his good friend Bruce. "Remember, dinner tonight!" handing the book back.

"You got it!" Bruce replied, shaking his hand again.

Bruce rushes back to his cabin. He was lucky to venture out looking for something to read. He didn't expect this at all. Finding out about Chuck's new book makes his day.

* * *

Going into town twice in one day is a first for Bruce. Usually, it's about once every other month. There are way too many people here, and already, he is uncomfortable. With all the traffic and noise, he wishes he had invited Chuck to come out to the cabin for dinner instead.

The Amangani Hotel is nothing but absolute luxury. Bruce is shocked, seeing how big and fancy this place is. Even the men's room is larger than his cabin.

Wandering through the hotel lobby, he finally sees Chuck sitting by a massive fireplace. "I see you like to live in style nowadays," Bruce said, "You must be making a fortune with the book."

"Hey, Bruce!" getting up to shake his hand. "You better believe it! First-class all the way. So, where are you staying?"

"I got a little cabin next to the lake. It's nice and cozy, just the way I like it."

"With all the money you got, you should be staying here with me. Hell, you could probably buy this place and still have plenty left over."

"Not my style... Although, I would like to try one of the fancy meals here. I'm getting tired of those TV dinners."

"Yeah, you ain't changed one bit. Come on... I got reservations."

Sitting in the huge open restaurant, Bruce feels so out of place here. This restaurant is too big, too refined, and too many people. At least he is glad to see his old friend again.

"Oh, I got you a little present from the others," Chuck said, pulling out a big gift-wrapped box from a sack.

"More surprises!" taking the heavy package.

"Go on... Open it," Chuck said with a big smile on his face.

"I feel bad not getting you anything," he replied, slowly opening the gift.

"Like hell! You gave me a best seller. If it weren't for you, none of this would have happened."

Bruce is surprised to see his present. "Holy shit! Karen and Jason got their book published. This must be Jack's. I haven't seen these in any of the bookstores yet."

"They sell out fast! I usually bring in a truckload with me on these book signings."

"Yeah, I noticed that today... I have never seen so many people in that bookstore. Everyone was there for your book, too! No wonder you guys got these published so quickly."

"It was a mad rush when Jack published. He jumped the gun on us, forcing everyone to publish ahead of schedule. His publishers really pushed it hard. They know a good thing when they see it. He's got people following his every word, and he's been doing this for decades."

"I know... I read all his books. Can't wait to read this one. Man, I got a lot of reading to do," glancing through both books.

"When he comes up with a new book, there are more than 100,000 people around the world, all ready and waiting. It was controversial, too. The media just ate it up. So, when we got ours out there, it didn't take long before someone discovered the link between us. And you heard about the mystery device?"

Bruce laughed. "The big mystery device scandal... The newspapers really played that up. After hearing about that mess, I knew it was time to leave."

"Good thing you did... It was a madhouse. We had the press following us for months. We've been doing interviews and been on the news all around the world. I did all the talk shows, and now it's the book signing tours. It's been one hell of a rat race. We're the hottest thing on the market. All thanks to you."

"Well, you guys did all the work. For me, it's all in the past now. I have moved on. I would rather be out fishing."

"That might be best for you... Since you've been hiding up here, obviously not watching TV or reading the newspapers, we still have a lot of people watching our every move. The news people are asking way too many questions. Luckily, you haven't been linked to the project. I guess it's a good thing you're up here and out of the limelight."

"Yep... That was a good move for me. I'm glad to be out of that fast-paced, high-tech industry. I'm now low-tech as one can get."

"You don't even have a cell phone, do you?" Chuck asked.

"Don't need one... Besides, they can track those things. I don't even use credit cards anymore."

"I taught you well," Chuck boasted.

"So, this is your new lifestyle?" Bruce asked. "Gourmet food and some of the best wine I have ever tasted," holding up his wineglass.

"You got that right! After months and months of hard work, it pays off in the end. Now, I can take it easy and see the world. I only stay at five-star resorts and eat at five-star restaurants. In these places, they treat you like royalty."

"How long are you going to be here?"

"This will be my last day... Tomorrow morning, I head for Aspen, then over to Vail and Denver. After that, it's New Mexico, Arizona, and Texas. I'll be hitting every major city, staying at the best hotels. Then I'm off to Europe."

"Sounds like one big vacation, and the publishers are paying the bill."

"You catch on fast, my friend! Maybe it's time for you to get out and see the world. Don't get too comfortable in that little cabin of yours. Look around... This is the life you need to be experiencing. You only live once!"

Bruce laughs after hearing that comment. "And maybe not."

Chuck notices the strange look on Bruce's face. "So, have you been experimenting with the other side?" starting to get worried.

"Since I have been up here, I haven't thought much of it lately. But there are a couple of things I wanted to ask you."

Chuck leans forward. "So, what have you been up to?" knowing every time Bruce asks for advice, it's always something good.

Bruce hesitates. "I seemed to have acquired a sixth sense."

Chuck just stares at him in disbelief. "A sixth sense? Are you kidding me? What the hell have you been doing up here? You can't be serious!"

"Unfortunately, it's no joke... I'm aware of people around me."

"How do you mean? Hell, even I'm aware of all these people around us," pointing around at the other people in the restaurant.

Bruce laughs. "I wish it were that easy..."

"So, how are you aware of other people? Can you read their thoughts?"

"Well, let's just say, if I had my eyes closed, I could count how many people are in this room. When I'm walking about, I can sense someone is nearby even though I can't see them. At least nowadays, no one can sneak up on me anymore."

"Interesting... How do you sense them, and how do you know they are there?"

Bruce has to think of a way to explain this. "It's like a compass pointing to the North. Except for me, it points to other people. Just think, having a whole bunch of compasses in my head, and each one is pointing to everyone in the room. I can even feel those two people walking behind me."

Chuck gasps out loud, seeing two people walking out of the room. "Those two are about 30 feet away and behind you! You're not joking with me, are you?" turning around, looking for a mirror or a reflection in the windows.

"Nope, no tricks or jokes," Bruce replied. "This is really weird for me, too."

"Damn, how far away can you detect people?"

"Out in the forests, when there is no one else about, I can tell when someone is nearby, maybe 100 yards away. In town, it's horrible. It's like having everyone talking at once. After a while, you just ignore it like you would for background noise. It took me a long time to learn how to block it out."

"When did you first notice this?" getting really concerned.

"Not long after I moved up here... At first, I thought it was the altitude or maybe the clean air. Going from Los Angeles to this place, yeah, your senses pick up a lot. The skies up here are so clear, and the flowers don't smell like smog. All that noise and pollution from the big city dulls the senses."

"Not in that way... It could be the side effects from your accident or the remote viewing. You were having a hard time with the aftereffects."

"That's what I was wondering... Have you or anyone you know had this problem?"

"Hell no! I never heard of anything like it," Chuck said, getting worried.

"That's not what I wanted to hear... There is more..."

"What else is there?" Chuck ask, now getting scared.

Bruce hesitates. "Since I have been up here, I haven't gone to the other side. I can tell the difference between dreams and the real thing, but there was one really odd dream. It really blew me away."

"Did you have any of the telltale signs? Exhaustion, flying, or the loud bang? How about a madwoman chasing after you?"

Bruce laughed. "Luckily, no madwoman... The loud bang at the end is the only thing that got me wondering. It could have been a dream, but it was so real with so much detail. I have been thinking about it for months and have been constantly searching for where this place might be."

"So, what did you experience? What was this dream about?"

Bruce explains the wild dream that he had in detail. The meeting with the strange people who lived up in the mountains and their cultural clash between the old Japanese world and the new modern technology. The old commune hippies were able to survive up at a high altitude in a remote location throughout the year. The most bizarre part of the dream is the way he got back.

After hearing about the dream, Chuck is also starting to wonder if it is real or not. "They called themselves gardeners or caretakers? Were they farmers?"

"I never saw any plants or anything. They didn't look like the type of people who got their hands dirty. The only thing I did see was a group of small cabins in the middle of the forest. I don't know how anyone like that could survive the winter. The way they talked was even worse. It was a throwback to the old hippie days."

"You started feeling tired, and he touched your forehead. Then you were back in your sleeping bag? You heard the bang?"

Bruce nods his head. "Yep... The other thing I remember that was odd. They kept using the word journey, or they were watching my progress. Initially, I thought they were watching me walking up the hill. Now, I'm starting to wonder what the hell they were talking about."

"Was it like they were spying on you when you were walking up there?"

"That's what I thought at first! They're isolated and probably don't like visitors. When I stood up on that ridge, I couldn't see anyone or any signs of people living there. But, from the way they talked, it sounded like they were watching me the entire time. It wasn't until I was by the lake. That's when this guy just showed up out of nowhere. That's the other thing that made me think that it was all a dream. I couldn't sense them being there."

"Then it was probably a dream, a really odd one, but a dream," Chuck explained. "If you can sense other people are around, then that would explain it."

"That's what I keep thinking, but it had signs that it wasn't. That's what keeps me going back and forth on this one."

"Yeah, it does have a few signs of it being a jump to the other side," Chuck said. "Then again, you were talking with them. That doesn't happen on the other side."

"I know... That's the weird part. When we are on the other side, we are just observers. People don't see us or even interact with us. These people did. I sat down with them and had tea and a lengthy conversation."

"The odd bit was when you discovered the missing time," Chuck added.

"Yeah... That's when things got weird. For me, it was all real. There was so much detail, not like any other dream. When they started talking about the stars, I remembered how I was looking up at the stars that night. That's when I realized that I didn't remember getting up that morning or how I got to the trail."

"Then you started feeling tired?" Chuck asked.

"It hit me like a brick... I was getting scared that I wasn't going to make it back home. It felt just like when I get back from the remote viewing. I was totally exhausted."

"He said he was going to help you on your journey back home. Then touches your forehead?"

"Yep, then I heard the bang! Next thing I knew, I was back in my sleeping bag."

"I don't know," Chuck said, shaking his head. "That's too many signs of it being on the other side than a dream. It's a little spooky too. Who could those people be? There are lost souls out there, but those people are definitely not like the madwoman you bumped into."

"During the accident, I did talk with the old man. Can you imagine if there were other people stuck between the worlds? If the lost souls are there, what about these people? In a way, they would live forever."

Chuck lets out a long sigh. "Never thought of that... No need for a job or worry about getting food or a place to live.

Damn, now you got me wondering about it. It's got to be one or the other."

"That's how I feel! I just can't get it out of my mind. I keep going over it, trying to make sense of it all."

"You remember the terrain and the lake? Would you be able to recognize it from a map or a satellite image?"

"That's what I have been doing for the last few months."

"Keep looking... When you find it, let me know. I want to be there to see it for myself."

"You think it's real?" Bruce asked.

He nods. "I think you might have stumbled onto something. If you can find that lake, then it wasn't a dream."

Bruce laughs. "I thinks I see another book on the horizon."

"You know me... You have to be one step ahead of the competition. I know that if I stick with you, I'll be publishing a new book every year."

* * *

The Lake

Months later, Bruce is at the local library, searching for what he now refers to as the dream lake. Taking advantage of modern technology, he spends hours searching Google Earth. He methodically searches the mountain regions around the world for anything that resembles the mysterious lake.

The lake was somewhat round, sitting deep within a mountain range, surrounded by trees. There are so many lakes out there that look just like it. The biggest problem is looking down at these lakes from a satellite image on the Internet. He only knows what it looks like from the ground.

Getting so frustrated, Bruce tries a different approach. Instead of using satellite images, he types in 'mountain round lake glacier.' Hitting the search button on Google, hundreds of images show up on the screen. Right away, he knows this will be more helpful. He can see them all on the screen at once, scrolling from one page after another. With everyone uploading their holiday photos from around the world, this is way better than satellite images.

After hours of looking at various lakes, one image stands out. He clicks on the link to open the original web page. To his surprise, someone uploaded their holiday photos from Switzerland. The vast gray mountain in the background is almost like the one in the dream.

After a little research, Bruce discovers that this is a popular holiday resort. Lake Oeschinensee, near Kandersteg in Switzerland. He can't believe he missed it after spending days going over all the satellite images of lakes in Switzerland. After studying all the maps and a few more photos, he now knows that using satellite images to find the lake was a complete waste of time. The satellite images don't even resemble what it looks like from the ground.

After seeing a photo of someone standing on that very same ridge, there is no doubt in his mind that this is the lake. Right away, he booked the next flight to Switzerland. Luckily, there is a small hotel situated right on the edge of the lake. He can check out the area and not have to hike very far like he did on his first trip in that crazy dream.

Going back to Google Earth, Bruce zooms in on the area. There are some similarities but vast differences. Most of the trees are gone. A small village is a few miles from the lake, with houses dotted all around the area. There is now a train station, plus a highway leading to the area. None of this was in his dream. What he remembers was an extremely remote wilderness area.

After booking his flight, Bruce is on the phone again. "Hey, Chuck! How are things on the bestselling book tour?"

"Good evening, Bruce! It couldn't be better. I'm having the time of my life."

"That's good to hear... Wait a minute. Good evening, where are you? It's almost noon here."

"I'm in Paris! What a place! I just finished a tour, so I'm going to take a break and do a little sightseeing. You need to check this place out. It's fantastic!"

"It's funny that you mentioned that. I just booked a flight to Switzerland. I'm going to be there in a few days."

"No, come to Paris! We'll hit the bars and have some fun. You need to check out the women here! This is the place to be!"

There is a long pause. "Chuck, I found it… It's real."

Chuck is a little confused. "Found what?"

"The lake in the dream… It's the Oeschinensee Lake near Kandersteg."

"You got to be kidding! In Switzerland? Are you sure?"

"That's why I'm flying out there," Bruce added. "It's the only way to make sure. It looks so similar to the lake in my dream. The only thing that's different is that this place is all built up. There is a small town nearby. You won't have to walk far. They even got a few hotels right next to the lake."

"Damn… You going to be there in two days?"

"Yep… Do you want to check it out? It's not far from Paris."

"I'll be there! But Bruce, you need to come back to Paris with me. You need a break!"

"It's a deal! I booked a room in the hotel right on the lake. I'll see you in a few days!"

* * *

The flight to Zurich is long and boring. Cooped up in a confined place, Bruce is getting claustrophobic. Living in the wilderness, he is not used to being stuck in a seat for most of the day. Luckily, flying first class makes things a little better. He knows he would have gone nuts all cramped up in the coach section.

Arriving in Switzerland, Bruce is so relieved. The best part of the trip is the train to Kandersteg. The train is slow-moving, with a great view of the landscape. Unlike on the flight, at least here, he can get up and wander about to stretch his legs.

Bruce has thought of nothing else since discovering the lake. He can still visualize the image as if it were yesterday.

Looking out the train window, he can now see the similarities with all the mountains, trees, and deep valleys. The entire area has been formed from old glaciers, gouging out the valley thousands of years ago.

The closer he gets to Kandersteg, the more familiar the area becomes. If he didn't know any better, these mountains are just like the ones back in Wyoming. Tall snowcapped granite mountains, surrounded by lush green pastures and dense forest, it all looks the same.

* * *

Arriving in Kandersteg is a big letdown. Standing at the train station, all he can see is a bustling town. From what he could remember, this was nothing more than a valley, covered with dense trees with a small creek meandering down the center.

Following the rest of the tourists, he has no clue how to get to the lake. From the maps, it's only a couple of miles, with several roads and trails leading up to the lake. After a 24-hour flight, plus sitting on the train, he is in no shape to hike up the 1,400-foot climb.

Bruce sees a woman holding up a sign for Oeschinensee Lake. "You give rides up to the lake?"

"Ah, yes! Are you staying at our hotel?" the woman asked.

He looks at his ticket and sees the same hotel name as on her sign. "Ahh, yes! That's the place I'm staying at," so glad that she speaks English.

"Our van is over there… Just give Lucas your backpack, and he will store it away. We will be leaving shortly."

"Oh, that's great! Thanks a lot!" so relieved that this long trip is almost over.

The van quickly fills with excited tourists from all over the world. Many are students traveling with nothing but their backpacks. In no time, it's standing room only. Safety is not a concern here. There are twice as many people in the van than what's on the sign for the maximum capacity.

As the van goes up the road, Bruce wonders if they are even going to make it up the hill with all these people. With all the grinding noises coming from the transmission, people are now looking at each other, getting scared.

The gray snowcapped mountain is a sight that he has seen before. Enormous walls are on both sides as the van drives up the hill through the valley. Now, he knows this place is just like the one in the dream.

The road follows along the gray rocky riverbed. Every minute that goes by, Bruce knows that this is the place. On his right side, there is a massive wall rising up over 1,000 feet above. On the left side of the valley is a steep hill full of tall pine trees. Seeing the waterfall coming down from the cliff face on the south side is one he has seen before.

When the van pulls up to the hotel, right away, Bruce knows this is the place. The scene is breathtaking. Many of the trees are gone, but the lake and the mountains surrounding it are still the same.

"This is indeed a beautiful place!" a familiar voice comes from behind.

Bruce turns around. "Hi, Chuck! You're already here?" giving his friend a big hug.

"I got here yesterday! So, how was your trip?"

"It was way too long. But the train ride was fantastic."

"That's the best way to travel here in Europe. The flights might get you there quicker, but you end up missing all of this. So, what do you think? Is this the place?"

Bruce nods his head. "No doubt about it… This whole area was covered with trees in my dream," pointing back to the hotel and the road leading back to town.

"Where were the cabins at?" Chuck asked.

"They were over there, just across from this small outlet opposite the hotels. That's the only part that looks different. That whole part used to be filled with trees, but the entire area looks like it's been pushed out into the lake. Let's walk over and check it out."

"Bruce, are you going to check in first?" pointing over to the hotel.

"No time for that. The room ain't going anywhere," grabbing the backpack. "Come on... I'll show you where they were."

Walking over to the south side of the lake, Bruce can't believe his eyes. Everything looks a little different as if returning home after many years. Walking along the sandy bank, he knows something is not right.

"It was not like this in the dream... This whole area wasn't here. It looks like almost a hundred feet or more of dirt has been pushed out into the lake."

"What do you think happened?" Chuck asked.

"It could be a landslide from the looks of things."

Chuck looks down at the water's edge. "I think you're right... You can see the difference in these two areas here. Further down, there are pine trees right up to the edge of the lake. This area around us is nothing but dirt and gray rocks, with no trees at all. It looks like a lot of this came down from up there," pointing up the hill.

"Yeah, it definitely looks like a landslide. It looks like there are a few more on the opposite side of the lake, too. If you look over there to the hotel, that's what it was like here. It was mostly flat, not steep as it is now. The whole place was covered with huge trees. That must have been one hell of a landslide."

"It's a shame," Chuck said. "If the cabins were in this area, they'd probably be deep underneath all of this dirt or pushed out into the lake. At least you know this is the right place."

Bruce is so frustrated. He came all this way to find everything had been buried under tons of dirt and rocks.

"Let's get you checked in, and we'll get something to eat. We'll ask around if anyone knows the geologic history of this lake. Maybe we can get some answers to when this all happened."

"Sounds like a good idea," Bruce replied, starting to feel tired from the jet lag.

* * *

Bruce and Chuck explore the area around the lake and the small town of Kandersteg. Finding a history book in one of the local stores, they learn that the small town goes back almost 600 years. The entire area was once a large forest. Most of the trees are now gone, probably used for firewood or to build the houses around here. The area was mostly used for herding and farming in the early days.

Bruce even retraces his first walk up to the lake. He can still visualize the path he once used. Dragging Chuck along, they spend hours on the 2.5-mile hike up the hill. Keeping to the original route, he avoids the roads and well-marked trails.

"Well, you retraced the path you took in that dream," Chuck said, so exhausted from the hike. "There's nothing else we can do."

"You're right... We've been over this whole area several times. It's all gone. I was hoping to find some remnants of the buildings, but they're long gone."

"People have been living in this area for hundreds of years. Even if there were something up here, someone would have found it years ago. Now, you have thousands upon thousands of tourists hiking up on all these trails. They would have found something long ago," pointing over at a group of tourists walking nearby.

"The landslide probably happened hundreds of years ago, or even more," Bruce explained, getting frustrated. "In the dream, none of this was here. No town or any roads, and the hotels sure weren't here either. This whole area was nothing but one big wilderness for miles around."

"That's the part I don't understand," Chuck remarked. "That meant that you were in the past and not the present. The remote viewing is always in the present."

"Maybe it was all a dream. None of it was real," so confused about it all.

"Yes, but you are here," Chuck said. "This place is for real. You were here long before the town was even built! You were in the past. Maybe a past life? I think it's time for Jack to put you under to see what's in that noggin of yours. You should give it a try."

"After hearing some of the things people went through, I think I'd rather not know about the past."

"You could have relived something that you experienced before. It kind of makes sense if you think about it."

"What? That was a past life? Remember, they had electricity. It wasn't just a light bulb, either. They had light panels that covered the entire ceiling. They even had flat-screen monitors and were using them as picture frames like people do now. It was extremely modern, even for today. Not too many places have that type of technology."

"Yeah, you're right," Chuck said, getting confused. "You said their accents sounded like they were from this region. That part makes sense."

"Oh, once I heard some of the locals talking, it's a dead ringer for that accent."

"The Asian part is still odd," Chuck added.

"That's why I spent most of my time looking around Japan for this lake. The Japanese influence was there, but they looked European. They were very pale but extremely tall as well."

"Damn, you seem to be getting yourself into some strange situations and meeting up with the weirdest bunch of people. I talked with Jack last night. He went nuts when I told him, and he wants in on this one. He also wants a detailed description of your conversation. The clothes they wore, the cabin interior, and anything else. Anything you can remember. He wants it all in detail."

"Oh, I bet he does... He sees another book deal as well."

Chuck laughs. "You got no one to blame but yourself. You started this mess!"

"So, where do we go from here?" Bruce asked, getting so frustrated with all of this.

"Well, it looks like this is the place, but now we need to find out the time. We need an expert in this area. Let's go back to the hotel and make some phone calls."

* * *

Visiting a local museum in Bern, Chuck uses his celebrity status to convince the curator to meet with them. They need someone to help go over some of the questions about the history of the area, especially in the area out by the lake.

As soon as Chuck and Bruce walk into the Natural History Museum, a man rushes up. "Welcome, Mr. Wilson! It's such an honor to meet you!"

"Ah, you must be Dr. Alex Gassner," Chuck said, shaking his hand.

"I read all about your work with Dr. Brown and Dr. Stewart. It's all so fascinating. Will they be joining us?"

"I'm sorry, but no... It's just me and my friend, Bruce."

"It's a pleasure to meet you, Bruce," Dr. Gassner said. "Are you part of Mr. Wilson's research?"

"Oh, no... I'm just here on holiday. We've been doing a little sightseeing together."

"Well, that's great to hear… Please come to my office," Dr. Gassner said, putting his arm around Chuck. "Tell me all about this new research you are doing here in Bern."

Bruce had to laugh. Chuck always uses his celebrity status every time he needs something. That does open many doors. What's even more surprising is how many people recognize him. That's one of the first rules of marketing. Always put your photo on the front cover of the book.

The curator's office is very small, resembling a library rather than an office. Every wall has a bookcase running from the floor to the ceiling, all filled with books. The desk and the work table also have stacks of books and papers. Bruce even has to move a stack of books to the floor to have a place to sit down.

"So, what brings you here to our part of the world, Mr. Wilson?"

"I'm doing some research here about the local history, mostly up by Kandersteg and the lake. I'm looking for some of the original people who may have lived up there, but I'm also interested in some of the geologic timelines of the lake."

"The history of the region is a simple one to answer," Dr. Gassner explained. "The area started out as seasonal herding and farming. Then there were the sulfur mines. In the first part of the 1900s, the big industry was the tunnel. After that, it's mostly tourism."

"We'd like to go back even further than that," Chuck explained. "What's the earliest known civilization?"

"Late Neolithic, which goes back 2,000 to maybe 4,000 years ago. Then there was the Bronze Age. The Romans were living in the region as well. About mid-1300, we joined the Swiss Confederation. It depends on how far back you are interested. Basically, it all goes back to the Paleolithic era."

Chuck turns to Bruce, looking for guidance. "What do you think?"

"From the sounds of things, people in this region go back to the stone age. Are there any out of the ordinary civilizations that you might have heard from old folklore?" Bruce asked, deciding a direct approach may get more information.

"Well, there are some old stories, but that's all they are."

"What about the landslide up at the lake?" Chuck asked. "That might get us to the era we are looking for."

"Yes, we noticed a landslide on the southern side near the outlet of the lake. Do you know when that happened?" Bruce asked.

Dr. Gassner is a little shocked by the question. "There is nothing in the records about a landslide. It's always been like that. The lake has always been the same going back hundreds of years."

Bruce pulls out a map of the lake that he drew. "This is what it used to look like years ago. See the old shoreline here. This entire area was covered with trees. We need to know the approximate time this all came crashing down."

Dr. Gassner is getting flustered. He keeps glancing back and forth at these two men, not knowing what to say. He knew of their research but was not expecting these types of questions.

"Would you know the geologic timeline of this event?" Chuck asked, seeing how the curator was practically speechless.

There is a long pause. "I need to ask one of my colleagues. We have a geologist who specializes in that area. He's not here today, but he may be able to help you. It may take a few days."

"That would be great!" Chuck said, standing up. "You have been extremely helpful. Here's my number. We're staying at the hotel by the lake."

Dr. Gassner gets up, reaching over to shake Bruce's hand. The moment he touches Bruce's hand, he feels a jolt. His eyes grow wide, staring at Bruce's face. It's almost as if this man is looking deep into his soul. He tries to let go but is unable to move. Images start flowing through his mind as if seeing his life flash before his eyes.

Bruce lets go of his hand. "Tell Dr. Reitnauer I'll be interested in his findings. It would be most helpful to our endeavor. We look forward to your reply."

Dr. Gassner is stunned. "You know of our Dr. Reitnauer?" feeling light-headed.

"No, you must have mentioned his name," Bruce added. "Well, we've taken up too much of your time. We don't want to keep you from visiting your brother, Albert, at the hospital. I hope he has a speedy recovery."

"Why thank you," Dr. Gassner replied. "It's nothing major," so confused how this person knows about his brother.

Bruce opens the door. "Come on, Chuck... I'm hungry! Let's check out some of the local restaurants."

"Yes, let's do that... Thank you again, Dr. Gassner!" Bruce added, making a fast exit.

As soon as they are far enough away, Chuck grabs Bruce's arm. "You want to tell me what happened back there?"

"Our friend Dr. Gassner knows more than he's telling us. There is the real science, and then there is the old folklore or unwritten science. He doesn't want to risk his job talking about fables and old wives' tales. He goes by the book, or shall I say the book of science."

"You came out of that meeting with a lot more information than what I did. He never mentioned this Reitnauer guy. You're keeping something from me!"

"Well, you remember that sixth sense I told you about back in Wyoming... It goes a little deeper," reaching up with his finger, touching Chuck's hand.

Chuck feels a jolt of electricity. Images start flashing through his mind. He is standing at the lake, and everything is different. The hotels are gone. Then he sees the forest across the lake. Inside the trees, he can see one of the cabins. He feels another jolt of electricity. A blinding white light slowly fades away, and now he is back in the museum again.

"That's what it used to look like," Bruce explained.

"What the hell did you just do?" Chuck asked, feeling woozy.

"It's a little trick I learned not too long ago. It comes in handy sometimes, like today. Oh, there is a nice little restaurant I want to check out. I also need to get a few souvenirs while we're here," motioning Chuck to follow.

"Damn, Bruce... You're starting to get a little spooky. Can you do that with anyone?"

Bruce shakes his head. "No, I just tried it on a few people so far. Lucky for you, it worked. The last time I did that, the poor guy dropped dead in his tracks."

Chuck comes to a complete stop, grabbing Bruce's arm. "You got to be kidding! The man died?"

Bruce laughs. "Chuck, you are so damn gullible!"

Chuck lets out a long sigh. "Karen is right... You need to get serious about this," not used to Bruce's sense of humor. "So, that was what you saw in the dream?"

"Yep... It's a shame that it's all buried."

"Karen is going to have a cow when she hears about this new trick you acquired. A sixth sense, like hell it is!"

"I thought it was an aftereffect from the remote viewing. I figured you would have known about stuff like this. Remember, you're the expert."

"Expert, hell no... Not after today. You're just full of surprises, aren't you?"

Bruce just laughs. "At least we are getting close... From what I was able to learn from Dr. Gassner, there were a lot of old stories about advanced civilizations in this entire region. Much of it is just old folklore, but sometimes there is always a little truth that started it all in the first place. Now we have to weed out the myths to get to the truth."

* * *

After a couple of days, Dr. Gassner comes up with the information. A geologic study was done decades ago, long before the hotels by the lake were built. The area across from the hotels was considered unstable because of the landslides. There was not just one, but many. From core samples taken near the lake and from the cliff face above, the study concluded that the first landslide was approximately 2,700 BC. That means the event happened almost 5,000 years ago.

Chuck is utterly shocked by the numbers. "Is that what you were expecting?" handing Bruce the documentation.

Bruce starts to laugh. "Seeing how they lived, you would have thought it was today. Not 5,000 years ago. It doesn't make any sense."

"Hell... That was when the landslide happened. That means those flower people were there before the landslide, not after. So, it had to be more than 5,000 years ago. No telling how long they were up there or when you were there. Damn, you hit a home run with this one. This opens up a whole new area for us."

"I don't know if the guys back home will be ready for this one," Bruce remarked. "I never expected this."

"Bruce, everything we've done so far has been groundbreaking. Multiple lives and the human soul, living for eternity. If you think about it, it's all coming together. There is always someone out there talking about advanced civilizations like Atlantis. Those stories go back hundreds of years. No one has ever found any evidence of it, but it doesn't mean it didn't happen."

"You're right... With all the things we've discovered, I'm surprised no one brought this up. Now that I think about it, the conversation I had with those people is not what I originally thought it was."

"How do you mean?" Chuck asked.

"When they referred to my journey, I always thought it was about the hike up the hill. Maybe they were referring to my jump to the other side."

"Could be... When we go to the other side, it's always in the current time. I have never heard of anyone changing time spans like that, especially going back 5,000 years. I read the transcript you did for Jack after hearing about the timeframe for all this. Yes, that conversation may have a totally different meaning now. You have to admit it. That was one weird conversation you had with them."

Bruce smiles. "You mean about the flowers and gardens. How they make them all grow and flourish."

"Maybe they weren't talking about plants," Chuck explained. "It's scary to think about it, but it could be people and not flowers. Damn, this keeps on getting better and better, doesn't it?" getting all flustered.

"Think about it... Extremely tall, fair-skinned people. Weird clothes and all that high-tech stuff, even for today. The UFO people will go nuts when they hear about this."

"It does lead to that conclusion... If your transcripts are correct, these people might have been messing about with our genetics thousands of years ago. The big question is, why?"

"The term gardeners," Bruce remarked. "Just think... If we had a garden and planted roses, we would do the same. Blending different ones together to get that perfect award-winning flower."

"Yeah, and we are the roses... I hate to find out what they did to the weeds or the imperfections. That's a scary thought. I think I'm going to go back and reread that transcript."

"It was all so weird!" Bruce said, thinking about that conversation.

"This puts things in a different perspective now. I guess they might not have been a bunch of hippies."

"I know... What was I thinking? I wish I could go back. I'd ask a lot more questions. What about all this stuff that's happening to me? Are they responsible for that, too?"

Chuck hesitates. "That's a good question... You are doing some strange things nowadays. You've gone further into the remote viewing than most people I know. You've also been able to do the jump after only a month. Most people spend years getting to that stage. Hell, you probably surpassed me long ago."

"Oh, that was just a fluke," Bruce said, trying to play it down. "Those days are long gone."

"Watching your progress... Could it be the remote viewing? It'll be kind of spooky if they've been watching you."

"You know... Now that I think about it. If they were watching my progress, how could they do it 5,000 years ago? It doesn't make sense!"

"I'm not sure either... Maybe you were living back then at that time. Jack said you probably have quite a few past lives. Hell, we all do. So that could have been a past life you were reliving?"

"I keep thinking about that... The only problem with that theory I mentioned was that I lived in California, and I was wearing my favorite hiking boots," pointing down to the shoes on his feet.

Chuck shakes his head. "This has got me so confused!"

"Me too... I think we'll let the guys back home figure this one out," Bruce said. "You got lots of data now. Let them analyze it and see what they can make of it. For me, it's over.

I can finally put this mystery to rest. I'm going to go on vacation!"

Chuck laughs. "Good for you! Come on… I'll show you Paris! You'll have a great time there!"

* * *

Old Friend

Years later, Bruce settled down in his small log cabin next to the lake. His days are nothing more than fishing, walking the trails, and painting. No one in the news media could connect him with Karen, Jason, Jack, and Chuck. He has been able to live a simple life, keeping out of the limelight.

Occasionally, going to town for groceries, Bruce is always surprised to see his old friends are still in the news. He makes sure to read all their books and news articles.

Jason's research is taken more seriously by the academic world with his publications in various medical and science journals. The peer-review process is still ongoing. With more and more people reviewing the data, the science community is now concluding this is not a fabricated story to sell books.

* * *

On a chilly Sunday afternoon, Bruce is on the porch trying to finish another painting. The cloud formations over the mountain and the fall colors of the trees always make a challenging project.

In the distance, far out on the lake, is a lone person paddling in a canoe. There is always someone out on the lake fishing or just enjoying the day. It's a perfect addition to his painting, and he quickly adds it to the scene.

The person in the canoe is different from the others. Not on any leisurely paddle, this one is making a beeline straight for the cabin. Not recognizing the canoe, he is getting a little concerned about strangers snooping around.

Bruce pulls out his binoculars. Focusing on the person far out on the lake makes him laugh. An old friend has come to visit. One he hasn't seen in a long time. The poor guy is struggling like mad not to tip over that canoe.

"Trust you to come in from the back way!" Bruce shouted out.

Chuck waves the paddle up in the air. "Hi, Bruce! How are you doing, old buddy?" then the canoe becomes unbalanced.

"You better be careful! That water is awfully cold!" running down to the shoreline.

"Yeah, I could use some help here! I'm not sure how to get out of this canoe without falling in!"

Bruce grabs the front of the canoe, pulling it up on the rocky beach. "It would have been a lot easier to drive… Where did you start out?"

"I got a campsite across the lake. I had to make sure no one was following me," carefully stepping out of the canoe.

Bruce gives his friend a big hug. "Still the same old Chuck. Nice to see you again. It's been a long time."

"Too long… Been trying to get up here for a while, but you know how things are."

"I hear it's still a big mess for you guys in the real world… Come on in. I'll get some beer. Looks like you can use a drink after that long haul."

"You read my mind."

"Have you eaten?" Bruce asked. "I was thinking about putting some steaks on the barbecue."

"That sounds perfect! That paddling was a real workout. I didn't think it would take that long."

"Have a seat, and I'll get you set up," Bruce said, rushing inside to get all the beer and food.

"I see you are still painting," Chuck remarked. "You got a good likeness of me out there," seeing the small canoe painted on the lake.

"Yeah, that's what this painting needed. Another damn tourist out paddling on the lake without a clue where they're going," handing out the beer, then lights up the gas grill.

Chuck laughs. "You got one hell of a nice place here. I can see why you moved out of the rat race. Have you got a phone yet?" sitting on the Adirondack chair.

Bruce nods his head. "I finally broke down and got me one… It's one of those unlisted pay as you go. It was a cash deal, so there is no link with me. The best part is that there are no names, addresses, or credit cards to trace. I leave it off most of the time. Just use it on Sundays to talk with the family. I still don't have a TV. No point up here since there is no cable or any good reception."

Chuck laughs again. "I taught you well… You are well dug in up here."

"The last thing I want is to get mixed up in that mess down there. I go to town once in a while to read the papers or watch the news at the cafe. It's horrible how these people are acting. That's why I never let my guard down, but I noticed you found me."

"I knew you were in this area when I met you here years ago during my book tour, but I didn't know exactly where your cabin was. It took me a long time to track you down. There are no records of you anywhere. You have literally dropped off the face of the earth."

"But you still found me… So, where did I slip up?"

Chuck couldn't help smiling. "I stopped by your parent's house and asked."

Bruce lets out a long sigh. "How many times have I told them?" shaking his head.

"Oh, don't worry about it… They know we go back. Actually, they are getting worried about you being up here all alone. Although, your dad still insisted on seeing a photo of us together before he told me. Good thing I kept that one from that bar in Paris!" and starts laughing.

Bruce laughed, remembering the great times he had bar hopping in Paris. "I'm so glad I kept out of it. I never thought it would blow up like this. I knew it was going to be big, but my God!"

"The whole world has gone nuts over this. We can't go anywhere without being followed. The news people are camped out in front of our houses. Every time we go somewhere, we're being chased by the press."

"Yeah, I saw that on TV last year," Bruce added. "Poor Karen was just going shopping, and this helicopter followed her every move, putting it live on TV. All she was doing was getting some bread from the grocery store, and that's breaking news?"

"Someone leaked the information to the news media that she is going to a secret meeting with Jack. When she showed up at the grocery store, they still followed her in. What a joke. There are so many people watching our every move. They think they can get some information and use it for their own work. The news people are worse. They just make stuff up as they go. We still have the corner on the market. I sold more books in the last year than what I did in the last forty."

"I know! A while back, I went to the bookstore and saw a whole row of books that were nothing but remote viewing and out-of-body experiences. At least the three main books were yours, Karen's, and Jack's, and they are still selling strong."

"I guess you haven't heard yet… They're about to release another book with additional data. Jack is discovering even more people that go way back. Through his work with regression, he is rewriting the history books."

"Any famous people yet?" Bruce asked.

"Not yet, but he's found one of the best ones… There is a woman who lived two thousand years ago near Judea while Jesus was alive. They are very careful with that one."

"You think that she might have met or seen Jesus?"

"Not sure… She does know of him, though. Right there is a new book in itself."

"So, how is the church dealing with all of this? When I left LA, they were looking at us as a bunch of devil worshipers."

"Oh, no... That's all changed. They like us now! They are all jumping on the bandwagon with the rest."

"Why would they do that?" Bruce asked.

"At first, they were all against us. Things they don't understand are always evil. When all those people camped out around the bank, making it some sort of a shrine, it got the church's attention."

"That's when they thought the Ark of the Covenant was there!" Bruce jokingly said. "If they only knew."

"Months later, people started going to church in droves, asking all about our work and what it meant to their religion. Mostly, they all wanted to know what the church's view on all of this was. It wasn't long before the Sunday service was standing room only. Some places had so many people showing up many had to stand outside."

"I bet the church people liked that!" Bruce remarked.

"You know they did! Next thing we knew, all those people who were calling us devil worshipers wanted secret meetings to discuss our work. Basically, they said they would endorse or give their blessing but at a cost."

"What did they want?"

"They wanted to set up all the rules. For their blessing, we would have to go through them for approval on any future releases or research. Also, they wanted to edit what we already published."

"So, you would be working for the church and play by their rules?"

"Exactly! The price was way too high. The bottom line is we don't need them, but they need us. Jason is the one who puts them in their place. He played up on their worst fears."

"What's that, money?" Bruce asked.

"Even better... Their fear of losing people to another church. When we go into a meeting with the Christians, they'd be coming down on us hard with all their restrictions. Then Jason starts talking about how the Jewish people were OK with that and how they were going to back us. He did that in every meeting. He played one against the other. The church people got so scared, and they even created a review committee to study it."

"All the churches? That's unheard of."

"They had to... They did a generic blessing just on certain aspects. They just picked the areas that would promote the heaven and earth thing. It's still ongoing. They'll be reading between the lines of all our books from here on out!"

"So, is everyone still trying to get in on the remote viewing?" Bruce asked, getting curious.

"Yep, everyone wants to roam the heavens. Remote viewing workshops are popping up in every town. Most of them are nothing more than a bunch of con artists taking people's money."

Bruce laughs. "So, you think it's going to get crowded out there?"

"No way... They are finding out that it's not that easy. After years of training, it takes a certain person to be able to do it. Back in the '60s, the military went through thousands of people just to find a small handful. It's no different today. It's probably less than one percent that can go to the other side. The people who do try and are successful don't ever want to go back again."

Bruce starts to tend the barbecue. "I know what you mean... So what about your world? Any big breakthroughs?"

"It's the same old thing for me... Although would you believe, every government is starting up their own remote viewing spy group! They think it's going to replace the spy satellites and be lots cheaper, too. Our government is now paying me big bucks to be their top consultant, mostly to prevent me from consulting with other countries. They sure don't want me helping out our allies with this stuff."

Bruce laughs. "They got their hooks on you... Now that they know this is real, I bet you they're scared. I guess the next big thing is finding out how to block it."

"You know it is! That's where all the big research money is going. Now they know it's real, and they are terrified."

"Yeah, with all the security the military has, and now anyone can just float on in and see everything!" Bruce added.

"Yep, they didn't see that one coming... Oh, did you hear how they got the camera?"

"No, I thought it was still in the safe deposit box?"

"With all the people camped out in front of the bank, it finally closed down. Too many people were scared to go in. They left everything in the vault and locked the whole building up. The government got a federal judge to seize it before anyone else got in there."

"And they all wanted the big mystery device!" Bruce jokingly said.

"It was great, almost like that Indiana Jones movie dragging out the Lost Ark. They brought in the military to handle it and even had it live on TV. They had no clue what was in there. Ended up hauling everything out and storing it all in the desert, just in case. In the end, they had to demolish the entire building. It's nothing more than a vacant lot."

"I wish I saw that on TV! That would be hilarious to watch. So they finally got their hands on the camera?"

"Oh yeah... They found the records with Karen and Jason's names on them. After that, they knew where to look. When they found the camera and tested it out, they were so disappointed. It was nothing more than a regular Hasselblad digital camera!"

Bruce smiled. "It was a good thing Karen put the original digital back that came with the camera in the safe deposit box. When I removed our sensor, I didn't want to leave any clues. All they found was nothing more than a Hasselblad camera. At least that fake ID and thumbprint kit you gave me got them off my back."

"Yeah, they are still looking for the third person who was with Karen and Jason. When they traced the thumbprint back to a guy who died ten years ago, it threw them for a loop. I'm still trying to figure out how the surveillance videos got messed up when you went in."

"Oh, that was me... I scoped it out a few times. When I saw they used old VCR tapes, I knew I didn't have to worry about the surveillance system."

"How the hell did you do that?" Chuck asked.

"Back then, I was wandering about on the other side... I just happened to go past one of those old ship's compasses in a museum. That thing started spinning like mad. I guess we are some sort of electrical field or something, and it affects the magnetic compasses."

Chuck is shocked. "I never knew that!"

"That's what gave me the idea... I got out my old VCR and did a little experimenting. So, when you are out traveling, all you have to do is pass through a VCR tape a few times, and it messes it up big time. I ruined some of my good tapes in the process. So, after I removed the sensor, I went back and messed up the surveillance tapes."

"Yep, you are the big mystery man everyone is trying to find. You know, you just gave me a good idea. Does it work on computers?"

Bruce nods. "It takes more work... Just don't go through the hard drive when it's spinning. I won't make that mistake again. If the hard drive is idle, then it's OK. You can also mess up the memory when the computer is running. I pissed off a lot of people with that one," then starts to laugh.

"The shit is going to hit the fan when the government finds out about that. If people are going out messing up all the computers and backup tapes, it'll be chaos in no time."

"Oh, yeah... That's got me scared, too. That'll be a hell of a military weapon to mess up everyone's computer systems. You need to warn them about that one. So, how far have you got on the flower people research?" Bruce asked.

"We are still trying to dig up more information on that group. What we have is sketchy. We started looking for ancient civilizations similar to what you found in Switzerland, whether it is fact or fiction."

"I read several of those books years ago," Bruce said. "It was the big craze back in the '70s. Ancient aliens type thing."

"Most of it fizzled out after all the scrutiny, but there are always one or two stories you can't ignore."

"Like having people building the pyramids? That's one hell of an achievement, considering how long ago it was."

"Exactly! What brought on such dramatic advances?" Chuck asked. "Why is it that certain areas had a head start?"

Bruce laughed. "You mean the aliens coming down giving us their technology?"

"Oh no, not that! We're trying to stay out of that mess. Remember what the flower people did? They tended the gardens to make sure the flowers flourished. Crossing them with others for new traits to make sure they survive."

Bruce thinks back to the conversation he had. "Survival of the fittest! They were creating the modern man. One that could use his mind to survive and to expand his knowledge."

"That's the best theory we got so far."

"So, what areas around the world did we get these dramatic advances?" Bruce asked.

"Would you believe the earliest ones were in Ancient China, Indus Valley, Mesopotamia, and Egypt? Later on, we got the Phoenicians and the Mayas down in Mexico. In a way, if you think about it, they all proliferated, or shall I say flourished into advanced civilizations."

"That seems to make sense... No Atlantis?"

Chuck laughed. "That's all people are talking about, Atlantis! Were these people from Atlantis? The big question is, who were they? From your description, they were advanced people. Maybe Europeans with an Asian taste?"

"They were extremely tall people. Fair-skinned and very polite, too. The Japanese-style cabin is something I always thought was really out of place."

"We did too... We got some good leads on that, but we are now leaning toward China and not Japan. We have people all over Japan doing research there. No one has found anything yet. China is the place we want to be, but we are having problems getting in. As soon as they find out who we are or what we are looking for, we are banned from the whole damn country. We tried to sneak a few people in, but as soon as they asked a few questions, it was over. Our people get arrested and kicked out of the country."

"Just our luck… What else do you have?" Bruce asked.

"We do have some leads, but in another area. With all this DNA research going on, we found a couple of universities that are using DNA to trace humans back to their original ancestors. So far, they got it down to six groups or species, Chinese, Mongoloid, European, Mediterranean, and African.

Everyone alive today is a descendant of one or more of those groups."

"That's only five," Bruce said, noticing one was missing.

"Oh, get this! The sixth one was a mystery for almost ten years. It was similar but didn't fit in with the rest. That's why it was kept separate. A few years ago, someone got their hands on some Neanderthal DNA. It just so happens that was the sixth group. It fit right into place."

"There are people alive today who are direct ancestors of Neanderthals?" Bruce asked.

"Well, from the sounds of it, yes! However, only Europeans have Neanderthal DNA traits. They probably got a little curious about each other and messed around. There were probably only a few offspring that survived. So when the Neanderthal eventually died out, their offspring did survive but probably looked European."

"So, how does this fit in with what you're doing?"

"It just so happens these six groups that they came up with in the DNA research almost match the areas of advanced civilizations. Originally, it was thought that everyone came out of Africa from one species. Now, they are thinking these six original species developed on their own in different parts of the world. There might have been more, but many probably died out like the Neanderthals."

"Survival of the fittest..." Bruce remarked. "Now that I think about it, those six types of people all do have different characteristics. I thought it was caused by their environment."

"That's what everyone thought before all this new evidence. DNA research is rewriting the books. From what I hear, they are coming to the conclusion that the six basic species all developed separately from each other."

"So, the Chinese were the first ones?" Bruce asked.

"From what I was told, the order is the Neanderthal, who was the oldest. Then Africans, Chinese, Mongoloid,

Mediterranean, and the Europeans are the youngest. There were probably a lot more, but they died out."

"Chuck, that doesn't make any sense?"

"There are lots of theories... But do you remember what the flower people said? There were other gardeners tending their flowers, too. These were probably totally separate groups dabbling with the human race. Each one was coming up with a unique species that was able to survive in that particular environment. Why were they doing this? Who really knows?"

"Now, I think about it," Bruce remarked. "They did say they had concerns about other flowers mixing in with theirs. And yes, they did say there were other gardeners. I wish I could go back and ask more questions. I feel so stupid now thinking that they were nothing but a bunch of hippies."

"Can you imagine more of those flower people located in different places throughout the world?" Chuck asked. "All basically playing God, trying to create people that could survive. The big question we have is, why are they doing this? Who are they, and where did they come from?"

"Yeah, that is a mystery. So, from the information we got, this could fit in with the DNA research."

Chuck shakes his head. "That's what I thought too... We just have a theory. They wanted hard evidence and were really interested in what we found. From some of the comments, they thought what we had would make a great science fiction novel."

Bruce is shocked to hear all the bad news. "That's just great... It sounds like you guys don't have much at all."

"We did have a major breakthrough last year, but it fell apart. The bastards locked us out."

"Kicked out again?" Bruce asked. "Sounds like you guys are not popular. What happened?"

"I have been talking with the university people in Zurich about the geologic survey of the lake they did all those years ago. They were having some major concerns about the stability of the landslide. With all the tourists in the area, they wanted to go back and do some new tests but didn't have the funding. They need some of those new ground-penetrating radar systems that will map the subsurface structures. That would give them a three-dimensional view of everything underneath the ground. So, I made a donation to pay for the survey."

"What did they find?" Bruce asked.

"Oh, they found plenty… There was not just one landslide but many over the years. Best of all, they found some unusual structures only 30 feet down. These didn't look like natural formations, but man-made."

"You think it could be the remnants of the cabins?" Bruce asked.

"I think so… I didn't tell them anything so that it wouldn't influence their conclusions. Just by their reactions, you can tell they were excited and wanted to excavate the area. Even they could see it was some sort of man-made structures or the foundations of something."

"So, they dug up the area?"

"That was the plan… When they went to get permission for an archaeological dig, everything was shut down. Everyone was excited about the dig until finding out where it was located. The first excuse they gave for not allowing it was because it was in an unstable area, and they didn't want to cause another landslide."

"Going down 30 feet is not much of a risk," Bruce added.

"All the geologists said that… Then it got rejected again because the lake is considered to be a natural treasure, and absolutely no one is allowed to alter any of its features."

"For an archaeological dig, that sounds weird."

"After that, they shut the door on us. They won't even return our calls."

"You think it was because of our other work? Maybe they don't agree with our research in past lives and such."

"This was strictly between the university and the government. They had no idea who was backing it. It was all funded anonymously. I made sure of that."

"None of it makes sense. Why would they shut it down?"

"It gets worse… They passed some new laws that made it a crime for anyone to dig anywhere around the lake or even in the town below. The entire area is now a natural landmark or natural treasure. You can't even bring a shovel to the area, or you will be arrested. The head geologist protested like mad. It just so happens he was from Canada. They revoked his visa and kicked him out of the country. After that, no one wants to talk about it anymore. So, we have been shut out by the Swiss government."

"It sounds like they don't want anyone to snoop around up there. You know what that means?" Bruce asked.

"Yep, they know what's up there! It'll just fuel the masses when this gets out."

"If they had let you do the archaeological dig and found nothing, it would have been over. We'll never know what's under there. Now, it means a cover-up, and that will sell lots of books. When do you think they'll publish it?"

"Oh, it'll be years from now. This is a new area for us. It's easy to publish when you have hard evidence to prove your theories, but with this one, it's all speculation. The one thing we had going for us was taken away. The information we got is small, but it's enough to warrant more research to get it right. You know how Karen and Jack are."

"Yep, if it's not perfect, then go out and get more information to persuade the non-conformist!"

"Every time we get close, we are pushed away!" Chuck said, getting so frustrated.

"If you can't get in the normal way, why not use other methods? You are the grand master of remote viewing. Have you tried to go in and snoop around?"

"Yeah, I tried a few times, but I must be getting old. I can wander about in some of their offices but can't open up file cabinets or look into the computer files. Most times, I just get lost."

"Keep trying... You'll find something."

"What about you, Bruce? Have you been dabbling with the other side much?" getting concerned about Bruce's health.

"Oh, once in a while... Not intentionally, though. Sometimes, I just nod off, taking a nap, and the next thing I know, I'm out flying around. Sometimes, I can't tell the difference whether it's a dream or an out-of-the-body experience."

"Damn... You're not even initiating it?"

Bruce pauses. "Sometimes it feels like I'm drifting in and out. Not long ago, I was thinking about Tuscany in Italy after seeing an article in a magazine. The next thing I knew, I was there going through the streets, wandering through all the museums."

"What's this thing you have about museums?" Chuck asked.

He shrugs his shoulders. "I visit a lot of art galleries, too. It's the best way to travel. It sure beats getting on a plane or driving across the country. However, the scariest part is when I find I'm in a strange place like it was years and years ago. Everything is so primitive, with no electricity or running water. The weird part is that I seem to recognize the people there, and I am even familiar with the place. Is it just a dream, or am I on the other side? At times, I don't even know."

"Sounds like you could be seeing your past lives. Maybe it's time for you to talk to Jack. He may help you in that department. You never did any of his regression sessions."

Bruce frowned. "It's the idea of reliving your own death. Hearing some of the things those people went through is a little too much for me."

"I don't know," Chuck said, getting really concerned. "I have never heard of anyone being able to jump over without going through a long process. It takes me forever, and I have been doing this for years. How are you doing when you get back? Are you exhausted or worn out?"

"No, not at all," Bruce said. "That's the thing… It's like waking up after a nap. It seems like I'm just drifting in and out without even trying. Is it all one big dream? I'm not sure about anything anymore."

"I'll talk with Karen… She might be able to help you. So, have you heard about US America? They sure didn't last long," trying to change the subject, seeing Bruce getting worried.

"Oh yeah! We saw that coming."

"They had a sure thing! How could they mess that up?" Chuck asked.

"Well, old Paul was a backstabber. We were always a little suspicious of his motives. We did all the work, and he was marketing and sales. He had the majority of the stock and overruled us on every occasion. So, when we hit the big time, we left out some key components of the processes and procedures."

Chuck busts out laughing. "The hell you did!"

"When he made the deal and promoted himself to vice president with a huge salary, he got rid of the rest of us. My accident is what saved me. When things went bad, they were hoping I'd stick around to help them out."

"So you just took the money and ran! Shit, I'd do the same. I told you this would happen."

"Yeah, you were right… We all cashed out. I knew it wouldn't last. What's the point of working for those bastards when you could live the good life? The rest of the team did the same."

"So, whatever happened to the sensor you removed from the bank? Jason has been asking about it. He could really use it for his research."

Bruce leans over, picking up a metal bowl from the table. "You can borrow it anytime you want!"

"Oh, hell! You didn't!" grabbing the metal bowl. "It's a shame…They were hoping to start back up again. With US America gone, there is no chance of getting another one!"

Bruce smiles. "Come with me… I got something to show you," motioning him into the cabin.

Bruce pulls up the rug and opens up a secret compartment on the floorboards. He reaches under the floor, pulling out a metal case. Putting it on the table, he slowly opens it.

Chuck is astonished. "Where the hell did you get these?" seeing six sensors in a protected foam case.

"When US America went under, the government seized everything and put what they didn't want up for sale. Most of the sensors were garbage because they didn't pass the quality control. When I saw the list of serial numbers, I discovered that these were from the last batch we made, and they are the best ones. Would you believe I got them for $10 each!"

"Holy shit! We are back in business again! Jason and Karen are going to have a cow when they hear this."

Bruce holds up the case. "Make sure you find a safe place to put these."

Chuck's mouth drops wide open. "You got to be kidding? These belong to you. This is your project."

Bruce shakes his head. "No... I'm retired. Fishing and painting is all I do nowadays."

"Damn... I didn't expect this," getting overwhelmed.

"Come on... Let's get those steaks off the grill. I'm getting hungry."

* * *

The Heavens

As the months passed, Bruce enjoyed the solitude of country life, but things were changing. With Christmas only days away, his family is showing up from all around the country. His log cabin on the edge of the lake is the epitome of a Christmas postcard. Surrounded by pine trees and covered with snow, it makes the perfect place for a family Christmas.

Bruce is frantically rushing about, trying to get everyone settled. Every day, he goes to town to buy more food, blankets, towels, and anything else to accommodate all the extra people. Only having a few friends staying over once in a while, now he realizes how little he has in the cabin.

After a few days, Bruce longs for the quiet country life. The cabin is a complete mess, with everyone always running in and out, tracking snow all over the carpets, especially with all the little kids. They are always yelling and screaming, playing in the snow, and having snowball fights. It's driving him nuts.

With so many people in the cabin, Bruce takes a few of the adventurous ones for long walks out on the trails. Since most of his family is from California and Florida, they've never seen snow. It is a big treat for them. To be able to walk through the snow-laden trees is something most people have never experienced in their entire lives. For Bruce, it's just another day.

* * *

With Christmas now over, things are settling down. On New Year's Eve, the fireworks are now the main event for all the kids. His family must have spent a fortune on the fireworks. The party goes on for hours, lighting one after another.

Bruce sits out on the deck with his family. Everything is so quiet now the fireworks are gone, and the kids are in bed. The stars are so bright, almost illuminating the snow. The sky is so clear that Andromeda is even visible to the naked eye.

After the long day, he starts to drift off to sleep. He slowly rises, moving toward the night sky. The horizon gradually changes as the Earth's curvature gets more prevalent. Looking down, he sees the cities all lit up, linked by highways.

Drifting higher and higher, Bruce is mesmerized by the beauty. So high up above the Earth, he can see the thin blue glow of the atmosphere. Distant cloud formations light up from a lightning storm in some remote part of the world.

The stars have never been so spectacular. Bruce recognizes a few constellations, following the stars to find obscure galaxies. The planets are out in force, seeing Jupiter, Mars, and Saturn. All the details on their surfaces can be seen.

One bright star stands out from the rest. This one is a little different, with a bluish tint. Looking at the stars around it, Bruce is having a difficult time trying to figure out which star this is. Being so bright, it should be one of the major stars. Then, the bright star slowly moves. Apparently, this is not a star or a planet, but maybe a satellite.

Seeing how quickly this bright light is moving, Bruce cautiously moves away. It is not a star, planet, or even a satellite. As he slowly moves away, the bright light becomes more apparent. Then he realizes whatever this light is, it's really close.

Out of nowhere, more of these bluish lights start swarming around him. He feels like he is inside a huge flock of birds, flying in synchronized patterns around him. Then, all at once, they dart off, leaving the one bright blue light.

As the bright light approaches even closer, it's about the size of a softball and is almost transparent. Being so close, Bruce reaches out, cupping his hands around it. For the first time, he realizes he is translucent and can see the stars through his hands.

A strange feeling comes over him. Small wisps of blue light slowly emerge from the object. Scenes of faraway places flash through his mind, and an eerie sense of serenity comes over him. He is overwhelmed with visions and a sense of familiarity. A pattern emerges of families and happiness, but mostly a woman, always smiling. As the scene changes, there is a different woman, but deep down, he knows it's the same person. For some reason, he feels as if he knows her.

The visions get more detailed, flashing by as if watching everything fast forward, only seeing major events. One by one, Bruce sees life from an early age, finding love with a woman, then a family, growing old together, and then the sadness of death. Then the scene starts all over at a different time, but it's always with the same woman, even though she looks different.

Bruce hears a faint voice that is difficult to understand, sounding like another language. He tries to talk, but even his voice is odd as if he is not speaking English.

The voice slowly becomes clear. "You are always too curious."

"Who are you?" Bruce whispers.

"I am Bashert, your destiny."

"Do I know you?" feeling a strange familiarity with this person.

"Yes, we are bonded together through the eons… You have not changed… Always too eager, never wanting to wait," then starts giggling.

Bruce is confused. "I don't understand… What is happening?"

"You are not supposed to be here… This is not your time. You must return. You are crossing over too soon. Be patient… Our time will come, my love."

The bright light expands and starts moving right toward his face. Unable to move, they merge into one. A wealth of information flows into his mind. Now, he understands, as the thousands of years of knowledge opens his mind to the world. The blue light slowly moves away from his face. Again, he cups his hands around it.

"Why are you here?" he asked. "I searched for you."

Another wisp of blue light comes out, touching his hand. He sees a vision of a little girl riding her bike. A car strikes her from behind, then speeds off without stopping. The family runs out. Her father holds her in his arms, frantically trying to revive his daughter.

"A beautiful life was taken too soon… They were a loving family. I miss being with them."

"I didn't know," Bruce said, feeling the grief from the loving family.

"You must now return… This is not your time… They are watching you," then the light shoots right toward his face.

Bruce feels a huge jolt, then a flash of bright light followed by a loud bang. The darkness is replaced by strange lights. Opening his eyes, he is unable to focus on anything. He can't even move his body, feeling trapped, as if something is holding him down.

An irritating beeping sound is all that he can hear. A dark image occasionally blocks out the light. Then he hears strange voices. People are yelling out in excitement.

Bruce hears his name over and over. The voice is so loud that it hurts his ears. His vision is starting to clear, getting used to the brightness. He is in a strange room. A woman is standing over him, shining a flashlight into his eyes.

"What the hell are you doing?" Bruce yells out, trying to push her away.

"Oh, my God!" the woman shouts. "It's OK! I'll get the doctor!" running out of the room.

Looking around, he is back in a hospital room. With tubes stuck in his arms and up his nose, this is an all too familiar scene for him.

The nurse rushes in. "He just woke up!" followed by several others.

"Well, Bruce... Nice to see you are back with us again. I'm Dr. Moore. We have been looking after you since your stay here," checking all the vital signs on the screens.

Bruce struggles to talk. "What happened, and why am I here?"

"We're still not sure what happened... You have been in a coma, and we couldn't get you out of it."

"You got to be kidding! Did I have a fall or something? Was I in an accident? I don't remember anything."

The doctor opens the charts. "Let's see... No, you were brought in by your family. They said you basically fell asleep, and they couldn't wake you. You were in the emergency room for a while, and then they brought you here."

Bruce tries to sit up. "Why do I feel like I have been hit by a bus? I feel weak all over! I'm hungry as hell, too. You got anything to eat here?"

"It's been a while... You're going to have to take it slow. Your body needs to get its strength back. You'll need some rehabilitation. We also need to find out what induced the coma. I'm going to have to set you up with some MRIs when you feel up to it."

"Sounds like a lot of trouble… I think I'll pass. So, where is my family at?" glancing over at the nurse.

"Oh, I'll go check your records. I'll give them a call to let them know about your condition."

Bruce is confused. "They're not here? They are probably at my cabin, playing in the snow!"

The nurse looks a little awkward. "Ahh, no… They're probably at home," glancing over at the doctor.

Bruce knows something is not right. "How long have I been in here?" staring at the doctor.

There is a long pause. "Bruce, you have been in a deep coma for 18 months."

"What! You got to be kidding! Why?"

"We're not sure… No one is. I consulted with Dr. Brown and Dr. Anderson in California. They said you were a special case. Not too sure what that means, but I was instructed to contact them when you come out of the coma."

Bruce smiled. "Yeah, I got a few questions to ask them… OK, first things first. Get all these tubes and stuff off of me, and I need something to eat."

"Get him something light to eat," the doctor said, jotting down a few notes in the charts. "Mr. Rollin, we're going to do a few quick tests to make sure you're up to it, then we'll move you to one of the other rooms."

"Another hospital room? Don't think so. I need to get back home."

The doctor smiled. "Let's do things one step at a time. You don't come out of an 18-month coma and go home the same day."

"What if I told you I don't have any insurance? You'll be kicking me out within the hour!"

"Nice try! You got the best insurance I have ever seen. We know all about you and your financial situation. Just sit back and let us do our jobs."

Bruce is so frustrated. The last thing he wants is to be stuck in another hospital. With no clue how he got here or why the coma thing happened, he needs to talk with Karen as soon as possible.

* * *

Upon hearing about Bruce's recovery, Karen gets the first flight to Wyoming. Everyone has been speculating about what went wrong. They knew Bruce had been having problems with the remote viewing. Many who have dabbled in the practice ended up in mental wards from the experiences.

"Hello, Bruce!" Karen shouts out as she enters the room. "Nice to see you're back with us again. So how are you feeling?" giving him a big hug.

"A little weak, but nothing major," Bruce answered.

"Yeah, right… You have been out for 18 months. We are trying to figure out what went wrong."

"I have no clue why I'm here. The last thing I knew, I was with my family on New Year's Eve. Then I woke up, and here I am in another hospital."

"You didn't go over to the other side?"

"No, I was watching the fireworks."

"Chuck told me you have been having problems drifting in and out. It sounds like you can't control it anymore."

"Yeah, it's been kind of weird lately… At times, all I have to do is think about going somewhere, and the next thing I know, I'm there."

"Damn, it's just like Chuck described… You're not even prepping for it."

"I have not done that in a long time. It's getting to the point where I wake up in the morning and remember having these dreams, but are they dreams? I'm probably going over to the other side, not even knowing it."

"That's a big problem… So, Bruce, what happened? It's got to be something bad to put you in a coma. Chuck thinks you might have gotten into trouble. He warned me about there being a dark side to all of this."

"Actually, I have no clue… I can't remember anything."

"You don't remember anything?" Karen asked. "No dreams at all?"

"Oh, no… It feels like I was only out for a few minutes. I was shocked to find out it was 18 months. So, what do the doctors think?"

"They have no clue… We've been here watching you for months. We even brought the camera in to do some scans. Your level is now so bright, actually twice what it used to be. We don't understand what would be causing that."

"I have no clue either... Everything else is normal?"

She nods her head. "Yes, across the board… You have no brain tumors. Your blood work is perfect. No one has any clue why you went into a coma."

"That includes me too," trying to figure this out.

"What did you see, and where did you go?" Karen asked, getting concerned. "It's got to be something."

"My mind is kind of a blank," Bruce explained. "I don't remember much at all. I had never experienced anything like this before. Usually, I remember everything in detail."

"I talked with Jack… He wants to do a regression. You've never done one, but now I think it's time. We have to find out what went wrong. Next time, you may not be so lucky. Chuck's been telling me about all the people who don't come back. Some of them had died or were in a permanent coma for the rest of their lives."

"Yeah, I have been wondering about that... OK, give Jack a call. I got to know what was going on to put me out for 18 months."

* * *

Regression

After several weeks of recovering, Bruce is feeling much better. Now more than ever, he is ready to take on one of Jack's regression sessions. Always avoiding these in the past, he makes sure to tell Jack that this regression is only for the period when he was in a coma.

Karen sets up one of the cameras to monitor the session. She wants to make sure he doesn't wander off to the other side during the regression. Jason and Chuck are in a separate room to watch the monitors just in case something goes wrong.

"Well, Bruce..." Jack said smugly. "I finally get a chance to see what makes you tick," giving him a big smile.

"Oh, I bet you can't wait to dive into all my past lives!" Bruce said jokingly. "You never know... I could have been your grandfather having to help change your stinky diapers."

Jack laughed. "My grandfather, like hell! You probably were my Uncle Ted. I heard stories of how he was known as the biggest fart in the county. Got a prize for it, too. He would light them up with a match, shooting flames across the room. That's how he died. He ended up burning down his own house."

Karen is not amused. "OK, you two... You need to get serious here."

Bruce hates having to do this. He has always been wary of having people dwell in his mind. With Jack's sense of humor, he wonders if he is going to end up barking like a dog whenever he hears a specific phrase.

"All right, Bruce, let's get started here," Jack said, glancing over at Karen.

Karen promptly leaves the room. All the cameras are recording. She joins the team in the next room to monitor the session.

"You guys need to get serious," Karen said, noticing how Chuck and Jason were still laughing.

"You got to admit it, that Uncle Ted joke was a good one," Chuck said.

Jack starts off the session, trying to get Bruce into the calm zone. Knowing that Bruce is a little nervous, this could take a long time.

Bruce lies back with his eyes closed. After listening to Jack's instructions, he gets a little tired but mostly bored and has this part memorized after reading all the transcripts. Never actually seeing this first hand, he is finding it hard not to laugh.

After a long twenty minutes, Jack finally gets Bruce into a trance. He knows Bruce has probably been fighting this the entire time, knowing his dislike of being hypnotized.

"He's a tough cookie!" Jason said. "I never seen Jack work so hard."

"Let's see how long he stays under," Karen remarked. "He doesn't really want to be doing this."

"Bruce, go back to when you were with your family," Jack instructed. "Right after Christmas, at your cabin. Can you remember that?"

There is a long pause. Bruce is obviously agitated.

"It's OK... Just relax. You do remember that time while in the cabin?" Jack asked.

"Sure…" Bruce mumbles.

"Can you tell me what went on?" Jack asked.

"Lots of noise… Absolute chaos."

"Your family was there… Is that correct?"

Bruce nods. "Lots and lots of people. Way too many."

Jack continues to ask simple, irrelevant questions to get him to open up. No different from any other conversation they had before while at lunch or dinner.

Eventually, Jack gets back to the ultimate question. "So, do you recall the night when you were in the cabin after Christmas?"

There is a long pause. "It was a busy night. Lots of fireworks," Bruce replied.

"What happened on that night?"

"Not much… We're all sitting outside watching the fireworks. It's a nice clear night. Lots of stars."

"Did you leave for some reason?"

"The stars were so bright that night… I had to check it out."

"You left your body to go see the stars?" Jack asked.

"Sure… Went up really high, too. Up to the heavens. It was nice up there. I can see lots of stars."

"How high up are you?"

"Not sure… I can see the earth far below. Higher than any cloud."

"Is it like being up on an airplane?"

Bruce shakes his head. "No… More like being in the space shuttle. The view is spectacular."

Jack is shocked by the response. "Why did you go up so high?"

"Don't know… See the stars… I found what I was looking for, or I should say they found me."

"What? Are you saying that you met someone? Are there others?"

Bruce giggled. "I wondered where everyone was."

"There was more than one?" Jack asked.

"Lots and lots of people... There are so many. It's like being in a flock of birds. So many glowing lights, all were flying about together. Bashert was there too."

"Who is Bashert?"

Bruce smiles. "My destiny... She explained it all to me. It's so clear now. I understand everything. It's all so simple," then starts to laugh.

Jason sees a massive fluctuation in the levels. "Oh shit! I think he's about to make a jump. I have never seen anything like this. He is moving way too fast."

"My God!" Chuck shouted. "You need to get in there and put a stop to this. It's too soon for him to go over. He is not strong enough to deal with it."

Karen types in the information to let Jack know, but he is not looking at the monitor.

"Get in there now!" Chuck yells out. "I think he's going. You can't let him go over while he is under hypnosis!"

Karen jumps up, rushing out of the room. "This is really bad! We shouldn't have done this!"

She burst into the room. "Jack, get him out! Now! Hurry!"

Jack immediately tries to get Bruce back. "OK, Bruce... That's enough. It's time to wake up. Can you hear me?"

Bruce does not respond. Still in a deep trance, in his mind, he is hovering high above the earth.

"Bruce, don't go there!" Karen shouts, slapping his face. "Stay here with us!"

Bruce is so confused, hearing Karen screaming at him. He doesn't know what's happening and is not sure if this is real or not.

"Bruce! Do you hear me?" Karen shouts again.

Bruce's eyes open wide. "Wow! I remember now… It's all so clear. I understand everything!" grabbing Karen's arm.

"It's OK! You're back with us now! Jack, get the doctor in here," seeing the pulse rate is way too high.

"So much out there…" Bruce mumbles, so delirious. "We just scratched the surface."

"What did you see?" Karen asked.

"It's all so wonderful… More than anyone could imagine."

Chuck rushes in. "Stay here, Bruce… Don't go over!"

Bruce laughs out loud. "Chuck, the flower people had it right... We can live one life to another. That's why we are so special to them!"

Bruce's body starts going into convulsions. The doctor rushes in. Seeing Bruce's vital signs, he orders the nurse to give him a sedative.

"Please clear the room!" the doctor shouts, pushing Karen out of the way.

Within seconds, Bruce falls limp, losing consciousness.

"What the hell did you give him?" Chuck shouted, grabbing the doctor's arm.

"It's just a simple sedative to calm him down."

"Oh, no! That's the last thing he needs. He'll slip over to the other side! We won't be able to talk him out of it."

"What are you talking about?" the doctor asked. "He needs rest more than this. He has been in a coma for 18 months. You shouldn't even be doing this in the first place."

Chuck grabs Bruce's shoulder, trying to wake him up. "Come on, Bruce! Stay with us! You need to keep awake!"

Bruce's eyes slowly open, struggling to talk. "I'm so tired... I need to sleep."

"No, that's the last thing you need!" Chuck shouts out. "Don't fall asleep!"

Bruce grabs Chuck's arm, fighting to stay awake. "They are not from here... The earth is nothing more than a communal garden. The gardeners are all from different places. They plant flowers everywhere, not just here..."

Chuck gasps. "Oh, my God! How do you know this?"

"Go see Lake Matilda... They are still here."

"Who are you talking about?"

"The flower people..." Bruce whispers. "Go there... You'll see the light. It's all so simple," closing his eyes, losing consciousness.

The doctor pulls Chuck away. "OK, that's enough! He can't take anymore. We are putting an end to this nonsense!"

The hospital administrator had just put an end to the session, and there will not be anymore. Bruce is rushed back to his room, still unconscious.

* * *

Bruce never regains consciousness. No one is sure what is happening to him. The information obtained from the regression indicated that he did go to the other side 18 months ago but may have gone too far. That might have been the cause of the coma.

The entire team analyzes every second of the session. Viewing the recording, Bruce didn't cross over but came close to it. What's even more concerning is how easy it is for him to go over at will without any effort.

Late into the night, Karen, Chuck, and Jack stay in the hospital room with Bruce. They all are wondering what went wrong. Still unconscious, Bruce's mental health is now in question. Everyone involved is questioning their own motives, wondering if they put their own interests ahead of Bruce's health.

"I should have done something sooner," Chuck said. "People go too far, and it's hard to get them to come back."

"How long has he been having problems?" Karen asked.

"Probably on his second time, when he was in his apartment. But, he crossed over several times before that, right after his accident. I knew something was odd when he was able to slip over to the other side so easily without even trying."

"I knew he shouldn't have gotten mixed up into this. It's just too dangerous. You should have known he wasn't ready."

"He knew what he was getting into," Chuck explained. "I constantly warned him, but he has been there before, so he knew what he was up against."

"Yeah, but you heard what he said," Karen added. "He was having a hard time trying to distinguish what he was dreaming and the real world. Apparently, it was all blending in together."

"After listening to the tapes," Jack said. "I'm even having a hard time trying to figure this one out. I never experienced anything like this."

"Have you known anyone else who had similar problems like Bruce is having?" Karen asked Chuck.

"No... Not like this. He told me how he has been drifting in and out without even trying. At times, I don't think he even knew he was on the other side. For me, it takes a lot to prepare so you know when you are there. I just can't imagine being able to move over without even trying, or worse, not even knowing you are there. It would be like being in one horrible dream, and you can't wake up. Especially hearing about that swarm of lights, it really gets me thinking."

"I noticed he always talked about the stars in his remote viewing," Jack mentioned. "Chuck, is that something you are familiar with in your travels?"

"No, not for me... For Bruce, it was his passion. A while back, I met his mother. She mentioned how he was interested in astronomy when he was a kid. He had all the telescopes, spending hours outside late into the night gazing up at the stars. That's probably the reason he did his research with those new sensors for the satellites. Being part of the space telescope project was his big dream."

"His dream did come true," Karen said. "He helped design the next generation of space telescopes."

"I'm worried about him going up too high," Jack said.

"That's true… He was always drawn to the stars in almost every one of his travels," Chuck explained. "I'm really concerned about that. I always stayed near the ground, but he goes up high, and it doesn't faze him one bit. Hell, he even goes up flying about through the clouds during a storm. God knows how high up he got on that one."

"You heard of the Aether theory?" Karen asked. "It would be something if that's where he has been."

Jack nods his head. "That's the old Greek mythology. The place of the mist of lights. The soul of the world, because that's where all life as we know it originates from."

"The well of souls!" Chuck added. "Where all the people go after they die. Some may even call it heaven."

"He said he was far above the earth when he saw all the lights," Karen said. "The swarms of lights flying about like birds. My God! Just think if he actually saw heaven."

"I saw some strange things, but nothing like that," Chuck said. "It was always a big mystery why some people don't come back... Maybe that's what happened to them."

"I'm wondering about that," Jack said. "Maybe he came close to doing the same. We need to make sure he doesn't leave again."

"We are still monitoring him," Chuck said. "He hasn't crossed over yet, and that's a good sign. I just wish they didn't give him that sedative. We'll have to wait and see if he comes out of it."

"What makes him so special?" Karen asked. "It's like he is a natural for this remote viewing thing."

"Bruce is the best I have ever seen. His ability to make the jump without even trying is just astounding. He has gone places no one else has. So, it doesn't surprise me that he might have seen the well of souls."

"I just looked up what the Bashert is," Jack explained, holding up his iPad. "This may be our problem. That's the old Yiddish word for a soul mate."

Karen gasps out loud. "If that's the case, no wonder we are having a hard time with him."

"He had a girlfriend a while back. What happened?" Jack asked.

"After the accident, they grew apart," Karen explained. "He became more isolated, keeping to himself. I think it got worse as time went by. When he started the sessions with me, he dropped out of everything, focusing on his recovery and his out-of-body experiences."

"If his soul mate is out there," Jack added. "It's no wonder he goes over so easily. This is not good. How can we prevent him from going to the other side?"

"There is nothing we can do," Chuck said. "Maybe talk to him and explain things. Just think about it. If you discovered that you had a soul mate and found out she is not alive, what would you do?"

"He probably wants to be with her," Karen said. "If this is true, then this is a person he has been with for generations. They always cross paths and end up together. For some reason, this time, they haven't found each other. I wonder what happened?"

"What do you do when you are born, and your soul mate is on the other side of the world?" Jack asked. "How do you eventually meet up with each other?"

"I think they are just drawn together," Chuck added. "If you read up on people like that, they seem to know at first glance. Shall I say, love at first sight?"

Karen lets out a long sigh. "If that's the case... We're going to have a bad situation here."

"What about all the other things?" Chuck asked. "The sixth sense and the other things like going back over 5,000 years... What brought all this on? Did we stumble upon someone who is extraordinarily special?"

"When he told me about that, I thought it was a joke," Karen said, shaking her head. "I gave him a few tests, and my God, it's real. How he was able to do these things, I don't know. What is happening to him? What brought all this on?"

"I think it all started when he was in Wyoming," Chuck said. "Especially when he had that encounter with the flower people. He was never the same after that."

"Is that when he started with this extrasensory perception?" Jack asked.

Chuck nods. "I think so... He could literally sense people from a long distance and even their emotions. I think that's why he lived out in the boonies. No people around for miles. Going into town must have been a nightmare."

"He told me how it was like being in a room full of people, and all are talking at once," Karen explained. "Apparently, it took him a while to learn how to block out the noise. What about the mind-meld thing he did with you?" glancing over at Chuck.

"That was straight out of Star Trek!" Chuck shouted. "My God! It was like I was standing out there, seeing what he had seen! The more I asked how he was able to do these things. The more he clammed up."

"He did the same with me," Karen added. "He would just give me that look and say you're not ready."

Jack laughed. "Yep, I heard that one too! He knew more than he was letting on. How he obtained these sixth senses, he wasn't going to tell anyone else. He didn't go about boasting about it either and always kept it to himself. I have a feeling it was something to do with those flower people."

"Yeah, what about the flower people?" Karen asked. "That's another big question. Who the hell were they?"

"The question would more likely be who are they?" Chuck asked. "From what he said, they are still here."

"That's one hell of a scary thought," Karen said. "If they were here for thousands of years playing with our genetics, I don't think I want anything to do with them. Why were they interested in Bruce?"

"He is an old soul," Jack said. "He might have lived hundreds of lives, much more than anyone else. The flower people probably knew of him and were monitoring his progress. I think even they knew he was special. If you were growing flowers out in your garden, you'd watch to see which ones were stronger and better."

"The common phrase they always used," Chuck added. "To ensure their survival, or make sure all the flowers grow and flourish."

"They weren't talking about flowers, were they?" Karen asked, starting to shiver. "The one thing I do know is there is something about him that's really different. You can see it on the monitors. The blue glow is now brighter than anyone else we have seen so far."

"No wonder he never wanted to do a regression," Jack said. "I think he knew all along. The only one we did, he made sure to limit the regression to the time right before his coma. I think we accidentally stumbled on those flower people, and they probably don't like it that we know about them and what they are doing."

"You are right about that," Chuck replied. "I can't believe what he said about them. That was something I sure wasn't expecting. This is now bigger than any of us ever imagined."

"I know," Karen said, still thinking about it. "We got more than we bargained for here. This is way out of our league. The idea that they might still be here scares the hell out of me!"

"This goes far beyond what we have been doing," Jack said. "Lake Matilda? I have no clue where it is, and I don't think I'd even want to go there."

"I agree," Chuck added. "I don't think I want to mess about with that bunch. If they really are what he said, I'd be overly cautious around them."

"We discovered so much in the last few weeks," Karen said. "I think it's time to stop and regroup. We have gone too far with this and have no clue what we just walked into here. It's too much for us to deal with."

"I think we got more to deal with here," Chuck added, pointing over at Bruce lying on the bed. "We got to figure out what's happening to Bruce and how to keep him down here."

"Yes, that's more important now," Karen replied.

"Can we tell by the monitors whether he is here or not?" Jack asked.

"The only time we know for sure is when we see the light leaving his body or returning," Chuck said. "As far as we know, he hasn't crossed over."

"So, what do we do now?" Jack asked, glancing over at Karen and Chuck.

Karen shrugs her shoulders. "Right now, there is nothing we can do but pray. They are monitoring his condition and hope he doesn't go into another coma," wiping away the tears.

* * *

Closure

After a week, Bruce finally regains consciousness but is unresponsive, almost as if in a daze. Most of the time, he looks out the window or takes naps. When someone is with him, he doesn't respond to questions but, at times, just stares with a grin on his face.

As the days pass, Bruce is getting weaker. The doctors don't know why. There is nothing medically wrong with him. Even with all the tests, nothing is out of the ordinary. The results are similar to when he was in a coma.

Bruce's condition is getting worse. The doctors made the prognoses that his body was shutting down. His family is notified. Most of his family is already in town to be with him. For reasons unknown, they feel that he has given up the will to live.

Two cameras are placed up high in the corners of the room. Monitors are brought into the room, displaying what the cameras are detecting. There are no more secrets. His family knows why it's being done, agreeing to the recordings.

* * *

At six o'clock on Friday, the doctor notifies the family. Bruce has only a few hours to live. Everyone rushes to the hospital to be with him. Karen, Jason, and Chuck sit in the back of the room, out of the way.

As the hours passed, Bruce's vital signs were slowing down. The doctor and nurses come into the room every fifteen minutes. They know time is running out. There will be no efforts to resuscitate Bruce at his time of death. His family knows he doesn't want to be a burden on everyone.

The soft beep from the pulse rate monitor gets slower and slower. Every breath he takes is getting slow and longer between each breath. Bruce's mother is at his bedside, holding his hand. Whispers of people praying fill the room. Everyone knows the end is near.

Bruce's body jolts, startling everyone. Slowly, he opens his eyes. He turns his head to look at all his family surrounding his bed. A tear flows from his eye. Everyone is so shocked, not expecting this.

He struggles to speak. "I'm so sorry... Don't be sad. It's my time, and it was meant to be. My destiny is already here, my Bashert," his eyes slowly close, then he smiles.

The alarms sounded. A long audio shrill replaces the beeping sounds of Bruce's pulse. The nurse rushes over, pushing the button to shut off the alarm.

"What's happening?" his mother shouted. "He was awake! He talked to me! He is all right. I just know it!"

The doctor pushes forward, placing his stethoscope on Bruce's chest. Then he put his hand on Bruce's neck, searching for a pulse.

"I'm sorry... He is gone..." the doctor quietly whispers.

"No! He is not gone! He talked to me! You all heard it!" his mother shouts out, crying profusely.

"Is there something you can do?" Bruce's father asked, grabbing the doctor's arm.

"I'm sorry... We don't know why his body was shutting down. We could put him on life support, but it's against his wishes."

Karen slowly pushes the monitor to the front of the room. "He is still with us, but just for a short time… He can still hear you," pointing to the blue glow on the screen.

They all have been told what the blue glow is and what it means. Seeing it on the monitor for the first time is still a little unnerving for everyone.

Bruce's mother starts crying again. She holds his hand, telling him how much she loves him, then a final goodbye. The rest of the family does the same.

The blue glow starts fluctuating, then the small white light slowly emerges. "See, Bruce's spirit is still alive," Karen explained, pointing it out to everyone.

They all stare at the monitor, so amazed to see the small white light slowly floating around the room. The light stops for a moment in front of each person. When the small white light approaches Bruce's mother and father, it slowly hovers right in front of them.

"Is that really him?" Mrs. Rollin asked. "Does he know we're here?"

"Yes, he can see you," Karen said. "I think he is trying to say goodbye."

Mrs. Rollin glances over at the monitor, then reaches out with her hand, trying to touch the small white light. "Don't go, Bruce… Stay here with us."

"Come back, son," Bruce's father cries out. "We love you so much," then starts crying.

The white light starts pulsating, getting brighter and brighter. Slowly, it starts to rise up. Then, the light begins dancing about in an odd way.

"What is happening?" Jason asked. "I never seen this before. What is he doing?"

Everyone watches the monitor as the light makes little circles, in odd ways, going across the screen. Then it jumps to the left side of the screen, continuing to dance about moving to the right. It went on for a while until it finally stopped.

The light slowly hovers above the bed. To everyone's astonishment, another light shows up on the screen. The two lights slowly circle each other, then merge into one bright light. Gradually, the brilliant light rises up and moves toward the window, vanishing off the screen.

"What's happening?" Mrs. Rollin cries out. "Where did he go?" not seeing the light on the monitor.

"I'm sorry," Karen quietly whispers. "Bruce is gone," putting her hand on her shoulder.

"Why did this happen?" Mr. Rollin asked. "Why couldn't he stay? He had so much to live for," wiping away the tears.

"Look at the monitor!" someone shouted out.

Everyone's attention is drawn back to the monitor. The blue glow slowly fades away. The room is now so quiet.

"It's time for us to go," Karen whispers, glancing over at Chuck and Jason. "Let's leave so the family can say their final goodbyes," turning off the monitor.

All three sit in the hallway, so drained from the experience. They lost a good friend and a colleague. Deep down, they blame themselves for letting this go too far. The warning signs were there, but they failed to act early enough.

Dr. Jack Stewart runs down the hallway. "I just heard! I got here as quick as I could. Is he OK?"

Karen slowly shakes her head. "Sorry, he passed away a few minutes ago."

Hearing the news, he goes limp, leaning against the wall. "Damn… Why did this have to happen? I wanted so much to be here with him."

Chuck pulls over a chair. "Come sit down. He is in a better place now. It's where he wanted to be."

"Did he ever wake up?" Jack asked.

"Only for a few seconds to say goodbye," Karen said. "Then, he was gone... It was so sad."

"He left his mark, though," Jason added. "He knew we were here watching. It was so beautiful. It was an experience I'll never forget."

Chuck stands up. "Come on! Let's not be sad. We need to go out and celebrate his life. I remember him telling me long ago, on his final day, to go out and look up at the stars. He'll be up there in all his glory," and all four stand up, hugging each other.

"I guess we shouldn't be sad," Karen said. "He is not really gone... He is just between lives. One day, he'll return to live among us again."

* * *

Days after Bruce's death, everyone is studying the recordings, trying to understand what they had witnessed. With the two cameras, they can view the entire event in three dimensions.

Nothing like this has ever been seen before. The entire event is still painful for everyone to watch. The white light slowly moves about, stopping in front of everyone in the room as if to say goodbye. Now, everyone fully understands the Bashert, seeing the other light enter the room. His soul mate was actually there to take him away so they could be together.

The wild dancing about is a big mystery. When Jason plays it back over and over, he starts to notice a pattern. The movements almost resemble cursive letters, as if someone were writing something. Realizing that Bruce probably knew he was being recorded, he might have left a message.

After a little reprogramming, Jason traced all the movements so it would be displayed as one long line on the screen. Seeing the results shocked everyone. This is the first evidence of a message from a spirit or soul.

Jason cleans up the image a little, then makes a big poster from it. He hangs it up on the wall for all to see and admire.

'I have been to heaven and back. It's more wonderful than anyone could imagine. They are all up there waiting for their turn. May meet you again one day in the future. For now, I'm back with the love of my life to live in eternity together. Don't be sad. Love Bruce.'

* * *

The Light

Months later, Chuck's curiosity gets the better of him. Lake Matilda is all he has been thinking about after all that time. Bruce's final message about the whereabouts of these flower people is too much to pass up. Many have been debating this since Bruce's death. With the little information they have, this may be their only hope. Unfortunately, no one else dares risk venturing to the lake to find out if these people really exist.

Searching the Internet, Chuck discovers numerous lakes named Matilda all over the world. One by one, he is going over satellite images looking for clues. Some are in populated areas, while others are incredibly remote. None of them look anything out of the ordinary.

Eventually, he makes a list of the most viable candidates. Some are in Finland and New Zealand, and several are in Canada and Australia. To his surprise, the one that does stand out is at Grand Teton National Park. It's not the exact name, but Emma Matilda Lake is close to where Bruce's cabin used to be.

Chuck sets out alone on his quest. He doesn't want to risk anyone else on this venture. He pulled out of the group and stopped promoting his books. Remote viewing is now a thing of the past. He doesn't want to be responsible for any more pain. Too many lives have been destroyed while experimenting with remote viewing. Losing Bruce is the one that hurts the most.

* * *

The first lake on the list is at the Grand Teton National Park. He finds it somewhat ironic that this is the place Bruce loved the most.

Arriving in town, he stops by Bruce's old cabin before checking into the hotel. Chuck is so depressed seeing the cabin, which is now empty. Bruce's family is still deciding what to do with it and all the surrounding land. While sitting on the old Adirondack chair, nothing has changed since the last time he was here.

He cannot believe it's been a couple of years since he was sitting here with Bruce. Looking around at the fantastic view and with everything so quiet and blissful, he knew right then what he was going to do. He has found his calling. This will be his new home, and he is going to make an offer they can't refuse.

Emma Matilda Lake is not far away. The hotel he is staying at is located right next to the Jackson Lake Lodge. So, he knows this can't be the one. The crescent-shaped lake does have some similarities. Lined with tall trees, with the backdrop of the Grand Tetons, it does make one spectacular view.

After talking with some of the local people, he finds there is nothing unusual about the lake. So close to the hotel and highways, there are always plenty of people walking around on the trails. There is no way that any strange people could be living out here without someone in the area knowing about it.

* * *

Early in the morning, Chuck sets off for a walk around the lake. The seven-mile hike will take a few hours. A helicopter tour would take a few minutes, but he knows the walk would be something Bruce would probably do.

The area around the lake is beautiful. Fields of lush green grass and tall pine trees surround the lake. The trails are filled with plenty of tourists out enjoying the day. He can imagine Bruce out here on a day like today, tramping on the various trails.

After circling Emma Matilda Lake, he is not surprised there are no secret cabins or extremely tall, fair-skinned people. Just a couple of miles north is the Two Ocean Lake. He figures since he is close by, he can explore that one as well.

By the end of the day, Chuck is heading for the airport. The whole area is beautiful, and the hike was invigorating, but it is not Bruce's lake. At least the time he spent walking on the many trails cleared his mind. He is now thinking about settling down. A place like this would be perfect. Traveling the world promoting his books is now a thing of the past.

Bruce's old cabin out by the lake is the ideal retirement home. He has already made the calls to acquire the property. Although, he knows he must talk with Bruce's parents personally about this to get their blessing first before all the lawyers get involved.

* * *

The next stop is Canada. The first lake is three miles south of Redditt and a mile from the nearest road. The other lake is in the remote district of Algoma. Each lake is extremely remote, with no trails, so hiking is out of the question. A helicopter will be needed to explore both lakes.

The lake near Redditt is a washout. After circling the lake several times in a helicopter, there is nothing to be seen. The entire area is an absolute wilderness covered with small lakes, and each lake is in the middle of a dense forest.

The most likely candidate could be the one in the Algoma District. Matilda Lake is so remote it could be the one. Even though it's only 30 miles east of Lake Superior and four miles from the nearest inhabitants, it looks like a perfect location for people who want to be left alone.

The nearest town is Sault Ste. Marie, in Ontario. With the lake 70 miles north of the town, a helicopter is the only way to get there.

Early in the morning, Chuck is on his way. The flight to the lake is long. The entire area is so remote. There is nothing around for miles but dense trees with a few lakes dotted here and there.

Arriving at Matilda Lake, there is nowhere to land. Hiking around the lake is out of the question. They circle the lake, hovering low, just above the trees. Using a heat sensor, he scans the area, seeing nothing but trees. There are no structures or buildings and no signs of anyone ever being out on this lake.

After spending several days interviewing the local people, it's more of the same. There is nothing out of the ordinary. After a week in Canada, Chuck strikes out again.

Lake Matilda, in Teijo, Finland, is more of the same. Even with most of the lake surrounded by a dense forest, there is a small town on one end. Hiring a small boat, he circles the lake, looking for clues, but there is nothing here. The area is too populated, and with all the tourists, this is not the lake either.

* * *

The next stop is on the other side of the world and a nineteen-hour flight. If Chuck fails to find anything in New Zealand, then Australia is the last stop. The lakes he looked at so far were nothing special. The people who lived in the areas near the lakes were very helpful. Not like the problems he had in Switzerland, where people stopped talking altogether.

Becoming discouraged, Chuck is wondering if this is all a wild goose chase. Bruce was drifting in and out so many times. Maybe he was seeing things in the past and not the present.

Arriving in the small town of Te Anau, on the South Island of New Zealand, Chuck is so exhausted. This is not the kind of traveling he is used to doing. On his book tours, he always goes from one city to the next, where the flights were only a few hours at most. A whole day sitting on an airplane is just too much.

* * *

After several days of rest, Chuck is taking a walk along the lakefront park. Seeing the local helicopter tour office, he decides it's time to check things out. Lake Matilda is only 26 miles away, so it shouldn't be too much of a problem getting there.

"May I help you, sir?" a man asked, seeing Chuck walking in.

"Yes, I'm looking to hire a private charter?"

"We have several packages. We can take you out to Milford Sound and Dusky Sound. We have about eight packages that cover the area. There are fishing or hunting tours if you are interested in that sort of thing. We do them all! How many are in your group?" showing him the brochure.

Chuck is impressed with the selection. "Only me... I'm more interested in this area here," pulling out a map pointing to Lake Matilda.

"Oh, that's near some of our package tours. You can do the Fiordland or Dusky scenic tour. They go right by that area. If you want to see the Sounds, it's the best way to go."

"I'm not really interested in the tours. I want you to drop me off right here next to the lake," Chuck said.

There is a long pause. "Not too sure we can do that... There are three to four-hundred-meter cliffs around that lake and lots of wind turbulence in those terrains. That's also a conservation area. We are also restricted to fly at 1,500 meters altitude around that area."

"You can't drop me off in this flat area right next to the lake?" Chuck asked.

"Sorry, sir... The winds up there are just too treacherous. Besides, you will need a permit from the Department of Conservation for us to land up there."

"I was afraid of that..."

"May I ask what's so important about this lake? There is not much up there. All our tours go to all the scenic spots. That's what most people are interested in seeing."

"I'm doing research on the Kea," Chuck said, hoping a fake cover story can help get him in. "I heard rumors that there might be some nests up there. I was hoping to get a few photos and counts of what's up by the lake. How about getting me in there as close as you can go without all the permits? Maybe circle around it?"

"We can get you close enough... I'll book you for our Doubtful Sound tour. I'll put down a note for the pilot to drop down near that lake. Oh, you're just in luck. The chopper is on the way back now. It should be here in about twenty minutes."

Chuck is so glad. "Thanks... I'm looking forward to it."

"If I can just have you fill out one of our forms," handing Chuck a card.

Chuck sits in the waiting area, reading the local paper. He has already studied the terrain around the lake. A helicopter landing next to the lake would be the best and fastest way to get up there. If he could get to the top of one of the mountains, he could easily hike down. The last option is to hike up to the lake from the road near Doubtful Sound. That would be one hell of a climb and one that he is not looking forward to.

* * *

More than twenty minutes have passed. No helicopter is in sight. Chuck is starting to notice a problem. There seems to be a lot of discussions going on between the manager and the person who booked his flight. The manager is always on the phone, looking somewhat irritated.

After another ten minutes, the manager walks over. "I'm very sorry, Mr. Wilson... We're going to have to cancel your flight. We're having some problems with our helicopter. It's going back to the hangar for maintenance. We'll refund your money."

"I hope it's nothing serious. You do have another helicopter?"

"Oh, yes... But it's fully booked."

Chuck notices that this person is really nervous. "When will I be able to book another flight?"

"I'm very sorry, but it won't be for a week or more. With one chopper down, we'll have to double up. It is the tourist season. Maybe if you leave us your number, we can call you if a seat comes available in the near future."

Chuck slowly turns, looking around the office. It's empty except for him. He already suspects a problem. Just by the way these people are acting, he knows they are lying.

"It's quite all right... I'll find other things to do to keep me occupied while I'm here."

"Thank you for understanding," the manager said. "I hope you enjoy your stay here," motioning him to the door.

Right away, Chuck knows something is wrong. Things were the same when he was in Switzerland. At least now he knows this is the right place. He can already hear the doors slamming in his face.

* * *

Walking back to the hotel, he sees another scenic tour office, but this one has a seaplane. He takes note of the number and will call later with a few minor changes in his approach. These people may already have his name on the no-fly list, or they know not to take anyone out to Lake Matilda. On the next booking, he'll make sure not to mention the lake or his name.

While wandering about the hotel lobby, Chuck finds the brochure for the tour company. Not wanting to make the call from his cell phone or the phone in his room, he uses the one in the lobby.

"Hello, I'm looking at one of your brochures," Chuck said over the phone. "I'm interested in one of your tours to Doubtful Sound. When would be a good time to schedule a flight?"

"Our next available flight is at nine tomorrow morning. The weather will be clear and calm. It'll be a great time to see the Sound. Would you like to book the flight?" the man asked.

"That's perfect!" Chuck replied. "Yes, put me down for tomorrow morning, please."

"Can I have your name?"

"The name is Roy Martin," Chuck replied, making sure not to use his real name.

There is a long pause. "How many are in your party, Mr. Martin?"

More warning signs. "There are three of us... Will all three of us be able to fit on the plane? We saw it land on the lake this morning and thought, what a great way to see the sites!" he really played it up as a tourist.

"That will be fine... No problem. We got you down for the nine in the morning flight. You'll need to be here 15 minutes early to sign in. Oh, make sure you have your passport or a driver's license. Some form of identification for our records."

"No problem... I'll make sure to bring them along. We'll see you tomorrow morning."

He already knows they have locked down all the flights. Luckily, he is prepared with several passports and identification cards, just in case this happens. Now, all he needs is two willing companions to join him on the flight.

After looking around the lobby, there are plenty of tourists to choose from here. An Asian couple is sitting nearby. That may seem a little odd and are too young. Anyone with kids is out of the question. He just has to find the right ones so he can blend in.

After several minutes, he notices two middle-aged women sitting on the far side of the lobby, looking over the brochures. Once he hears the English accent, he knows they will be perfect.

Chuck slowly walks over, taking one of the brochures from the shelf. "Excuse me... I couldn't help noticing you're looking at the tour flights. Are you planning on booking one?"

"Oh, yes... We're thinking about it! They are so expensive. It's way too much for our budget. I'm Diana, and this is my friend Janice."

"Nice to meet you... I'm Roy. It sounds like you're from England?" reaching out to shake their hands.

"Yes, we're on holiday... We've been planning this for years! You must be from America?"

"I'm from California... We did the Hobbit tour and decided to come down here and see the famous Sounds."

"Are you planning to go on one of these tours?" Diana asked, holding up one of the brochures for the flights.

"Yes, I got one booked for tomorrow."

"Not sure if I'm ready to go on one of those helicopters," Diana said. "Looks dangerous."

"That's why we booked a plane," Chuck explained. "It's much safer, I think. Although, I'm in somewhat of a dilemma. My friends had to leave a day early, and I got this flight booked for tomorrow. We already paid for the flight, and it seems a waste having two empty seats. Would you two be interested? The flight is tomorrow morning at nine."

They look at each other, wondering what to do. "Oh, I don't know," Janice said. "We're not sure if we can afford it."

"Yeah, we're on a tight budget," Diana added.

"It's already paid for, so it'll be no cost to you. You know how these places are, and there are no last-minute refunds. My friend paid for it anyway. He has plenty of money to throw away. I hate to see it go to waste and end up going alone. I hear it's one of the best scenic tours. I'm staying here at the hotel, so if you're interested, let me know."

"I think it would be great!" Diana shouted, taking only a few seconds to reply. "We'd love to go! Thank you so much!"

"Are you sure you don't want us to give you some money to help with the cost?" Janice asked.

"It's no money out of my pocket, so don't worry about it. We have to check in fifteen minutes early and walk a block down the street to that plane sitting in the water. So, maybe we'll meet here in the lobby at 8:30 tomorrow morning?"

"That sounds fine!" Diana said. "You really made our day!"

"We'll have a good time tomorrow. I'll meet you here in the lobby then?"

Things couldn't have worked out any better. Now, he has two real tourists to help mask his identity. He knows he'll blend in well with these two lovely ladies.

* * *

The next morning, Chuck is up early. Dressed in his Hawaiian shirt, Bermuda shorts, black knee-high socks, and sandals, he is ready to play the typical American tourist.

Once on the plane with Diana and Janice, he is home free. He knows it'll be best not to mention Lake Matilda at all. The lake will be on the right side, so he hopes to get some good photos to help find a way up there.

The one thing he needs the most is to see what the terrain is like around the lake. From looking at the maps, it's hard to tell how steep the cliffs are. Without a helicopter, hiking up there may be his only option.

He couldn't have picked a better day to do this. There is not a cloud in the sky, and the visibility is more than 20 miles. Already, he can see the vast mountain range in such detail. These mountains are huge, coming right out of the ocean. Seeing how steep the cliffs are, it's no wonder that some of these lakes are over a thousand feet deep.

The airplane starts dropping altitude as they approach Doubtful Sound, flying right along Wilmont Pass Road. The remoteness of this place is absolutely stunning. Some of the peaks are over a mile high. The cliffs are almost vertical, going straight down into the water. There are so many lakes high up in these mountains. Nothing more than huge natural bowls filled with water from the rain and snowmelt. Seeing how steep the mountains are, he knows that this is far worse than he anticipated.

Coming up to Wanganella Cove, Chuck looks back to the right. Tucked away in a large valley of these remote mountains is Lake Lucy, and behind it is Lake Matilda. Almost 3,000 feet above sea level, these lakes are surrounded by 1,000-foot cliffs. Looking down, it's practically a vertical cliff down to the ocean. Climbing to the lake from down there is not an option.

Chuck takes as many photos of the lake and the surrounding area while he has the chance. In less than a minute, the lake is obscured by the other mountains. He now knows hiking up there is going to be treacherous. Maybe it was something he could have done in his younger days. This is not the kind of hike a person can do all alone. He needs to look for other options.

* * *

Days later, Chuck is still looking for ways to get up to the lake. There are several options, but the best one is driving up Wilmont Pass Road. Stopping by Stella Falls would be the start of the brutal climb. The first obstacle is a 400-foot cliff to get up to the base. After that, it's a two-mile hike going from a 1,400-foot elevation to a 3,600-foot ridge above the lake. The last part up to the ridge is another 400-foot climb up a steep cliff.

Once at the top of the ridge, it's a 500-foot drop down to the lake down a 45-degree cliff. The only option is to try to scale down the side of the cliffs using ropes, but that's going to take a team of young, experienced climbers. Getting a team together for a climb like that will attract way too much attention.

Going over all the options, each one requires a brutal climb. Getting up to a 3,600-foot mountain in only a couple of miles is just too much. He knows he is just too old and out of shape to attempt the climb.

Looking for other means to get to the lake, his only option is to go back to his old CIA days. There is always someone who will do anything for money and will not ask too many questions.

Walking around town for some ideas, he finally sees what he is looking for, skydiving. Even though it's been way too many years, Chuck signs up for a few jumps. Since the owner, Colin Moore was part of the Special Forces in the Royal Marines, Chuck blends right in.

Every night, Chuck and Colin are in the bar talking about old war stories. During the day, they are out doing two to three jumps, showing up all the young guys. With all the modern rectangular 'ram-air' canopies having better directional control, these are far superior to what he was trained on in his Army days.

With the local canopy piloting skydiving competition coming up, it gives Chuck an excuse to practice every day. Even on windy days, he is out there training when no one else will.

His goal is to come down from a 13,000-foot altitude and land on the east side of the lake. The turbulence over the mountain range can be treacherous. An early morning jump is the best and probably his only option.

* * *

When the weather is looking perfect, Chuck schedules an early morning flight. The pilot is one that he chose carefully. The price is high for a flight over Doubtful Sound instead of the usual practice skydiving over the airport. An additional bonus was added for the pilot, so he would not ask why someone was skydiving out by the Sound.

The flight is recorded as an early morning photo session for a tourist and not for skydiving. The pilot is instructed to land at another airport right after the jump. So no one will be asking any questions about why he is flying back without any passengers.

Chuck couldn't have picked a better day for the flight. The morning is exceptionally calm, with clear skies. No one else is around this early in the morning. Even better, there is no one around to see him get on the plane.

The flight out to Doubtful Sound is breathtaking. The soft orange glow to the east indicates where the sun is about to rise. The timing has to be just right. A few minutes before sunrise, there is enough light to be able to land safely. Once the sun pops up over the horizon, he has to be on the ground. Even with a black parachute, he can't risk being spotted.

"We're coming up to the target!" the pilot shouted. "Good luck!"

"Thanks!" Chuck said, checking his gear. "I'll contact you in a few days."

"You sure you want to do this? It's really dark down there."

Chuck laughs. "I have been doing this for a long time. It'll be a piece of cake," slowly opening the door.

A blast of ice-cold air rushes through the small airplane. Chuck turns in his seat, sliding the door wide open. The pilot slowly turns the aircraft to the east. There is just enough light to see the outline of the lake far below.

The pilot taps Chuck's back as the sun peeks above the horizon. "OK! It's now or never!"

Chuck gives him the thumbs-up sign. "Thanks for the ride!" leaning forward, then falls into the darkness.

The cold air on his face is invigorating. Seeing the sun coming up over the horizon never looked so good. Falling more and more into the darkness, he sees nothing. A loud buzzing sound is really bothering him. He wonders if it's from a loose strap on his helmet, but it's too late to deal with it.

A vicious crosswind hits him, coming out of the west. Going into a flat spin, he gets light-headed, and his vision is blurred. This is the one thing that he doesn't need at such a low altitude. He struggles to get back in control, knowing there are only a few seconds to spare.

Surrounded by darkness, he finds it impossible to get back into a steady free-fall. The sun, coming up over the horizon, is his only hope. Seeing it flash by several times, he now knows he is spinning to the right. With a quick adjustment, luckily, he is back in control. All those practice jumps have paid off.

Looking down, to his relief, the outline of the lake comes into view. Seeing the reading on his altimeter, he pulls the canopy release. Immediately, the canopy pops open. Now, the difficult part of his journey begins.

Slowly circling, he keeps an eye on the tall mountains that surround the lake. The ambient light is enough to see where he is going. With the valley only 1,500 feet wide and steep walls of more than 1,000 feet above, there is no margin for error.

Passing within the walls of the valley, he reaches down, turning on his landing lights. With lights strapped onto his boots, helmet, and arms, he is hoping it's enough. This is not the flat grassland of the airport where he has been practicing his landings. Any rock or boulder will put an end to this real quick. The trees are another problem to deal with once he gets down there.

At 3,300-foot altitude, he sees his landing zone. The landing lights illuminate the small grassy area just east of the lake. With one last turn, the lake is to his back, so he prepares for the final approach. Gliding just a few feet above the grass, he pulls down on the control lines. Slowing down to a crawl, his foot touches the ground. With a few quick steps, he is on the ground without any problems.

Just like in his old army days, the first order of business is dragging in the chute. Running to the nearest trees, he stashes everything away. With the sun coming up, he knows it won't be long before all the helicopters and airplanes will be flying by, filled with tourists. The last thing he needs is to be spotted up here.

Seeing the lake and the tall vertical cliffs towering a thousand feet above it's absolutely breathtaking. Chuck feels like he is standing at the bottom of a bowl surrounded by all these steep cliffs. There is no beach at all on the north and south side, just a straight drop off into the water.

The one thing he really notices, this place is very similar to the lake in Switzerland. The entire area is a big u-shaped valley with an opening on the west side. It was probably formed from glaciers many years ago.

The first order of business is to check out what's on the east side of the lake. After storing everything away, Chuck grabs his binoculars. A quick scan of the area leaves him somewhat confused. Even though there are a lot of trees, the steep cliffs would make it impossible for anyone to live up here.

The only possible area is either the east or the far west side of the lake. On the east side, it's somewhat barren. Nothing but a few small trees and shrubs. Mostly grass and rocks on this side.

Walking along the edge of the lake, he reaches a small group of trees. The trees go up the hill over a hundred feet above the lake. There are no signs of anyone here or even having been here. Nor are there any footprints or man-made structures.

He pulls out his infrared camera, hoping to see heat signatures from people or buildings hiding up within the trees, but there is nothing. Even across the lake, there are no signs of any man-made structures.

After surveying the area for several hours, he finds the west side looks more promising. There are huge trees on that side, and the cliffs are not as steep. Seeing how bad the terrain is, Chuck is prepared. A raft is the only way that he is going to be able to get to the far side of this lake.

Dragging everything out of his backpack, he grabs the inflatable raft. Pulling on the release cord, a burst of air inflates it within seconds. Quickly assembling the paddle, he drags it all out to the water.

The raft is small, but it'll do the job. With the water being ice-cold, Chuck is hoping not to fall in. Keeping close to the shoreline, making sure no one could see him out on the water. Hearing all the flights going out to Doubtful Sound, the last thing he needs is to be spotted and be arrested by the Government for trespassing.

He reaches the west side in just a few minutes. This part of the lake does appear more promising. A small ridge separates Lake Matilda from Lake Lucy. Over the years, the water cut a small creek between the two lakes. The water spills from one lake into the other, then finally down the far side into the ocean.

On the north side of Lake Lucy is a 500-foot wall going straight up. The south side is covered with huge trees. The cliffs are not as steep, but it still would be a challenge for anyone to live up here.

Spending hours surveying the ridge between the two lakes, but he sees nothing out of the ordinary. There are plenty of trees on both the north and south sides. Again, there are no signs of anyone ever being up here. He starts to wonder if he is the first person ever to come up to these lakes.

Getting frustrated, Chuck stands on the edge of Lake Lucy, staring at the enormous trees on the south and west side. For some reason, this should be the lake and not Lake Matilda. He wonders why Bruce didn't say anything about this one. These lakes are right next to each other, only separated by a small 75-foot ridge. If it weren't for this little ridge, this would be one big lake instead of two.

Running out of options while he is here, he might as well explore this lake. He goes back to retrieve the raft, dragging it across the ridge to Lake Lucy. The more he thinks about it, this has to be the lake that Bruce was referring to.

Halfway across the lake, Chuck gets tired and ready for a short break, pulling out a few snacks and a drink. This lake is beautiful. The water is so clear he can see the rocks at the bottom, and it must be over 50 feet deep. Surrounded by tall cliffs hundreds of feet above, he feels so small. Closing his eyes, he longs for a short nap, knowing he is too old to be doing things like this.

After several minutes of drifting on the lake and admiring the view, he notices an open area between two huge groups of trees on the south side. Not far from the edge of the water, he spots a small trail. He quickly grabs the infrared camera. Just within the trees, he sees a faint warm spot. Adjusting the camera's sensitivity, he notices a small plume of warm air rising out of the trees.

Chuck quietly paddles to the open area. It could be nothing, but he still needs to check it out. Reaching the shoreline, he pulls the raft out of the water, tying it to one of the trees.

The dirt path is not far from the water and cuts across the open area between the two groups of trees. There are footprints in the dirt. So, people have been up here. It might be nothing more than a trail that tourists have used over the years.

Walking along the trail, it leads right into the trees. Slowly walking through the dense trees, Chuck tries not to make any noise. Then, he starts scanning the area with the infrared camera. The small trail leads right up to the heat signature.

Walking another twenty feet, he sees the source of the heat. A cave is tucked behind a small bush. With the infrared camera, he can clearly see heat flowing right out of the cave. The entrance to the cave is so well-hidden that no one walking by would have ever noticed it.

With no warnings, a voice comes from behind. "Welcome, my friend... We were not expecting you so soon."

Chuck quickly turns around and sees a tall, pale man standing a few feet behind him. "Oh, hello! I didn't know anyone was here," so shocked being discovered.

The man smiles. "We understand your concerns... I am Julian. Marcus mentioned you might be stopping by to visit.

We don't encourage guests, but Marcus can be, at times, persistent."

"Oh, sorry... Were you expecting me? I'm not sure who this Marcus person is. You might have confused me with someone else. Oh, my name is Chuck," holding out his hand.

Chuck is very cautious, not sure who this person is. He was expecting to find a few people out in this wilderness. There are always some extremist tourists in the most unexpected places. Although, this person didn't look like your typical tourist. The clothes he has on are very odd. From his mannerisms and the way he talks, it seems as if he is some sort of old hippie.

Julian clasps his hands together. "My apologies... It is not our way," not wanting to shake his hand. "Marcus goes by many names. He speaks well of you. You may have known him as Bruce during that lifetime."

Chuck is absolutely stunned, not expecting this at all. "Oh, my God! You are one of the flower people!"

Julian laughed. "Such an amusing term he associated with us."

"Is Bruce here? Can I talk with him?"

"Unfortunately, no... Marcus is between worlds. He informed us of your interest. We have agreed to enlighten you on our ways."

"You mean I can ask you questions? I have so many!"

"Yes, you may ask any question, but you will leave only with the knowledge you arrived with."

Chuck is a little confused with the response, but he is already trying to think of all the questions he wants to ask these people. "Where do I start? There are so many!" his mind is going blank.

"First of all, please come inside. You had a long journey. You will find it more comfortable," motioning Chuck inside.

"Wow! I saw the heat source, but I wasn't expecting a cave!"

"Yes, we must adjust our entrance since you discovered the warmth flowing from our shelter."

"You don't have the cabins anymore?"

"Oh, you are referring to the ancient times. With your new enlightenment, we must now seek shelter within the terra firma. We must not interfere with your development."

"Like the Prime Directive?" Chuck asked as he entered the cave.

Julian laughs, hearing the phrase. "Marcus speaks the same terms. He has opened our minds to some of your ways."

Chuck can see this is no natural structure. The floor looks like Italian marble. Even the walls are smooth as if they have been polished. Light panels run along the ceiling. This is no simple cave. A massive door at the end of the cave slowly opens, revealing an underground city. These are indeed extremely advanced people.

* * *

Chuck sees nothing but darkness. His body aches all over, and his arms and legs are numb. He feels a sensation of motion as if swinging back and forth. Strange voices are in the distance. An odd mechanical sound gets louder and louder.

"Are you OK?" a strange man's voice shouts into his ear. "You still with us?"

Chuck is confused. He opens his eyes, seeing nothing but blurred colors. In the distance, he sees flashing lights. Then, a strange, horrible smell jolts him awake.

"Just keep calm," a man said, waving smelling salts under Chuck's nose. "We'll have you down in a few minutes. We'll cut you free once we get you tethered. Don't worry. You won't fall!"

His vision is clearing. A man is right in front of him, wearing a bright yellow jacket. He feels like he is being turned around and someone is pulling on his arms and legs.

"What the hell is going on?" Chuck asked, pushing away the smelling salts from under his nose.

"Don't worry! We're going to get you down," the man replied.

Looking down, Chuck is absolutely stunned. He is high up in the air. Far below is a fire truck, and the man is up on a ladder, putting a harness around him. Looking above, he sees a parachute tangled up in a tree.

"Holy shit! How did I get up here?"

"Looks as though you've been doing some illegal base jumping. It's not a smart move with all these winds. Where are your companions? How many are with you?"

"None... Just me," Chuck answered.

"That's bullshit! No one goes out base-jumping alone. You need to fess up, man. No telling how many of your buddies are up in the trees like you. You're damn lucky you didn't kill yourself with a stunt like this. Hell, we would have never found you in these forests. It's a good thing you landed near the road."

Chuck keeps his mouth shut. He has no clue how he got here or why he was out with a parachute. His lines are cut and slowly lowered to the ground. As soon as he is on the ground, the paramedics are all over him.

After a few minutes, he is on a stretcher being hauled away. Police cars and rescue trucks line the road. A heavy thumping noise drowns out all the voices and sounds. A helicopter slowly descends, landing in the middle of the road.

Once inside the helicopter, the medic is checking his vitals. "Looks like you got some minor scrapes and bruises. I see no signs of exposure or malnutrition. You are damn lucky. You'll be back on your feet in no time!"

A man in the back steps forward. "How can that be? Check him again! I want to make sure he doesn't die on us! I got a lot of questions that need answers!"

Chuck looks over at the man. This is no medic. Seeing the 'New Zealand Security Intelligence Service' badge on his jacket, he knows he is in trouble.

"Well, Mr. Wilson... We finally caught up with you. You think you can hide from us forever. After we interrogate your ass, then we're going to kick you out of the country. Hell, you might be spending some time in jail for that little stunt you pulled."

Chuck smiled. "I'm just on holiday. Came down to see the Hobbits!"

"Hobbits, like hell you have! We checked your background. You're an old CIA man. Your boys back home told us you retired, but we know better. What are you doing in our country, and where have you been for the last four months."

"Four months? I have only been here a week. Like I said, I'm on holiday. What kind of crap are you pulling here?"

"Your Visa expired a long time ago. We can get you on that one alone."

Chuck is confused. "What do you mean my Visa is expired? I told you, it's been a week. You can check with the hotel where I'm staying."

"A week, like hell... You checked into that hotel back in October. We got word that you were snooping around, and then you disappeared four months ago. Some people thought you were dead until they found you hanging from that tree. We knew you'd show up sooner or later!"

"What the hell are you talking about, and what day is it?" looking up at the medic.

"It's Tuesday," the medic replied. "The 18th of February."

"That's bullshit!" Chuck shouts, then looks at his watch. "What the hell is going on?" seeing the same date on his watch.

"That's what we want to know, Mr. Wilson... Where have you been for the last four months?"

"Are you here doing research on remote viewing?" the medic asked. "I read your last book, and it was great!"

"Keep quiet, and do your job!" the security officer yelled at the medic. "Mr. Wilson, I don't want to hear anything about that mumbo jumbo crap you have been peddling. That remote viewing bullshit is nothing but a convenient cover story for what you are really doing. Don't think you are fooling us. We've seen your travel plans for the last few years. A lot of countries have marked you as an undesirable. I guess we'll be next!"

* * *

Chuck spends the next couple of days in the hospital. He is under house arrest until the deportation orders come in. The doctors are the only ones who are keeping him from being deported due to concerns about his health.

His past with the CIA is not helping things. New Zealand officials are demanding to know the true nature of why he is in the country. The American Embassy and the State Department deny knowing anything, which makes matters worse.

* * *

"Hi, Chuck!" Karen shouts as she enters the room. "You had us all scared for a while."

"Oh, it's nothing... Welcome to my prison cell," glad to see a familiar face.

Karen pulls up a chair. "So, how are you feeling?"

"Not too bad... I'm getting too old for the base jumping. I'm still a little sore from that mess."

"What the hell happened? You've been gone for four months. We have all been down here looking for you. You literally disappeared. Everyone thought you were at the bottom of one of these deep lakes or out lost in the vast forests they got down here."

"I have no clue... My mind is blank. I don't even know why I'm here. The doctors think I might have had a concussion or something."

"You don't remember anything?" Karen asked.

"The only thing I do remember is being at the hotel. I don't have any recollection of why I'm here. All I do know is that I was stuck up in a tree near Doubtful Sound. Luckily, it was near one of the roads. They say I was base jumping up there."

Karen doesn't understand any of this. "When did you start this parachuting thing? When we were here looking for you, we heard you had been out practicing for some competition. You're too old to be doing dangerous things like that. So, what did you find down here?"

"That's the big question... Tell me why I'm here. I have no clue."

"You are kidding?" Karen asked. "Let me look at your chart," giving it a quick run through it.

"There is a question about a possible concussion, but all your blood work is fine," Karen explained. "You show no signs of exposure to the elements or being malnourished. There is nothing here to explain the memory loss or the four months out in the wilderness. From the looks of things, you have been taking it easy for those four months and not wandering about lost."

"So, what am I doing down here? I don't remember anything other than being on holiday seeing the Hobbits. Is that why I came to this country? Then I lost four months. How did that happen? It's all so confusing."

"Right before Bruce died, he mentioned the flower people and something about a Lake Matilda... There are several lakes around the world with similar names. That's why you have been traveling to all these places to check them out. That's why you are here in New Zealand."

He looks at Karen, so shocked. "You know this for a fact? I don't remember any of that. None of this makes any sense."

Karen laughed. "I have a feeling that you found the lake. You disappeared off the face of the earth for four months, but other than a few cuts and bruises, you're healthy. I guess that's a sign that things went well."

Chuck starts thinking about all this. "You are telling me Bruce sent me here?"

"Yes... You might have found what you were looking for out here. Based on how much memory you lost, they don't want you talking. Maybe Jack can put you under, and through hypnosis, we can learn what happened?"

"I don't know why, but I got this deep down feeling we don't want to do that. If they are here, then they are still in business and don't want people snooping around. I made it out alive, so that is a good sign."

"If that's the case, then we're getting into things that are bigger than we could have ever imagined. These are probably extremely powerful people who have been around for thousands of years or more. I think it's best just to leave things be for now."

"You are right... I must have been with them for four months. For some reason, I don't remember anything."

"Maybe they wiped your memory," Karen suggested. "You are lucky to be alive. I don't think I want anything to do with those people."

"I don't know why, but I have a feeling it went well," Chuck said, trying to remember things.

Karen laughs. "Your time with the flower people may have gone well, but not with the Government here. I'm here to take you home. They are kicking us out of the country. We're being deported. Our whole group has been banned from New Zealand, Japan, China, Brazil, India, and Switzerland."

Chuck laughs out loud. "When did they do that?"

"I found out when I got off the plane... We got 24 hours. Then we're being escorted to the airport."

"Looks like we hit a home run!" Chuck added. "They just told us where the rest of them are hiding."

"Not much we can do about it... When we get back home, the FBI will be seizing our passports. None of us will ever leave the country again."

Chuck laughs again. "You guys may not leave the country, but for the others like me... They will never stop us. I now have a new outlook on life. A new goal!"

"What are you going to do?" she asked.

"I'm going to go back and live in a cabin by the lake. You remember Bruce's old cabin out in Wyoming. I'm going to buy the place, and then I'm going to be a florist!"

"What! You're going to live out in the boonies and sell flowers?" Karen asked, confused by his statement. "I don't get it."

"Oh, you will... It was something that Bruce had taught me. Believe me, this is not the end, but just the beginning. Bruce was the first of a new generation."

"How do you know? Did they tell you that? I thought you said you don't remember anything."

He shrugged. "I don't remember anything, but it seems like I know about certain things... It's like trying to remember something that's on the tip of your tongue. I have no clue why, but it's still there deep down somewhere in my memory."

"They might have done something to make you forget the last few months, but you may still have some of the knowledge. Does it feel like trying to recall a distant memory?"

Chuck smiled. "Yes, it does... All I know is that they have done this for thousands of years. Bruce was the first, and we were there to witness the event. The one thing I do know is that it's something wonderful. This is the beginning of the human transfiguration. I envy the children of tomorrow. What a wonderful world they will live in..."

* * *

The End